Murder In Gemini

Murder In Gemini

A Write Club Mystery

MICHELLE CORBIER

BOOKS BY MICHELLE CORBIER

Write Club Mystery

Murder Is Revealing

Murder Between Neighbors

Mwindajis

Dark Blood Awakens

Standalone

Hollow Voices

Michelle Corbier
415 Pisgah Church Road, PMB 342
Greensboro, NC 27455
For more information: www.MichelleCorbier.com

This is a work of fiction. Names, characters, places, brands, media, and incidents are either the product of the author's imagination or are used fictitiously.

Cover and interior design by Karen Phillips at PhillipCovers.com
Murder In Gemini

978-1-7375252-8-8 Murder In Gemini, eBook
979-8-9870408-0-5 Murder In Gemini, paperback
979-8-9870408-1-2 Murder In Gemini, hardback

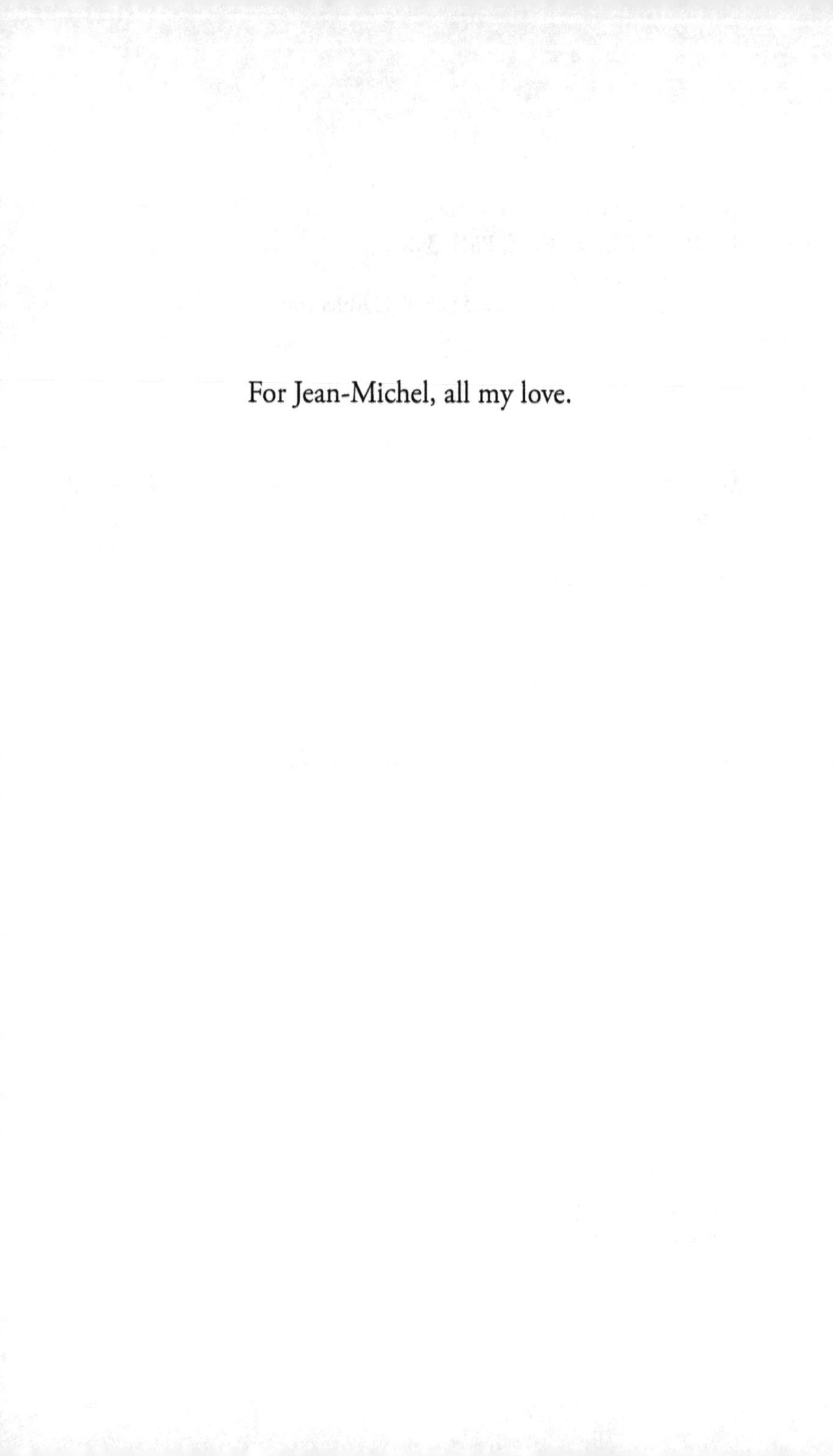

For Jean-Michel, all my love.

Acknowledgements

Special thanks to my family and friends who encouraged me every step of the way—particularly Jerusha for her suggestions and enthusiasm.

Epigraph

"One person can't be responsible for another person's happiness." *An Unwanted Guest* by Shari Lapena

PROLOGUE

How much time had elapsed?

After one final tetanic spasm, Robin's back arched. A minute later, she became flaccid. Her dead body lay sprawled along the beige carpet like a broken doll. Blood oozed out her mouth, pooling underneath thick box braids.

Careful not to slip in blood splatter, she bent down and checked for a pulse but detected nothing on Robin's warm wrist. Fingerprints. *Could police get prints off skin?*

She scanned the living room and considered what she had touched. It didn't matter. Her prints were all over the house, and there wasn't time to wipe everything down. *Need to get out of here and think.*

In reaching for the doorknob, she noticed blood droplets on her knuckles. Without thinking, she reached into her coat pocket for a tissue. *Damn.* Blood smeared along the sleeve. Time to go.

At the front door, she paused and glanced around once more. Certain nothing was left behind, she dashed outside for the car. *Had the neighbors heard anything?*

Across the neighborhood, street decorations heralded the upcoming holidays. Plastic reindeer and inflatable snowmen dotted lawns. Christmas ornaments promised gaiety and good cheer.

Inside the car, dread pressed down upon her. *Was there time to drive away without being seen?*

It was the middle of the day. Most people in this middle-class neighborhood were at work, and their children were in school dreaming about the pending holiday break.

Tinsel rustled in the wind. Cold December weather created an empty street. From the rearview mirror, the neighborhood looked vacant. She had a chance.

With a deep breath, she started the engine and reversed down the driveway—not too fast or too slow. *Don't attract attention.*

But when Robin's body was discovered … *Would anyone identify her car?*

With a sigh, she rested her head on the steering wheel. This was supposed to have been a quick errand. *How did it end like this?*

Chapter 1

Laughter danced around the Green Pastures Café conference room like leaves on a spring breeze, but it was actually a Saturday autumn afternoon in downtown Greensboro. Peppermint and cinnamon scented the air, announcing Thanksgiving had passed and a new year stood on the threshold. Already, people were wearing the festive colors of Christmas.

Myaisha noticed a café server wearing an elf's cap passing around receipts. She searched in her wallet for loose change, preferring to tip in cash.

In the conference room, standing before a brick wall of shelves containing books and assorted bric-a-brac, Tina stood on tiptoes, straining above the din of conversations.

"Don't forget *Think It, Ink It* is on Thursday evenings at the library."

"Ladies, please," René said, her eyes boring into the attendees. "We're almost finished with the announcements."

Tina's round face lit up. She wiped a few strands of thick black hair off her forehead. "Remember, next month we vote on whether to join the women's national writing organization. Complete your ballots and we'll tally the results before our next meeting." She pivoted toward René and lowered her voice. "Anything else?"

Shaking her head, René dismissed the attendees, and the Greensboro Women of Color Writing Group meeting concluded.

Myaisha and Deniece rose but remained beside their chairs. Most women exited from the conference room's rear door leading into the café. Once the room emptied, Myaisha donned her fedora while approaching Tina and René.

At that moment, another group member was speaking with Tina. While she waited, Myaisha observed René's necklace.

"How unusual." With her fingertips, Myaisha probed the figurine dangling along a gold chain. "Is that a lion with a goat's head?"

Grimacing, René retreated, causing the figurine to slip from Myaisha's fingers.

"Yes, it was a gift."

"Sorry." Myaisha smiled. "It's unique."

Before she could inquire further, René's sister, Robin, skipped over, linked her arm with René's, and interrupted.

"Chi, you ready to go? I have an appointment."

A bloom crested over René's freckled face as she extricated her arm from Robin's embrace.

"Hello," Myaisha said, extending a hand forward.

Robin faced her. "Oh, hi. I'm sorry. Did I interrupt?"

"No, it's quite all right," Myaisha said as they shook hands.

"Haven't we met?" Robin's forehead wrinkled with thought. "I think … Oh, yes. You're the doctor."

"Yes. I believe you attended our November meeting."

"Of course. It's nice to see you again. Chi speaks about you all the time. You helped launch her childcare business."

"A little," Myaisha said, glancing at René.

"I'd love to speak with you sometime about business opportunities. If Chi wasn't busy, I'd stay and chat now." Hollywood white teeth contrasted against Robin's slick red lips, accentuating her ebony skin. "Well, we should be going." Without allowing René an opportunity to reply, Robin headed for the exit.

"I'm coming," René said. Then she addressed Myaisha. "Excuse me. See you Thursday." Pivoting on her back foot, René jogged behind Robin and left.

Myaisha stared at the departing sisters—something about twins intrigued her. She shrugged and turned around to find Deniece conversing with Tina. The other group member had departed.

"So, when is your book coming out?" Deniece asked.

Tina's face glistened. "Oh, not 'til sometime next year. I finally got an agent."

"How long does it take to traditionally publish a book?" Deniece asked, her forehead creasing.

Chuckling, Tina gathered her purse and several folders off a nearby table. "A year, maybe two. Getting an agent is simply the first step. It'll be a long time before I publish anything."

"Why query for an agent then?" Deniece grumbled.

While discussing the pros and cons of traditional publishing, the women snaked between abandoned folding chairs and exited the conference room into the café.

"Tina, you're the first person in our group to get an agent," Myaisha said, bringing up the rear. "We're behind you. Any support you need, let us know."

"Are you guys going to get something to eat?" Deniece asked.

"No," Tina said. "Ian's dropping by. My aunt is visiting from the Philippines and tonight she's making his favorite dishes."

A vision of Detective Ian de Jesus flashed across Myaisha's memory. She recalled enormous biceps.

"Mmm." Deniece licked her lips. "I have dibs on leftovers."

Tina threw back her head and laughed. "There won't be any leftovers. If you want food, you better stop by."

"How long is your aunt visiting?" Deniece asked.

While Tina and Deniece conversed, Myaisha sauntered over to the café counter and ordered fried okra, red beans and rice, cornbread, and fried chicken.

Christmas music murmured from hidden speakers, playing *What Christmas Means to Me* by Stevie Wonder. While waiting for her order, Myaisha admired the black and white photos of Civil Rights-era icons hanging on the red brick walls. She remembered Boomer, her black Labrador, and requested two servings of chicken.

Since she didn't have to work at the urgent care clinic tonight, Myaisha had planned a quiet day at home reading a book. Because her medical office was closed this Saturday morning, her entire weekend was patient-free.

"Bye." Myaisha waved, completing her order as Tina departed.

"Did you want something?" she asked Deniece, who stood beside her at the counter.

"No, I ate earlier."

"That was a snack." Myaisha accepted the takeout containers from the server. As they headed toward the exit of the café, Myaisha checked the bag to verify its contents.

Deniece held the door open. "It'll have to be enough. I have a few pounds to work off. My pants are strangling my hips."

Myaisha's drooping eyes considered the food containers. "I could afford to lose some weight too. We can exercise together."

They crossed the street toward the parking lot. On the right, in a corner of the lot, Myaisha observed René and Robin standing beside a car, arguing. She stopped and watched. However, Robin detected her scrutiny and tapped René's arm. Their conversation paused as they eyeballed her.

Myaisha raised her voice to compensate for the traffic noise. "Everything okay?"

Without responding, both sisters waved, jumped in their car, and zipped out of the lot.

Half a minute passed as Myaisha observed their car stopped at a traffic light. Hands flew back and forth between their faces as each sister gesticulated animatedly. Though she couldn't hear anything, it was clear Robin and René were quarreling. *But about what?*

The traffic light flashed green, and the coupe sped forward and through the light.

As she started toward her own car, Myaisha spied a white Camaro whip out of the lot and rush across the intersection behind René's car before the traffic light changed.

Odd. The Camaro had been idling in the parking space as Myaisha and Deniece exited the café. *Why would someone be following* René?

Myaisha shook her head free of suspicion. *You read too many mysteries.*

"Have you noticed a change in René?" Deniece asked, holding the food containers as Myaisha unlocked the car doors.

After settling behind the steering wheel, Myaisha checked traffic before exiting the lot. "Possible. She's been reserved since—"

"Donald dumped her—yeah, real hush hush about it. But what can you say when your sister steals your man?"

"Robin didn't steal him. You can't steal a man."

"But you can date someone other than the guy your sister was seeing." Deniece opened the smaller food container and crunched on a piece of okra.

"Close it. I don't want the okra to become limp."

"Kinda like Donald." Deniece laughed.

Myaisha side-eyed her. "That's not funny."

"Not to René either."

Twenty minutes later, Myaisha steered her car into the cul de sac where she lived.

"I don't know what I'd do if my sister dated my ex."

"I'd kill her." Deniece grinned and popped another piece of okra into her mouth.

CHAPTER 2

Tires screeched as René's small coupe weaved between the parade of cars on the used car lot. Cardboard yellow sticker signs advertised '*Deep Discounts*' on car windshields.

Robin gripped the door handle and glared at her sister's profile.

René shifted the coupe into park and idled in front of double glass doors leading into the Evans Used Cars dealership showroom.

"There," René said, staring out the windshield.

Part of Robin hoped Donald would exit the dealership at that moment and the three of them could discuss the situation.

Older than her by five minutes, René had always been the dependable sister. Nothing reckless or unexpected about her. She'd been on the school honor roll consistently since grade school. Accepted to college on scholarship, and not once had she given their parents a moment of consternation.

During an eighth-grade school assembly, their father had beamed with delight at René's achievements. He had regarded Robin with questioning brows. "Why can't you get good grades like your sister?"

Instead of replying to his comment, Robin had cried. Though he apologized, he had asked a good question. *Why hadn't she done better in school?*

Robin wasn't stupid. No, she simply didn't believe it mattered. She had no interest in attending college. Early in life, she had decided comfort and ease would be her mantra. Like the lilies of the field in Matthew 6:28, neither would she labor or toil.

Still avoiding Robin's gaze, René said, "This has gotta stop. I'm not dropping you off here again. He's gonna hurt you."

With a surly grin, Robin released the seatbelt and opened the passenger car door. "This is real love. Donald wants to take care of me—and I'll take care of him."

"It's just sex."

"Was it only sex when he dated you?"

René's jaw clenched as the car door slammed.

Robin bit her lip. She'd gone too far. As she leaned toward the window, René stepped on the accelerator and peeled out of the lot.

Though her actions were selfish, Robin knew she was a better judge of male character than her sister. Donald was wrong for René. An older man wanted excitement, adventure. Traits she possessed.

Sure, he'd dated René first. But once they'd met, Donald had realized his mistake. *Why couldn't René get over it?*

On espadrilles laced up her shimmering dark legs, Robin pirouetted toward the entrance. "Forget it."

A man exiting the showroom held the door open for her.

She bestowed a lascivious smile upon him. "Thank you." Her back straightened, feeling him ogling her behind as she entered the brightly lit showroom. Her full hips sashayed her appreciation.

Inside the building on the right, a man leaned against a desk watching an enormous television screen positioned on the far wall broadcasting a sports game.

"Hello, Milton. Is Donald in?" Although Robin asked, her strut continued toward the rear offices.

"Hey, Robin. Yeah, I think he's with someone."

His last sentence was spoken to her back because she had already proceeded toward the wide hallway leading to the offices.

Out front, the building contained a small showroom. In the rear were four rooms—two on each side. Donald had designated the smallest as an employee break room. The others served as business offices.

Bypassing the restroom, Robin chuckled at the site of Cynthia—Donald's bookkeeper and nursemaid. Seated before a large calculator with her head bent over a ledger, Cynthia stared at a computer screen. Robin didn't stop to speak with her.

On the opposite side of the hallway and one door down, loud voices seeped under a flimsy plywood door.

For a moment, Robin's hand hesitated above the doorknob as she eavesdropped.

"Dad, I can't live on this salary."

"Well, you'll have to. Your sister does."

"She doesn't work for you. Besides, I'm also in school."

"There's a recession coming—in case you haven't heard. I've already let most of the staff go. I—"

Uninterested in family drama other than her own, Robin rapped on the door, simultaneously opening it.

Tap, tap, tap.

"Am I interrupting?"

Neither man had an opportunity to reply before she sauntered across the room and rested on the desk in front of a heavy-set dark man seated in a plush leather chair. Her curvaceous legs crossed as she leaned across the desk.

Donald grinned. Fluorescent lights glinted off his gold-capped left front tooth.

"Hey, babe." Large lips swallowed her mouth as they kissed.

On the other side of the desk, a younger man—the spitting image of Donald—grimaced and rose.

Robin ended their embrace and ambled behind the large leather chair as her hands caressed Donald's shoulders. "I'm sorry, but I had to see you."

"No problem. Junior was leaving." Donald's weighty gaze glowered at his son, hinting toward the open door.

Junior, his lips tight, glared at Robin. "What do you want? Haven't you taken enough of his money?"

The leather chair slammed against the back wall as Donald stormed forward. "Look here—"

Because he vaulted out of the seat, Robin scooted backward away from the desk and bumped against the window.

"You better learn some respect." Donald's beefy finger darted before Junior's face.

Nostrils flaring, Junior eyed his dad. "Or what? You'll fire me. Go ahead. I never wanted this dumb job anyway." Junior marched away.

Walls shook as the office door banged shut behind him.

Donald bolted for the door, wrenched it open, and dashed from the room. In the hallway, Cynthia accosted him, impeding his pursuit of Junior.

"Mr. Evans," she said, "we need to discuss these expenses."

For a moment, Donald stared over her shoulder, watching his son depart. His shoulders heaved as he brushed against her and headed back toward his office.

"Not now. I told you I'll get to it later."

"But Mr. Evans, the bills …"

Her voice trailed away as Donald re-entered his office and the door banged shut.

During the exchange in the hallway, Robin sat in the leather chair rummaging inside desk drawers. When she heard Donald returning, she quickly shut them and pretended to be reading on her cell phone.

"What did Cynthia want?" she asked.

"Business. Nothing you need to worry about."

Beside his desk, Donald opened a mini refrigerator and removed a carafe. He poured a sea-green thick fluid into a mug, followed by a dollop of protein powder.

"Do you like the smoothies I made for you?" Robin asked, extending her legs along the desktop.

Donald strolled up to the desk, rubbing his thick fingers along her calves. "They taste like grass, but they give me energy." His hungry mouth smiled down at her. A drop of green smoothie clung to the corner of his lips.

Robin swung her legs off the desk, rose, and allowed him to retake his seat. She relaxed against the corner of the desk again.

"I'll make a fortune selling them in my yoga shop. When are we going to talk about starting my business?"

After a deep inhale, Donald sipped more smoothie. "I told you, babe. It's gonna take a while."

"How long?" Her slick red lips pouted.

"Why do you need a place in Charlotte? Greensboro is—"

"Provincial. I want to be in a city."

"This is a city."

"A larger city." She ambled around the room. "Maybe I should go back to Chicago."

Donald's gaze simmered. "Back to your ex?"

The corner of her lip curled. "There are other people in Chicago than Terrence. People who will support my yoga business. Or maybe I should be alone for a while—like René suggested—before settling down with another man."

Green contacts made her cat-like eyes glimmer. She peeked toward Donald, before her gaze darted away. In front of the mini fridge, she pretended to read ingredients on a container of powdered protein.

Not a minute elapsed before Donald—as she expected—hustled to her side.

"I told you, I'll take care of it." His hand rested on her hip.

Like a slow wave along the Carolina coast, her shoulders dipped. She slipped away from him and sauntered around the room. "You seem to have your hands full, and I don't have time for family drama. First, take care of your personal business, then call me when you're available."

She headed for the door but knew he would intercede.

On cue, he bustled in front of her with open pleading arms. "Don't go. I promise. Give me 'til the end of the month. You can stay at my place for now."

Slender arms crossed over her ample cleavage. "I'm not staying in another woman's bed."

"I'll buy another mattress."

"I want another place."

"Fine. Stay with René until I figure things out. It'll take time to get an apartment *and* start a business. I need to move some money around."

She feigned a pouty lip as her sinewy arms embraced him around the neck. She simpered, her voice solicitous. "Okay. I'll wait."

Donald's rough hands brought her hips against his pelvis. She allowed him to explore her body as she teased a flickering tongue along his neck. His cheap cologne reminded her of rubbing alcohol. She would have to buy him a different scent—with his money, of course.

Excitement grew inside him. He pressed her up against the wall.

A giggle trickled from between her lips. He lifted the corner of her skirt. Heat escaped her mouth as she panted into his ear.

"And Donald, you better not disappoint me."

For the moment, he did not disappoint. His moaning throbbed in her ears. Robin hoped though, he had more to deliver. If not, perhaps Terrence …

CHAPTER 3

The rhythmic beeping of the pulse oximetry machine mimicked the child's heartbeat, echoing throughout the urgent care clinic. Myaisha auscultated his chest and smiled up at the parents.

"Once the breathing treatment finishes, I'll discharge him home," she said, dropping the stethoscope into her coat pocket. "The RSV and flu tests were negative. Give him plenty of fluids and follow up with your doctor tomorrow. The medical assistant will give you a handout on what to watch for tonight."

Screech.

A muted green curtain slid across the metal rod, dividing the toddler from the other bed in the trauma bay.

Myaisha peeked into the other compartment and gazed over at the nurse. "Are we ready?"

"Yes, Dr. Douglas. I cleansed the wound. He's ready for stitches."

With a wave to the child whose face was covered by a nebulizer mask, Myaisha closed the curtain and approached a somber man lying on the gurney. These were the last two remaining patients after a long, busy Sunday clinic. She washed her hands before slipping into sterile gloves.

The man reclined along a stretcher with his head on a pillow, while she considered different options for stitching the wound.

"You okay, Carl?"

"Yes, ma'am. I'm fine." The paleness under his tan contradicted his comment.

She fought to hide a grin and considered the six-foot-tall, 230-pound Carl lying on the gurney with a laceration along his lateral arm. *The bigger they are, the harder they cry.*

Bending down, she scrutinized the wound, inhaling scents of wood and paint. "You're doing fine. Face the curtain."

Once Carl averted his gaze, Myaisha injected lidocaine with epinephrine around the wound where she intended to insert sutures.

"He'll be fine," AJ said, grinning up at her from a seat beside the gurney.

Myaisha gave him a slight smile. She and AJ had dated consistently since their meeting six months ago during an ACLS recertification class. He impressed her with his intellect and passion for history and museums. Now, she admired his patience and caring for a fellow firefighter.

"It's a flesh wound," AJ said, "but I thought he should get it stitched up. I'm glad you were working tonight." A corner of his mouth curled up, slightly revealing his dimples.

Myaisha ignored his banter. Besides treating a patient, she didn't want the clinic staff aware of her personal relationships. She segregated private and work life.

The nurse arranged a suture kit on a portable metal tray. Forceps pinched the skin around Carl's arm as Myaisha tested to determine if the anesthetic had taken effect.

"Can you feel that?"

"No," Carl said.

"Good." She began closing the gash.

"What happened?" the nurse asked Carl while handing Myaisha a pair of scissors.

"I slipped and a 4x4 slammed into my arm."

Seated on a low wheeled stool, AJ peered up at Myaisha, observing her handiwork. Aware of his gaze, she concentrated on stitching.

"We're making modifications to his house," AJ said to no one in particular, "and instead of making two trips, Superman here tried carrying drywall *and* his tools."

"I didn't want to drop the automatic drill," Carl said, his blanched face glaring at AJ. "Anyway, I tripped and cut myself on the corner of a piece of wood."

Using gauze and antiseptic, Myaisha cleansed the skin and evaluated her work. "Not bad, but you'll have a scar. The inner layer of sutures is absorbable, but the top layer should be removed in ten to fourteen days. Instructions will be on the discharge papers."

The curtain parted as the nurse departed to retrieve paperwork.

Myaisha ripped off the gloves and washed her hands. "What renovations are you making?"

Less squeamish now and regaining color, Carl sat up, tossing the pillow aside. "We're not remodeling but fixing it up to be habitable."

AJ answered the frown on her face. "Carl bought a 'fixer-upper' from Evans Realty. Have you heard of them?"

"No," Myaisha said, wrapping Carl's wound in bandages. "What's wrong with the house?"

"I can't believe it passed inspection," Carl said as his face sagged.

"Humph," AJ huffed. "There was no inspection. That piece of crap should've been condemned."

Myaisha considered AJ's attitude. He acted more upset than Carl. *What was their relationship?*

"Did you complain? To the city, I mean."

While AJ chuckled, Carl moaned.

"We've done nothing but complain," the latter said. "Reggie's been down to city hall so often, they might start charging him rent."

"Reggie?" Myaisha asked.

"My husband." Carl laid his discharge papers from the nurse on the gurney while he slipped his arms into a sweater.

She nodded, detecting a piercing glare from AJ. *What was that about?* "It sounds terrible."

AJ said, "Real estate is nothing but chaos right now—people losing their homes. The city can't address all the problems even if they wanted to."

"Friends have been helping us get the house in order," Carl said. "Even some of the guys from work." Once dressed, Carl shook Myaisha's hand. "Thank you, ma'am."

A line exited the trauma room as Carl proceeded toward the front desk, followed by the nurse. Myaisha brought up the rear with AJ hovering at her side. She perceived he wanted to speak privately but waited for him to take the initiative.

He leaned toward her ear. "Thanks. I wasn't sure how you'd react about him—"

"Being gay." She rubbed his arm. "I'm not homophobic."

He smiled. "Thanks for stitching him up. I—"

"Dr. Douglas," the medical assistant interrupted, "someone came in as the last guy left. She insists on being seen. I told her we closed ten minutes ago."

Myaisha's shoulders slouched. "That's fine. I'll see her."

When the medical assistant hustled away, AJ whispered, "Call you later."

Before sprinting to the computer to complete charting, Myaisha gave him a tepid grin.

Five minutes later the nurse returned, her lips in a flat line.

Myaisha's brows lifted at the nurse's scowl.

"She walks in late and can't pay," the nurse said.

Deep breath. Myaisha stretched her back and draped the stethoscope around her shoulders. "There's a sliding scale for uninsured patients."

"Yeah, but the billing clerk left, and we don't know what to charge."

"Not our problem. Collect her information. The biller will figure it out in the morning."

Minutes later, Myaisha tapped twice on the exam room door then entered. She gaped.

"Hello, Robin. What ..." Surprised, she used the seconds it took to wash her hands to judge the situation. "How can I help you?"

"I didn't know you worked here. Chi said you had an office in Greensboro."

While drying her hands, Myaisha said, "I work here to make extra money."

Robin's gaze narrowed. "I would've thought a doctor made enough money."

"It also keeps me up on my suturing and splinting skills. I don't get a lot of experience in the office. But if you're uncomfortable, I can suggest another clinic." There wasn't another urgent care open at that time of night within fifty miles, but she didn't want Robin to feel obligated to stay. An ER was ten miles away.

After nearly a minute, Robin said, "No, it's fine. Medical care is confidential, right?"

"Absolutely. I never discuss patient care outside the office."

Robin exhaled. "Good."

"So, how can I help you?"

"Well, for the past month, I've developed these bruises—especially on my back."

Myaisha regarded Robin's outstretched arm. The two-centimeter bruise on her forearm was blackish purple. Robin denied any pain on palpation. Four other bruises of similar color and size covered Robin's upper extremities.

It was going to be a longer night.

After handing Robin a cloth gown, Myaisha said, "I'll step out while you get undressed. I need to examine your entire body."

Chapter 4

The clinic clock chimed ten o'clock as the nurse exited the exam room carrying two vials of blood labeled with Robin's demographics. Myaisha re-entered the room and perched on a stool.

"Remember what I said, if you're being abused—"

"I'm not in an abusive relationship." A fluffy soft pink sweater slid over Robin's head. "At least not anymore." She spoke the last bit before departing the room.

Myaisha stared at her departing back, vacillating between following Robin or leaving the matter alone. During the twenty-minute office visit, she'd questioned and cajoled. But Robin had remained steadfast about not being assaulted. *How many patients had she treated who made similar assertions?*

People needed support, despite their denials. The handout she provided Robin included numbers and resources to assist abuse victims—including her private office number.

In the charting area, where the nurse prepared the blood specimens for the laboratory courier, Myaisha sank into a chair and completed Robin's chart. Afterward, she massaged her temples. Her mind became thick. *Maybe she should approach Robin privately outside the office.* If she was careful not to refer to the office visit, it shouldn't skirt HIPAA restrictions. It would require more thought.

With her eyes glued to paperwork, the nurse asked, "Did someone hit her?"

The computer monitor blinked off as Myaisha shut it down. "She denied it."

"The front door's locked," the medical assistant said, returning from the lobby.

Dropping the stethoscope into her tote bag, Myaisha asked, "Ready?"

Both the nurse and medical assistant nodded and en masse they departed from the building's rear exit, huddled together against the cold weather. The back door locked behind them, snapping shut.

"Good night, Dr. Douglas," the medical assistant said, dashing into a nearby idling car.

With a hurried goodbye, the nurse drove off too.

Zipping up her leather jacket, Myaisha held onto her trilby and bolted for her car. Once inside, she circled around to the front of the building prepared to enter the main road. Down the street, a signal light changed green.

When Myaisha craned her head right to scan for traffic, she glimpsed movement near the urgent care center entrance. In the building's front parking lot, she noticed Robin—who wasn't alone. Myaisha reversed and drove toward the entrance.

Thrum.

On the car's console, her cell phone shimmied. She snatched it up and hit answer. "Yes?"

"Is this a bad time?" AJ asked. "I thought the clinic closed at 9:30."

Even as she spoke, Myaisha observed Robin speaking to an unknown person in a Camaro. "It does, but we had a late patient."

"Are you on your way home?"

"No. A woman is outside the clinic speaking to someone in a car. I want to make sure she's okay."

AJ's voice raised. "What's going on?"

"Nothing. I—"

In an instant, a hand jutted out of the car and grabbed Robin about the wrist. She struggled against the person's grasp.

"Oh, no."

"Is there a problem? Call 911."

The Honda accelerated as Myaisha raced toward the melee, dropping the cell phone onto the passenger seat. AJ shouted questions and advised her to call the police. Before she reached Robin, the Camaro's engine revved, and the car exploded out of the parking lot.

Pulling up beside Robin, Myaisha scrolled down the window. "Are you all right?"

A plastered grin crept along Robin's face. "Yes. It was nothing."

"We should call the police," Myaisha said, viewing Robin's wrist for signs of bruising.

"No, forget it." Robin shook her head and hurried away. "I'm fine."

"Do you want me to drive you home?"

Robin's jaw clenched. "No, thank you."

"Where are you going?" Myaisha scanned the area as they spoke.

"I'm staying with René."

"I'll follow you home."

"No," Robin sniped, biting her bottom lip. The plastered grin returned. "I'll be okay."

Robin charged into her car, started the ignition, and sped off.

Monday evening traffic between Kernersville and Greensboro was steady. However, Myaisha managed to remain two to three cars behind Robin even on the freeway.

Because the phone was still on, Myaisha placed it on speaker. "AJ?"

"I'm on my way. What happened?"

She watched Robin signaling to exit the freeway and duplicated those actions while answering.

"The last patient was arguing with someone in the parking lot. I wanted to make sure she was okay, but we've both left. You can return home."

"I don't like you working at night. You should carry a gun or learn self-defense."

"We aren't allowed to bring weapons into the clinic."

"Then you need to learn self-defense. I—"

"AJ, I'm fine. I need you to write something down for me."

Robin turned off Interstate 40 onto state Highway 68 in High Point—not Greensboro.

"What is it?"

"A license plate." She gave him the information.

At the bottom of the off-ramp, Robin caught the green signal light and turned right. The car in front of Myaisha slowed down long enough for the light to turn red.

"Dammit," Myaisha swore, slapping the steering wheel.

"What happened?" AJ asked.

She finally turned right onto Highway 68, but Robin's car was no longer in sight. "I lost her."

"That plate's not from North Carolina," AJ said.

"No, it's from Illinois."

CHAPTER 5

Howling winds tossed around long pine trees framing René's High Point office window. December's winter tempest bled through the cement walls. She shivered and tightened the sweater over her shoulders, studying budget figures provided by her accountant.

Careful management and judicious spending had brought her childcare business into a positive cash flow for the past two quarters. She reclined into the cushioned chair. It had been a long, arduous journey.

René, obsessed with organization, had calculated her business and household budgets to the penny in anticipation of opening this second location. Although the High Point office hadn't opened as planned—nothing in business or life ever proceeded on schedule, Robin's unexpected arrival added another level of complication.

For three years, René had struggled to establish a childcare business in the Triad region of Winston-Salem, High Point, and Greensboro. Although she'd grown up in Chicago, René had fled the Windy City once she'd completed her undergraduate degree, placing distance between herself, her family, and especially Robin.

In Greensboro, she had developed a sense of security, built new friendships, and a romantic relationship—until her sister's unannounced arrival.

The idea of refusing to help Robin had danced along the edges of René's mind, but of course, she hadn't. Older by five minutes, she felt obligated to protect Robin, despite any inconveniences. Even if she wanted to refuse, her parents wouldn't allow it.

Their differences were biblical. She, the older twin, was loved and adored by her father—they were both intellectual high achievers. Dark, svelte Robin resembled their mom in appearance and attitude.

Like Esau and Jacob, they'd fought for attention and favor all their lives. Though the birthright technically belonged to her, bubbly, beautiful Robin had eclipsed quiet, reserved René from the moment they'd abandoned the womb—except in the eyes of their father.

However, her father had acceded to the wishes of their mother, and René had always been expected to make sacrifices for Robin. But when Robin stole Donald—

Crack.

The pencil twisted between René's fingers snapped.

"Ms. Jones?" An office assistant hovered in the doorway.

René jerked to attention as the pencil crumbled onto her desk. "What is it?"

"A parent would like to speak with you."

As the assistant held the door open, René exited her office.

Over the next fifteen minutes, René conducted a tour of the childcare facility, assuring the new mother they could be trusted to care for the shy toddler.

Back in her office, René opened a drawer full of menus and considered where to order lunch. Her cell phone rang.

The screen read Robin. For a moment, she considered ignoring it, but she didn't.

"Yeah?" she asked.

"What's wrong?"

"I'm working."

Melodious tones drummed in the background of Eartha Kitt singing *Santa Baby*. Robin giggled. "It's lunchtime. Even great businesswomen eat."

René bit back a rejoinder. "What. Do. You. Want."

"You're my sister. I thought we could spend lunch together."

A high school memory flashed across René's mind. A time when she'd been eating lunch alone on the bleachers. Her friends were a small tight group, but they were solely focused on their GPAs. During lunch, they congregated in the library, studying class notes in preparation for the next exam or quiz.

But that day, René had wanted to enjoy the sunshine. Chicago winters were brutal, and she loved spring. She had asked Robin to join her for lunch.

"Where are you going?" Robin had asked.

"Nowhere. I want to sit outside. Come on. We're sisters. Let's do something together for once."

Gazing over René's shoulder, Robin had said, "Not today. I'm going to the pizza joint around the corner with some friends."

"Can I come?"

A moment of incredulity suspended between them, then Robin chuckled. "You wouldn't fit in. We talk about fashion, not fractions."

Robin had disappeared into a boisterous crowd of giggling teenagers.

Swiveling her chair around, René glanced out her office window. "Would you turn down the music? I can't hear you."

The music died away. "Happy?" Robin asked.

"I don't have time for this. Tell me—"

"I need a ride."

"Where are you?" René asked, glimpsing menus scattered across her desk.

"At Donald's."

"Why—"

"Not now. We can argue about it later. It's important. *Please*."

The last word shot home. Robin never begged. It must be serious.

"Give me ten minutes." René slid the menus into a desk drawer. She donned her coat, checking in the pockets for her gloves. *What trouble was Robin in this time?*

Chapter 6

Tall, knobby trees shaded the suburban neighborhood street. Lack of sunlight further decreased the temperature. René appreciated shade during the summer, but it made winter's bite harder.

She counted five homes on the street with Christmas decorations. A six-foot Santa waved to her across a green lawn studded with reindeer. A blow-up snowman saluted beside a gloomy crepe myrtle. People decorated earlier each year. Soon holiday decorations would go up after Halloween, she mused.

Her mind circled back to last winter. She and Donald had lounged together on his patio deck, admiring the winter foliage while planning their future together.

There had always been an excuse why he wouldn't—couldn't—marry her. His divorce was new. His kids would cause drama. Finances were complicated. But she wasn't concerned because she loved him, and he her. Whether or not they married hadn't mattered. The institution meant little to René since Donald belonged to her.

Then she'd made the mistake of introducing him to Robin. Her twin sister had arrived unexpectedly and needed a job. Donald knew people and René had requested his help.

René hoped her boyfriend would find her sister a job. But like a dial moved by the magnetic pull of earth's core, Donald's feet—and heart—gravitated toward Robin. Men had always been enamored by Robin. Not simply her beauty, but her buoyant character.

People described Robin as charismatic. To René, her sister acted silly and immature. *Would they consider Robin charismatic if she had a hooked nose without an hourglass figure?* Probably not. Charisma was a generic term bestowed upon the young and beautiful who were forgiven for being slack and selfish.

At first, René hadn't worried. She figured Donald and Robin were engaging in harmless flirting. Sisters honored certain boundaries—until they didn't.

Within days of meeting Donald, Robin had slept with him—deliberately flaunting their tryst without confessing their mutual attraction. René resented Robin but forgave her. As for Donald … *Had he ever loved her?*

René questioned every moment of their relationship. *But did she have a right to be upset?* Her relationship with Donald had begun during his marriage. And René had heard rumors of his prior infidelities. In fact, Donald had admitted to an indiscretion with his office assistant. Still, like a fool, she'd loved him. Trusted him. Made certain—

Once she'd learned about Robin's affair with Donald, René had spent nights devising torture mechanisms to castrate him before slowly killing him. When she'd confronted him about Robin, he'd deflected. Then he ghosted her calls.

Over the past month, her murderous rage had dwindled to a simmering anger. More crucial things now occupied her mind. She focused on business and writing.

Poetry provided an outlet for her repressed anger. Dark, ugly thoughts flowed from her mind and onto the pages of her journals. She hid those words from prying eyes, afraid to acknowledge the hurt festering inside her soul.

René had had enough of driving Robin to and from Donald's home and office. When she picked up Robin this time, she'd explain things would change. If Donald wanted to see Robin, he could loan her one of his trashy used cars. *How long would their affair last when Donald tallied up the expenses associated with keeping Robin happy?*

After parking in the driveway, René trotted up to Donald's home and tapped on the wooden front door. She rang the bell. Seconds later, she jiggled the knob. The front door glided open. René gasped.

Robin was splayed along the floor of Donald's beige carpet, convulsing. As if in a wind tunnel, time swooshed around her. She grew faint.

Rallying, René rushed to Robin's side. Her shoe slipped in splattered blood surrounding her sister's head like a syrupy lake of death.

With one hand, she pushed thick black hair away from Robin's forehead. She gazed into the fluttering green eyes rolled back into her sister's head. René's fingers brushed against a scar behind Robin's ear from when they'd tried to pierce their own ears. She wiped blood away from Robin's lips, smearing makeup grotesquely along her cheeks.

Helpless, she frantically looked around the room but found nothing likely to help. She grabbed Robin's hand, but convulsions ripped it away. Removing the cell phone from her handbag, she dialed 911.

While it rang, she cried, "I'm so sorry. Please don't die."

The phone dropped onto the ground as she attempted CPR at the direction of the call center operator.

Robin's back arched and gurgled blood spewed from her mouth.

Like pistons, René's arms pumped on Robin's chest. Her mind swirled. *How did this happen?*

CHAPTER 7

Positioned in an established neighborhood closer to downtown Greensboro than not, the weathered brick home buzzed with police and rescue personnel. Todd's gait stalled as his gaze canvassed the nearby homes and scenery. A quiet neighborhood awaiting Christmas.

A police officer greeted him. "Detective, the first officers to arrive on scene are inside."

He frowned. "Why are we here? I heard the woman had a seizure."

"I never heard of a seizure causing massive bleeding." The officer led him into the house.

Before Todd reached the front door, he evaluated the area for any disturbance or irregularity. Upon entering the home, he observed a light-skinned, freckle-faced woman off to the left huddled on a recliner sobbing. He blocked out the woman's sorrow and examined the scene.

A different uniformed officer approached. "Detective Gamble?"

He acknowledged the officer with a slight nod.

"I thought you'd want to know …" The officer relayed information about what had occurred prior to the first unit arriving.

Todd's thin fingers tapped along his long, lean legs. While listening, he assessed the crime scene.

"If she was seizing, why didn't the paramedics take her to the hospital?"

"She was dead when they arrived."

On the floor five yards ahead of him lay a dark-skinned woman, her body bent awkwardly with one arm across her chest and the other strewn limply beside her face. Around the woman's head and torso, the once-beige carpet resembled a Jackson Pollock painting. Todd's stomach clenched.

Paramedics circled the area, gathering tubing and miscellaneous items discarded during resuscitation efforts.

"The victim's a Mrs. Robin Jones-Collins," the uniformed officer said, regarding a notebook. His head tilted toward the couch. "Over there's the sister, a Ms. René Jones. She came by to pick her sister up for lunch, found her seizing, and called 911."

While the officer consulted his notebook, Todd viewed the woman on the couch again, taking time to give a more comprehensive look.

"Can you believe they're twins?" the officer said. "The one in the chair could almost pass."

Though he nodded, Todd didn't speak. He considered the officer's assessment of Ms. Jones' fair skin and whether anyone would think she was White. Those thoughts retreated in his mind as he examined the victim up close, careful to avoid puddles of blood surrounding her body.

The women shared facial characteristics. In fact, he noticed a resemblance, save for the diametrical differences in their skin tones. The victim on the ground, despite the blood splatter congealed around her head, had been a beauty. Death hadn't disfigured her appearance—yet.

A large, muscular hand clapped Todd's shoulder. He glanced up at his partner, Detective Ian de Jesus.

"I'm going outside to interview the neighbors," Ian said, before bustling away.

Todd kneeled beside the body and inspected the victim's manicured bedazzled fingernails. On her fingers were three rings but no bruises or scars. One nail was chipped and another bent. He couldn't be sure, but it looked like blood under her nails. There was a bruise on her left wrist. The victim wore gold earrings and a thin gold necklace. *Had there been a fight? Did Mrs. Jones-Collins strike an attacker?*

Smacking his notebook along his palm, the uniformed officer returned. "Can they take the body away, Detective?"

"Who's in charge of forensics?"

The officer directed Todd to a woman standing in the kitchen wearing surgical gloves and scrubs. Before approaching her, Todd directed the officer to check the perimeter of the home and garage.

"And the trash cans," he shouted as the officer departed.

Two people with jackets displaying the words *FORENSICS* gathered the dead woman onto a litter.

"Before you take her away," Todd asked, "what have you got for me now?" Even as they reported, Todd scrutinized the foyer and living room.

Ian re-entered the house as forensics departed.

"The neighbors didn't hear anything until the sister …" Ian consulted his notepad. "René Jones—quote—began screaming her head off like a banshee."

"And the victim?"

'They've seen her around. Apparently, she was dating the homeowner."

Before Todd could reply, Ian answered his questioning brows.

"A Mr. Donald Evans."

Todd's gaze widened. He laid a hand on Ian's arm. "*Donald Evans?* The guy who owns the used car lot?"

"You know him?"

"Not personally, but I've seen his cheesy commercials. Big, ugly guy, balding with a monogrammed front gold tooth."

Ian winced. "Oh, yeah. I know who you mean. People still do gold caps?"

"I guess old guys do," Todd said, shrugging his shoulders and walking further into the living room.

"I asked one of the desk officers to contact him."

In concert, they inspected the living room.

With a hand movement, Todd halted a departing EMT. "What did you find when you arrived?"

A thick woman sporting a brown-blond ponytail clamped shut a plastic container resembling a toolbox. She said, "The victim stopped seizing before we arrived. But we got some oxygen on her and delivered a dose of valium and Narcan. You can never be sure."

"It didn't help though," the other EMT interjected. "She had vomited a lot of blood."

"I thought she was coughing up blood," Ian said, sizing up the EMT.

"We can't be sure, but it was a mess," the woman EMT answered. "By the time we got her hooked up, it was over. Fire got here within fifteen minutes of the call, but she was already gone. Flat lined. You guys arrived next. We stayed and treated the sister."

"She was in shock," the other EMT said.

Once they answered a few more questions, Todd dismissed them and addressed Ian. "You want to lead with the sister?"

"Sure," Ian said, dropping the notepad into his suit coat pocket.

In a recliner near a living room window, the sister rocked absently. Her reddened, swollen eyes drifted into the ether. Her fingers tightly gripped a limp tissue.

Ian trod over to her, squatted down beside the chair, and gazed up into her face. "Ms. Jones, we need to ask some more questions."

She didn't flinch.

Five feet behind Ian, Todd stood against the wall, observing, wondering if he should call the paramedics back.

With a pen, Ian lightly tapped the woman's hand.

Todd identified dried blood on her knuckles and palm. He frowned but then remembered the first officer on the scene reported the sister had performed CPR after calling 911.

In a slow pivot, Ms. Jones faced Ian. Her mouth didn't move but her eyes enlarged.

Todd frowned. *Was she about to lose it again?*

In a low, soft voice, Ian said, "I can call the paramedics over if you don't feel well."

Ms. Jones' chin trembled. "No, I …" Her gaze wandered around the living room, landing on the bloody patch of carpet. Her shoulders quivered.

In one swift motion, Ian stood and guided her from the recliner. He led Ms. Jones outside, keeping his body between her and the rest of the living room—namely the blood-soaked carpet.

After checking in with the forensics team and other officers, Todd followed Ian outside. Refreshed by cool night breezes, he surveyed the neighborhood, evaluating whether any of the gawkers looked suspicious.

A minute later, he sauntered over to where Ian interviewed Ms. Jones. Todd arrived in the middle of a question.

"So, your sister invited you over," Ian was saying.

Leaned up against the garage door, Ms. Jones dabbed her nose with a tissue. "Invited isn't—she needed a ride. Her car's in the shop."

Todd handed her a fresh tissue.

"Thank you." She spoke automatically. Her gaze remained on Ian.

"And when you got here?"

"The door was open. I came in and she was ..." Ms. Jones' gaze extended beyond Ian.

Concerned she might faint, Todd inched closer.

But her back stiffened and eyes sharpened. She eyed Ian as if seeing him for the first time. "Robin was on the floor having a seizure. I called 911 and performed CPR. Then the paramedics arrived."

The abrupt change in her demeanor hadn't been missed. Todd detected a distant, rehearsed tone behind her explanation.

Ian shot him a glance and a brief nod. His partner snapped the notebook closed. "We'd like you to come downtown to give a statement. Our car is by the mailbox."

Ms. Jones' body shrank from his outstretched hand. "No, I have to go to the hospital. Robin needs me."

With a somber face, Todd came forward. "Ma'am, she's dead. There isn't—"

"I want to be with my sister." Her chin thrust forward, and Ms. Jones bounded away, toward what Todd presumed to be her car.

"She's going to the ..." Ian stopped, perhaps aware of his insensitivity.

Todd caught up with her. "Ms. Jones, can we call someone for you? A family member or friend?"

He observed the emotion behind her watery eyes. She paused though, suggesting she considered his offer.

"I have my own car. I want to go home."

Todd placed a hand on the car door. "You shouldn't drive in the state you're in. We can give you a lift."

Her gaze landed on him a second before darting away. She pushed the door open, shoving him aside. "No, I want to be alone. I don't need help."

Without another word, she hopped in the car and drove off. A second later, Todd and Ian trailed behind her in the direction of the hospital.

Focused on traffic, Todd asked, "Did you notice something peculiar about her behavior?"

Candy wrapping paper crinkled as Ian crunched into a chocolate bar. "Yes."

"Twins supposedly have a special connection," Todd said, careful not to lose sight of Ms. Jones' car. "But she's afraid."

"Of being alone?"

"Or something else." He gave Ian a side glance. They both nodded.

Todd followed Ms. Jones out of the subdivision and onto the main road. However, the direction she turned was not toward the hospital. *Where was she going?*

Chapter 8

In a small room at the back of a craftsman-style house she'd converted into a medical office, Myaisha typed up patient notes. A December storm rattled the office windows, causing her to glance outside.

The door cracked open and Yvette, her office manager, sauntered inside.

From the gaping doorway created by Yvette's entrance, Myaisha spied a toddler running down the hallway. She laughed and pointed with her chin.

"There's someone behind you."

Once the toddler had been corralled by his mom, Yvette again approached Myaisha's desk.

"Mrs. Doctor, you need to complete these forms. I also signed for a certified letter." After depositing the envelope on the desk with other correspondence, Yvette exited the room and shut the door.

Pitter-patter of tiny feet, along with the shrieks and wails of children seeped under the door. With a letter opener, Myaisha slit open the document.

Her shoulders shrank, followed by a deep exhale. Another letter from the Greensboro Black Professionals Alliance. This missive read the organization—specifically their president,

Derrick Jenkins—was suing the estate of Candace Knight for one million dollars.

Their allegation of fraud seemed ludicrous given the indictments filed by the North Carolina state prosecutor last month against *their* organization. Three fraud allegations against the Greensboro Black Professionals Alliance, and one separately against Mr. Jenkins. Rumors circulating around town stated the organization was disbanding. In fact, the city of Greensboro had opened a separate investigation into the Alliance following … Myaisha tossed the envelope into her purse. Another item to discuss with the estate lawyer.

In June, her college friend, Candace Knight, had been murdered. After being designated executrix of the estate, Myaisha had investigated the homicide and helped the police catch a murderer.

However, her appointment as executrix had been less than ideal. In addition to fielding multiple lawsuits against Candace's estate, Myaisha had to contend with Knight family drama. Last month, she finally completed negotiations involving Candace's 1950s ranch home. Myaisha adored the house and was happy with the settlement.

Noises from the office quieted. A glance at the clock alerted her to the late hour. Grumblings from her stomach confirmed she had neglected to prepare anything for dinner. On the computer, she pulled up a list of local restaurants. A ping from her cell phone interrupted dinner arrangements.

"Hello?" she asked, having forgotten to first check the caller id.

"Hi. You have plans for dinner?"

AJ's deep voice made her smile. "No, I was looking over menus."

"How about I grab something and bring it over to your place?"

"Zoey coming?"

He laughed. "Of course. That's the only way your mean Labrador will let me in."

They discussed various eateries before she hung up.

She grabbed her handbag off a side chair and locked the office door.

"Good night." She waved to the staff on her way out.

"Good night, Mrs. Doctor."

The moniker Mrs. Doctor added a bounce to her step. Before her husband died from a stroke, the medical staff had distinguished them by the monikers Mr. and Mrs. Doctor respectively. She loved the sentimentality the words conveyed.

As she navigated home, her cell phone buzzed again. At the signal light, she hit the speaker button.

"AJ?"

"No, it's Deniece. Where are you at?"

"I'm on my way home. AJ's picking up takeout."

"Sounds like you have a nice evening planned."

Myaisha didn't want to discuss her relationship with AJ, not right then—even with her best friend. "What's up, D?"

"Did you hear about Robin?"

Focused on executing a left turn, Myaisha didn't reply immediately. "No, what happened?"

"She's dead."

***

It took less than five minutes for Myaisha to set the table. Because it had rained last night, the deck furniture was damp—not to mention it was cold, windy, and December. Instead, she set plates, cups, and utensils on the dining room table located in front of an expansive bay window overlooking the backyard.

By her side, AJ opened food containers. He stepped over Zoey, his brown Labrador, and added morsels to the dogs' food dishes.

"I can't believe she's dead," he said.

When AJ arrived, Myaisha explained what Deniece had shared about Robin's death.

"She was the lady you followed home last night, right?"

"Yes," Myaisha said, staring out the bay window. For a minute, she observed trees buoyed on the wind. Her thoughts flowed in another direction though.

Once the dogs began chomping on their food, AJ relaxed into a dining room chair. He also gazed out over the yard.

"You think it has something to do with the guy who assaulted her last night?" he asked, slurping up noodles.

A fork hovered before Myaisha's mouth. She recalled what had occurred outside the urgent care center. "To be honest, I don't know for sure it *was* a man. I didn't see the driver's face."

"Humph." AJ speared a shrimp and munched.

They ate in silence.

Minutes later, Myaisha said, "I should call the police."

"It couldn't hurt. Want me to look up the number?"

She scanned her contacts list. "No, I'll call Todd." She noticed AJ's brows rise. "Detective Gamble. He investigated Candace's murder."

"Um. How do you know he's assigned to this case?"

"I don't. But he'll know who to contact."

AJ nodded and completed his meal.

After what happened in June, Myaisha wondered if the homicide detective would be pleased to hear from her.

CHAPTER 9

People milled around the hospital lobby. An odor of sour milk hovered around a man with disheveled hair and tattered clothing sleeping across three plastic chairs. A line of people extended before a plexiglass window, waiting at the registration desk.

Todd and Ian strode to the front of the line, displayed their official police credentials, and were buzzed back into the emergency room triage area.

"Hello, ma'am," Todd said, addressing a woman in dark blue scrubs. "I'm looking for a Mr. Donald Evans. I was told he's in bay two."

The woman directed them toward the left side of the emergency room where partitions sectioned off smaller examination areas.

Rip.

Curtains sliced along a rod. Todd viewed an older Black man reclined on a gurney, a blood pressure cuff squeezing his left arm and a black brace on his right wrist. His chest slowly rose and fell.

Tick, tick, tick.

Like a clock, numbers on a cardiac monitor climbed, displaying blood pressure readings. The man sat up in bed and tore off the cuff.

A small thin man with hound-dog eyes, wearing blue scrubs reached across the hospital bed. "Your blood pressure is still high, Mr. Evans." A clear plastic badge clipped to the man's shirt identified him as a physician. "But it has decreased enough to discharge you home. Follow up with …"

Todd evaluated Mr. Evans, drowning out the doctor and beeping medical equipment.

With effort, Mr. Evans pulled down his shirt sleeve and buttoned it at the wrist. "Yeah, well, I'm ready to leave. I'll call my doctor tomorrow."

The ER physician departed, closing a heavy gray curtain behind him.

Ian stepped forward, handed over a business card, and made introductions. "Mr. Evans, I know an officer has already informed you about what happened at your house regarding Mrs. Jones-Collins—"

"I don't understand," Mr. Evans interrupted, wiping his damp brow. "Robin is—was—so young. How did she die?"

"There are a couple questions we'd like to ask. We can give you a lift home or to the station, whichever you prefer."

Todd winced at Ian's indifference to Mr. Evans' grief. Though his partner could be abrasive, this was unusual—even for Ian.

Mr. Evans scowled. "Do you know what happened to Robin? What caused her seizure?"

"We've just started our investigation, sir." Ian removed a notepad from his suit coat. "Would you like to answer questions here or at the station?"

"But you're homicide detectives," Mr. Evans said, reading the card and apparently weighing this new information. A minute passed as Mr. Evans sized up him and Ian, and they likewise scrutinized him.

"Was Robin murdered?"

Ian placed the pad and pen into his suit coat pocket. "We don't know. This is routine."

Not really. But Todd didn't flinch as he perceived Ian had a reason for approaching Mr. Evans in this manner.

"I … I can't go home," Mr. Evans stuttered. "Not yet. Not with …"

Recalling the bloody carpet in the living room, Todd understood the man's reticence.

"We can drop you off," Ian said. "Where would you like to go?"

Mr. Evans climbed off the gurney. "My office."

***

On leaving the hospital, Ian sat in the back of their department-issued car with Mr. Evans while Todd drove. His partner asked Mr. Evans routine background and demographic questions. Not until they pulled onto the used car lot had the questions approached the time of Mrs. Jones-Collins' death.

Preliminary information confirmed Mr. Evans had been at work when Ms. René Jones called EMS. Although the evidence would eliminate Mr. Evans of possible involvement, Todd maintained an open mind.

Cause of death hadn't been determined, but the bloody crime scene suggested an assault. Todd recalled broken fingernails but no blood on the deceased's hand. It was possible she'd fallen, hit her head during the seizure, and the bleeding had resulted from a massive head injury. *Too many possibilities.* He would have to wait for the autopsy.

Inside the building, they trekked single-file toward the rear offices. Mr. Evans invited them inside a square room with a large desk centered under a rectangular window.

Todd accepted a seat in front of the desk while Ian stood off to the side, away from the door.

A college dorm-sized refrigerator stood beside a small folding table. On the latter were a coffee machine and a half dozen cups of various sizes. From the refrigerator, Mr. Evans removed a clear plastic pitcher and poured a thick green slurry concoction into a cup.

"Want some?" he asked. "Robin made this for me. She planned on selling it to health food stores, and eventually marketing it to a beverage company." His voice trailed off as he stared at the cup.

Both Todd and Ian declined his offer.

Once he scooped a heap of protein powder onto his shake, Mr. Evans settled behind the desk.

"When was the last time you saw Mrs. Jones-Collins?" Todd asked, wincing at the grass-colored beverage.

Licking slurry from his thick lips, Mr. Evans said, "I knew her as Mrs. Jones."

Todd remembered the sisters were twins. *Ms. and Mrs. Jones.*

"Right. Mrs. Robin Jones. Do you know why she used her maiden name?"

"After the divorce, Robin rejected her husband's name. She applied to have it legally changed."

"When did you last see her?"

Mr. Evans slurped smoothie while glancing at the open doorway. "She spent the night."

"Was that usual?"

With a dry, bent hand, Mr. Evans wiped his mouth. "Not as often as I wanted."

Todd frowned.

Next to him, Ian perched on a chair with a notepad resting on his knee. "Go on."

"I asked Robin to move in. She … You know women." Mr. Evan's gaze tottered between them, but neither Todd nor Ian acknowledged his statement.

Mr. Evans shrugged. "Or maybe you don't. Well, Robin wanted a place of our own. She didn't want to stay in the house where I had lived with my ex-wife."

A tight grin from Todd's mouth encouraged Mr. Evans to continue.

"I was working on getting us a new place, but with this housing market it was taking time. She rotated between my house and her sister's place."

"What about her ex-husband?" Ian asked. "You have any interactions with him?"

Shaking his balding head, Mr. Evans said, "Nah. He stayed away from me. I don't think Robin saw him after she left Chicago."

"Do you know why they divorced?"

Ian's eyes lifted from the notepad at Mr. Evans' hesitation. Todd leaned forward. "Mr. Evans?"

"He abused her. She filed for divorce and was granted alimony."

"Was she afraid of him?"

A gloom spread across Mr. Evans' graying face. "No, Robin wasn't afraid of him—at least, that's what she said."

***

Forty minutes later, Todd and Ian exited the car lot. As Todd merged into traffic, he glanced over at his partner.

Paper crinkled as Ian opened a bag of chips.

"Seriously?" Todd grimaced, stopping at the traffic light. *Crunch, crunch.*

"Yeah, man. I'm hungry. We didn't get lunch." Ian handed him the bag. "Want some?"

Todd declined. "I don't understand how you can look like that," he pointed at Ian's biceps, "and eat such crap."

A smirk curled on Ian's lips. "I told you. I work out." Ian's biceps jiggled as he flexed.

Their laughter roared throughout the car as Todd steered toward the downtown police station.

"What did you think about Mr. Evans?"

Crumbling the paper bag, Ian tossed it into the cup holder.

"He ended up on a gurney when they told him Mrs. Jones-Collins died. His blood pressure soared to the roof. You can't fake that."

"No, you can't." Todd stared ahead at traffic and considered their interview. "But he's hiding something."

"Yeah. I picked up on his hesitation. It's probably more to do with their relationship than the murder though."

"Their relationship may be the motive behind the murder."

Ian nodded and plucked a black muscle ball from the center console. "An older man dating a recently divorced younger woman. You bet."

"We're getting ahead of ourselves. Mrs. Jones-Collins' death hasn't been classified as murder yet."

A minute passed.

"You were easy on the questions," Ian noted.

Todd parked in the police employee lot behind the station. "Laying a foundation. Let people establish their alibis, then look for inconsistencies."

Not until they strode toward the police station did Todd speak again. "You were brusque in the ER. That's not like you."

Ian massaged his shoulder. "Was I? Not on purpose."

They entered the station and ambled over to their desks, stacked facing each other in the middle of a long rectangular room housing over a dozen other desks. The police station hummed with activity. Officers on telephones, typing, or chatting with each other.

Todd circled around his fellow officers, greeting some, and avoiding others. At his desk, he placed his gun in a side drawer and booted up the computer. He glanced at Ian but didn't broach the ER interview again.

Ian addressed him from across their desks. "So, did you notice any inconsistencies in his story?"

"Maybe. I believe there's more to his girlfriend staying the night."

For over an hour, they discussed their interviews with Ms. Jones and Mr. Evans, and how to proceed. It ended when Todd received a call on his cell phone.

"Personal?" Ian grinned.

Todd sighed as he read the number on the screen. "Maybe." He pivoted his chair around, turning away from Ian. He answered on the third ring. "Hello?"

"Todd? This is Dr. Myaisha Douglas. I don't know if you remember me?"

His shoulders slumped. "I remember. What can I do for you?" From his periphery, he saw his partner rise. He motioned for Ian to get him a beverage from the machine. He covered the phone with his hand. "And not a cola."

She said, "I thought you might want to know …"

Watching Ian amble way, Todd realized he'd missed something and asked her to repeat.

"I witnessed someone grab Robin's hand from inside a car."

He bolted upright. The phone cradled on his shoulder as he reached for a pen and writing pad.

"Tell me again what happened."

"Robin came to the clinic last night. When I left, she was still in the parking lot out front, speaking with someone."

"Did you see who it was?"

Right then, Ian returned with a beverage. Todd mouthed he was speaking with someone about the case. Since their desks faced each other, Ian watched as Todd scribbled on a pad.

"No," she continued, "the other person was inside a Camaro. They grabbed Robin by the forearm. That's when I started to drive over, but the person in the Camaro sped off. I spoke with Robin, but she insisted it was nothing."

"Thank you—" He hesitated, not wanting to use her first name in front of Ian. "This is good information. I suppose you can't tell me why Robin came to the clinic?"

"No, I can't. HIPAA."

"That's okay. This helps." Todd leaned back against the chair rest. "Well, you take care. I have to go." He started to hang up.

"Wait. Don't you want the Camaro's license plate number?"

An expletive dripped from his lips. "Yes, of course."

She gave him the information.

This time, instead of being in a hurry to end the call, he extrapolated every detail.

"Thanks again," he said, once satisfied she had no further information to provide. "If you remember anything else, please call."

"Of course, Todd. Enjoy your evening."

Though she'd been helpful, he relaxed once the call ended. While he appreciated the information, Todd hesitated to encourage her curiosity. Although she gave off a strong maternal aura, he liked the doctor—and didn't want her involved in another homicide.

Once the call ended, Todd shared what he'd learned with Ian.

Pop.

With his head thrown back, Todd drank long and deep from the soda can while Ian reviewed the police database for the Camaro's license plate information. Five minutes later, the computer pinged.

Todd weighed Ian's pause. "Let me guess. Ex-husband."

Ian smirked. "Suspect number one."

Scooting his chair closer to the desk, Todd swallowed the remaining soda before chucking it into the trash can.

"All right. Let's start a suspect list."

"Ex-husband, Terrence Collins."

"Right. We need to find the details of their divorce. Do you have any contacts in Chicago? We need information about domestic abuse, any priors."

"On it," Ian said, grabbing his desk phone.

Somehow, after speaking with Dr. Douglas, Todd's mood soured. Her involvement suggested this case wouldn't be straightforward. Even without speaking with the medical examiner, he suspected Mrs. Jones-Collins *had* been murdered.

CHAPTER 10

On Wednesday morning, the outside of Evans Used Cars lot was deserted. Inside, Donald slogged from behind his office desk. At the small refrigerator, he poured the remaining smoothie Robin had prepared for him into a travel mug.

"I told you I'm not paying for another college degree," his voice bellowed, shaking the boxy office walls.

Seated in front of the desk, Junior flicked absently through a circular. "I'm not working with you anymore, Dad. Selling cars isn't for me."

"What is?" Behind the desk, Donald collapsed into an oversized leather chair. "You better find a way to support yourself and that ghetto rat you live with."

Junior's palm slammed down on the desk. "Don't call her that."

"Where did you pick her up? At a Fayetteville strip club?"

"I guess my girlfriend isn't from a place as sophisticated as Chicago's south side."

His eyes boggled. "Robin's dead. How dare you slur her name?"

"She was about to dump you. Once she realized you had no intention of buying her a yoga studio in Charlotte."

Words hissed between Donald's teeth. "You don't know what I'm capable of."

"Of course, I do. I'm your son." Junior bounded out of the chair.

A mug shattered as Donald hurled it at Junior's back, striking the wall adjacent to the door. Like slime, the smoothie trailed down the wall, pooling onto the floor.

Cynthia entered as Junior fled.

Like a bull, Donald charged after his son, flattening Cynthia against the door frame, and barely avoiding a collision.

"Mr. Evans, are you all right?"

Donald grunted, ignored her question, and chased after his son.

In the showroom, Milton leaned against a table, watching television. The broadcaster announced the death of his boss' girlfriend. Milton startled when Junior raced passed him and out the front door.

Trailing his son, Donald stood by the double doors, panting, as Junior sped off.

Quiet returned to the showroom and Milton continued watching television.

Donald's chest heaved. He remained at the entrance, staring after his son.

Minutes passed before he stormed back into his office, sank into his chair, and pivoted around, glaring out the window. He stared at the cement wall surrounding the sides and rear of the building.

In his absence, Cynthia had picked up the broken mug fragments. Now, while wiping up smoothie from the wall and floor, she said, "The bank called. They had a question about a withdrawal."

"I'll call them."

"Several clients left messages about their rental properties."

"They aren't clients," he grumbled, and swung around, eyeing her.

Cynthia was now seated in the chair Junior had vacated, cleaning her hands with a sanitary wipe.

"They're customers," Donald said.

"Either way, today, two people called to say they couldn't pay their rent. They requested an extension. Carl Bryant left a message about his property. He's threatening to sue."

Donald chuckled. "Good luck with that. The courts are busy with evictions and foreclosures. Besides, he can't prove I promised to make those repairs."

Cynthia grimaced and straightened her back. "Mr. Evans—"

"Is Milton outside or in the lobby?" Donald stood.

Peeking down the hall, Cynthia said, "He's inside."

"With a customer or watching TV?"

She didn't reply but followed him out of the office.

A lumbering stride brought Donald into the front showroom in seconds. He marched up to the television dangling from the wall and pressed the off button.

Suddenly at attention, Milton grinned. "Hey, boss. Slow day."

From the wallet in his back pocket, Donald counted out fifteen hundred-dollar bills, which he handed to Milton.

"That's your salary for this week and another two. Get your stuff, you're fired."

A gaping Milton stared for a couple seconds then began blubbering. "But … Mr. Evans, I was watching TV because things were slow. I need this job."

"Inventory's not moving. I can't afford to keep you on."

In Milton's trembling hand, the bills fluttered. "But, sir, you can't afford to let me go. I'm the only staff—"

"You're done. Clear out."

A fist formed around the wad of bills in Milton's hand. He sneered. "This is bulls***. I won't forget this, Mr. Evans. You ain't being fair."

With the speed and ferocity of a tornado, Milton snatched his personal items from a desk drawer and roared past Donald, elbowing him aside.

Donald shook off the hit, bustled to the front door of the showroom, and secured the lock with a key dangling from a hook beside the door. He trudged back down the hallway, halting beside the door of Cynthia's office.

At the doorway, he asked, "You heard that?"

Slowly, she nodded without speaking.

"It's this housing market. Credit's trash, and people can't pull money out of their homes anymore. No money for rent, no money for cars."

He leaned against the door frame, wiping his sweaty forehead with a handkerchief. "I arranged to sell the inventory for a little above my costs. The rental properties will go to the bank—unless I can offload them too."

Cynthia's shaking hands rested on the desk. She squared her shoulders.

He appreciated she understood what was coming.

"I'll pay you up to January. No reason for you to come in the rest of this month. I can handle the paperwork."

Like a thief, he slid into the office, dropped a wad of hundred-dollar bills on her desk, and left without meeting her gaze.

He entered his office and shut the door as sobs reached his ears.

CHAPTER 11

A uniformed officer handed Todd a paper. "Detective, this came over the fax. It's from the medical examiner."

"Thanks." Todd accepted the paper, leaned back in his chair, and read the report—twice.

Ian frowned. "Come on. What does it say?"

Todd sailed the paper across the desks toward Ian's waiting grasp. He waited a minute, giving his partner time to read the report. His fingers wriggled along the desktop as if he was playing piano keys.

"She died from pulmonary hemorrhage," Ian read aloud.

Like a leaf, the report floated back toward Todd, who propped the document next to his computer and typed the summary into his case notes.

"The medical examiner wrote Mrs. Jones-Collins aspirated on her own blood. Nasty."

"Gruesome," Todd said, "but not consistent with an assault."

Staring up at the ceiling, Ian bounced a black muscle ball on the desk. The bouncing stopped when he began squeezing the ball. "Could someone strike her hard enough in the chest to cause a pulmonary hemorrhage?"

His brows knitted as Todd considered the possibility. "Don't know. Sounds improbable." Again, he scanned the medical examiner's report. "Bruising on the chest wall. Broken ribs—but the medical examiner associated those with attempted resuscitation."

Ian tore open a candy wrapper, scrunching the paper before tossing it in the trash. "Weren't there bruises on her face? Maybe that's how she swallowed the blood."

"No, not from a nosebleed." Todd continued typing. "But Dr. Page did mention several bruises on the victim's hands and left wrist." A quick glance at the report confirmed what he remembered. "A ten-by-three-centimeter bruise on the thoracic paraspinal—"

"How big is that in inches?"

Todd shrugged. "I don't know. Look it up. It sounds big."

Computers keys clicked as Ian searched online for a conversion calculator.

"What did you find?"

"About four inches. The back is an unusual location for bruises unless they're deliberately inflicted."

"Wait a minute." Todd re-read the report. "The doctor mentioned nasal tissue damage."

"Someone punched her in the nose?" Ian eyed him.

For a moment their gazes locked.

Todd said, 'The ex," at the same time Ian said, 'The boyfriend." With a synchronized nod to each other, both detectives took up their respective desk phones and made calls.

***

Two hours later, Ian handed Todd a paper plate with two slices of pizza.

In answer to his raised brows, Ian said, "A new joint down the street dropped off ten pizzas. Gratis. I thought I'd grab a few before the swarm descended."

"Free food to cops is like blood in the water for sharks." Todd chuckled.

"You're not kidding." Ian sank into his chair, chomping on one of three pizza slices on his plate. Because his mouth was full of food, his voice was garbled. "You set up any interviews?"

"Yes." Todd searched his side drawer for a napkin. Not finding one, he wiped his mouth with a tissue. "I have a phone interview later today with the deceased's mom. She's trying to find a flight out of Chicago, but it might get scratched. The divorce lawyer will call back tomorrow."

With his chin, Todd motioned to Ian. "You?"

The trash can clunked as a pizza crust crashed inside. "I called Donald Evans' ex-wife and kids. No one answered the office phone, but it was nearly lunchtime. I'll try again at one. The office staff should be back by then."

"Confirming his alibi?"

"And getting any dirt on him and his relationship with Mrs. Jones-Collins. Someone put those bruises on her back."

"Humph."

Ian glanced up at him but continued eating.

A thought marinated in Todd's mind, but he finished the pizza before giving voice to his thoughts. The crumpled paper plate landed in the trash can as Todd wiped his fingers on another tissue. Then he resumed typing.

"I have an idea about the sister."

Tossing his food scraps into the trash, Ian said, "Go on."

"Did you notice the scratches on her hands?"

Ian rubbed his chin. "No. I remember dried blood."

"There were scratches on her knuckles."

"That's from doing CPR."

"You use your palms for chest percussions, not your fists." Todd saved his computer document before glancing at his partner. "Besides, a bruise is different from a scratch."

"So, you think what?"

Todd's lean head with sharp military haircut nodded. "A fight between the sisters would explain the deceased's facial and nasal bruising."

"But not the pulmonary hemorrhage."

"No," Todd grimaced, "pulmonary hemorrhage is a wild card." He wheeled his chair away from the desk and popped up from the seat. "Let's go speak with Dr. Page."

Ian locked his computer and removed his badge and gun from a desk drawer. "Fine with me. I'd like some fresh air. I can still smell pineapple from one of those pizzas." He jogged to catch up with Todd. "Who puts pineapple on a pizza?"

Todd hadn't registered Ian's comments. His mind recalled the pathology report. Mrs. Jones-Collins suffered facial bruising and a nosebleed. *How did those signs correlate with pulmonary hemorrhage?* And the seizure.

The sister had denied any family history of seizures or neurological problems. It seemed unlikely Mrs. Jones-Collins had acquired a seizure and lung problem the day she'd died.

Could the twins have fought, and Ms. Jones accidentally struck her sister hard enough in the face to cause a seizure and subsequent lung bleed? Todd had no idea, but he hoped the medical examiner did.

CHAPTER 12

Out of a stained-glass window inside the church sanctuary, Myaisha watched leaves in nearby trees toss about on a gentle breeze. Light momentarily shone through the window in a radiant spectrum as the sun descended.

Myaisha imagined her son, Josiah, returning home from college. Winter holiday was special for them. Instead of traveling to California to visit extended family, they hunkered down in Greensboro with Boomer, devoured a large meal, and discussed their personal lives. She valued their time together.

A heavy gray cloud crossed over the sun. The sudden dark sky made Myaisha shiver. Her attention returned to the Bible study class about to begin.

***

Pastor Matthew's bowed head bobbed as he closed Bible class with prayer. A second after he said "Amen," the sanctuary swarmed. People abandoned the pews and socialized before leaving.

Scanning the sanctuary, Myaisha gathered up her tote bag and Bible. She spotted Mary in a front pew on the opposite side of the room. Other attendees streamed passed her out the rear double doors. Once traffic decreased, Myaisha approached a group of four people conversing near a piano.

"Hello, Mary." She hugged her friend and exchanged greetings.

"Are you on your way home?" Mary asked, entwining her arm with her husband, Greg, who leaned forward and hugged Myaisha.

"Did you enjoy the lesson?" she asked Greg.

"Yes. I've always enjoyed the story of Daniel, Shadrach, Meshach, and Abednego. People don't appreciate—"

"Greg, the lesson ended." Mary tugged on his arm. "Time to go home."

Biting her cheek, Myaisha hid a grin.

As the trio departed, they discussed weather and current events.

Slapped in the face by a sharp, harsh wind, Myaisha rapidly zipped up her jacket. Mary and Greg did likewise.

Myaisha inclined toward them, tilting her head away from the wind. "Have you heard about Robin Jones?"

"Terrible," Mary said. "Have you spoken with René?"

"I thought her last name was Collins?" Greg asked, his gaze jumping between both women.

"She returned to her maiden name," Mary said, quickly returning her attention to Myaisha.

"Not yet," Myaisha said, jamming her hands into jacket pockets.

They huddled together and headed for their cars.

"I wanted to ask if you would write a poem for Robin," Myaisha asked Mary. "The writing group is holding a memorial for her. I'm going to René's place now to discuss it."

"Of course. I'd love to. Has any family come down from Chicago?"

"Not sure. I left several messages but René hasn't called me back yet."

Greg's hand reached around Mary as he opened their passenger car door. "She's probably still upset. I read in the paper René discovered her sister's body."

Mary entered the car and scrolled down the window.

Greg turned and faced Myaisha. "Do you know where she goes to church? Maybe I should go pray with her."

"She's an atheist, Greg," Mary said from inside the car. "Can we go home without your proselytizing, please?"

Myaisha laughed and hugged Greg. To Mary, she said, "Let me know when you finish the poem."

Once inside her car, Myaisha dialed René once more. Five rings, no answer. A message announced a full mailbox. She started the ignition and exited the lot, headed for René's townhome.

***

The doorbell chimed as Myaisha's knees quivered. She hadn't dressed for such cold weather. The morning temperature had been decent, but it had dipped precipitously in the evening due to the howling wind.

Leaves fluttered across her shoes. She stomped her leather loafers to warm her feet while pounding on the door with her fist. Suddenly, the door opened, causing her to jerk backward.

A short dark woman glared up at her under thick false eyelashes. "What do you want?" the woman asked, while one hand rested on her hip and the other barred entry.

"I'm Dr. Myaisha Douglas. A member of René's writing group. I came by to pay my respects."

The woman's face slackened and her shoulders drooped. "Oh."

From inside the house. a familiar voice beckoned. "Come in, Myaisha."

"Thank you," she said, hurrying inside.

In the foyer, square tiles gave way to carpeting. The living room was overfurnished with heavy, dark furniture. An older television cabinet housed the entire far wall.

René reclined in a wooden rocking chair with a knitted comforter covering her legs. She gazed up with weepy eyes.

Myaisha hurried over and embraced her warmly. As she rubbed René's back, she spoke words of condolence. Minutes passed before she pulled up a chair and sat beside her friend.

"This is my mom, Angela Jones," René said, her speech clouded by tissues surrounding her nose.

"I'm sorry we have to meet under these circumstances." Myaisha stood and shook Mrs. Jones' hand.

"Thank you. Were you Robin's doctor?"

Myaisha paused. Technically she wasn't Robin's doctor, but she had treated her the night before ... *Damn.* She suddenly remembered she needed to call Todd again. Not wanting to lie, she avoided the question.

"I hadn't known Robin long."

Tears streamed down Mrs. Jones' cheeks. "She was such a beautiful child. Why would anyone kill her? This is ... I can't believe it."

A box of tissues caught Myaisha's eye. She handed it to Mrs. Jones. Two minutes passed before she broached the topic for her visit.

"The writing group wants to hold a memorial for Robin. Mary agreed to write a poem for the service and Harriet said we could hold it at her café, but I wanted to get your permission before we proceed."

Like a jigsaw puzzle, René's expression evolved. Myaisha detected surprise, doubt—maybe even … *What?* She couldn't describe the expression on René's wide-eyed, slack face. If she didn't know better, Myaisha would've guessed it was fear. *Ridiculous.* Robin's death was an accident.

Before René answered, Mrs. Jones leaped from the couch.

"Oh, how wonderful. Yes, that would be very nice. Robin would appreciate being remembered by her friends. I could provide pictures—and we must play Robin's favorite songs."

They weren't actually Robin's friends but were conducting a service because of their friendship with René. However, Myaisha didn't mention that to Mrs. Jones because it didn't matter. Instead, she asked, "If you know of any other friends here in Greensboro—or North Carolina—let me know and we'll invite them too."

In a flurry, Mrs. Jones besieged René. "Chi, you should contact Robin's friends. They would want to know what happened. We need to call them right away. You should've thought of this already."

"Can you contact her friends in Chicago, Mrs. Jones?"

Wrinkles crisscrossed the mother's forehead. "I'm not sure I know how to reach them."

Myaisha's gaze bounced between the women. She detected an uncomfortable undercurrent as René avoided looking at her mother.

"Their numbers should be in her cell phone. Did the police return it to you?" Mrs. Jones asked René.

"Did the police give you the phone?" Myaisha also glanced at René, whose gaze fell.

Seconds passed without a response.

Mrs. Jones strode over to the chair and smacked René's arm. "Chi, what's wrong?"

René jumped. "No, they didn't give it to me."

The two Jones women glared at each other. Silence hung like a funk, fouling the atmosphere.

Myaisha remained quiet and observed. A minute passed. Detecting her presence was no longer appreciated, she retreated towards the door.

"Let me know about the memorial. We'd like to have it Friday night, but we could hold it over the weekend if you prefer. Will Mr. Jones be able to attend?"

"No," Mrs. Jones sniffed. "He's *too busy* to travel. But we'll have a service in Chicago when we take Robin back home."

"Of course." Myaisha turned to leave.

As if in a trance, René rose and accompanied her to the door.

"Thank you." Moving closer, her head touched Myaisha's. "I'm sorry I didn't return your calls. I had to pick up my mom, and ..." René's trembling arm brushed up against her. In a rush, René hugged her tightly, kissing Myaisha on the cheek.

She rubbed René's arms. "Call if you need anything, or if you simply want to talk. I'm here for you—anytime."

A second after the front door closed, raised voices erupted from the townhome, amplified by the quiet evening.

Not exactly eavesdropping, Myaisha hesitated on the doorstep, careful to zip the jacket up to her neck. When the front window curtain fluttered, she trotted to her car. As she reversed down the driveway, she watched the window.

An unspoken tension had arisen between René and Mrs. Jones regarding Robin's friends. *Why?*

Myaisha hadn't known her long, but Robin acted friendly if a little insincere. Despite many invitations, Robin had never accepted her lunch or dinner requests. Since Robin didn't have a job, it couldn't have been because she was busy.

What was the relationship between the sisters? Twins supposedly shared a unique connection, though not always positive. Personally, Myaisha enjoyed a comfortable relationship with her sisters.

On her way home, Myaisha wondered if Robin's death *had* been an accident—especially given the urgent care center lab report she'd received this morning. The results suggested something else. *Was she dreaming up sinister possibilities because of her penchant for murders?*

Writing mysteries could be a liability for a physician with a twisted imagination. Those test results weren't imaginary though, and they could be relevant to Robin's death.

What could she deduce from the odd behavior between Mrs. Jones and René?

Myaisha sat up straight and turned off the car radio. She needed to think.

Chapter 13

On Thursday morning, Todd arrived at the station later than usual. A tan beverage carrier tottered precariously in his right hand. Carefully, he lowered it onto the desk while balancing food containers with the other.

Like bees to honey, police officers surrounded him, relieving him of the containers. As the crowd diminished, Todd straightened his desk, now strewn with abandoned coffee lids, plastic utensils, and napkins.

"You're welcome," he shouted to the room.

"Yeah, man. Thanks." A few officers expressed generosity, while others exited too quickly to hear his comment.

"That's the last time I make a coffee run." Todd sank into his chair and sipped from his own cup.

Smack.

Ian dropped a thick black binder on his desk before grabbing a large white bag. "This my breakfast sandwich?" he asked, peering inside before taking his seat.

The police station hummed with a multitude of conversations and food wrappers opening.

Todd frowned. "You too? Doesn't anyone around here know how to say thank you?"

A mumbled thanks dribbled from Ian's mouth as he snacked on the sandwich. "What you got?"

Perceiving Ian's comment was directed at the paper in his hand, Todd slid it across the desk. Ian caught the paper before it drifted onto the floor.

"It's from the medical examiner. Dr. Page said something's wrong with Robin Jones-Collins' lab work."

"Lab work?" Ian wiped his mouth and swallowed. "She was DOA. They did lab work on a corpse?"

Todd shrugged. "Probably from the paramedics. It doesn't take long to draw blood. Anyway, because the lab work was abnormal, she ordered a tox screen."

"Jones-Collins was struck in the head."

"Her nose was injured, but no other head trauma. No skull fracture or brain hemorrhage."

Neither spoke as Ian read the report. "She died from pulmonary hemorrhage causing asphyxiation."

Caffeine ignited Todd's brain. He slurped up tart Arabica goodness. "Did you read the part about bruises?"

"Yes. Over—"

Chirping from Todd's phone interrupted their conversation. He pulled the phone from his coat pocket and read the screen.

DR. MYAISHA DOUGLAS.

A crease bent his brow.

"Who is it?" Ian asked before biting into the sandwich.

"The doctor again."

"The medical examiner?"

"No, the doctor from the Knight case—back in June."

Ian frowned. "Why?"

"I don't know."

"She's a pain."

"Yeah, but she gave us a good tip about the Camaro. Remember?"

Empty containers thumped into the trash can.

"You think she's got another tip?"

"I don't know." He texted a message.

WILL CALL LATER

He slid the phone into his suit coat pocket. "Let's go. We've got interviews lined up."

Ian tilted his head back and gulped the remaining coffee before tossing the cup into the trash. He joined Todd, and together they exited the station.

****

Inside the Triad Travelers Hotel lobby, Todd sauntered over to the registration desk. A minute later, he pointed Ian toward a thick Black man with locks sitting in a corner of the hotel's restaurant.

With Ian leading, they strode over to a small square table in front of an enormous paned window overlooking the front parking lot. Hovering over the man, they displayed their police badges.

"Terrence Collins?" Ian asked.

From under plucked eyebrows, Mr. Collins asked, "Yeah?"

Without waiting for an invitation, Todd and Ian grabbed chairs and sat around the table.

"Wait." Mr. Collins popped out of the chair and backed away. "What's going on?"

Ian glanced up. "Would you prefer to speak in a police station?"

With a deep sigh, Mr. Collins regained his seat. "No, let's do this. What do you want to know?"

Over five minutes, Mr. Collins provided background information: his address, phone number, and occupation.

During the preliminaries, Todd reclined in his chair, observing Robin Jones-Collins' ex-husband.

Under a polished veneer of moisturizer and facials, Todd detected a heaviness in Mr. Collins' demeanor. *Sadness?* Not unexpected given his ex-wife's sudden death. A divorce didn't mean he didn't care for her. In fact, Mrs. Jones-Collins had instigated divorce proceedings. Mr. Collins might have remained deeply attached to his ex-wife.

But Myaisha said the person in the Camaro grabbed Robin's arm. *Could that person have been someone other than Mr. Collins?* Todd had arrested many murderers who mourned the people they had killed. But this wasn't a murder case—not yet anyway.

Who was responsible for assaulting Robin Jones-Collins? Those bruises might not be related to her death but after speaking with Dr. Page, Todd had a deep suspicion they did.

"Where were you Monday night?" Ian asked.

Mr. Collins' posture stiffened and his hands fisted. Todd braced, prepared to intervene, but his partner didn't need help. Seconds passed as Mr. Collins glowered at Ian.

Undeterred, Ian met the stare and leaned forward. "Sir?"

With a clenched jaw, Terrence inhaled deeply before answering. "I spoke with Robin."

"Where?"

Under the table, Todd's fingers drummed along his thigh. He understood Ian was testing Mr. Collins's veracity. *But would the latter admit to assaulting his ex-wife outside an urgent care clinic?*

Mr. Collins spat the words out. "Fine. I followed Robin to a clinic outside Greensboro." He glanced outside into the parking lot. "We argued."

"That's all?"

"We fought."

"We?"

"I didn't hurt Robin—at least, I didn't mean to." Mr. Collins unclenched his fists. Perhaps he noticed Todd's gaze because he extended his manicured fingers along the table. Another minute elapsed before he continued.

"Look, I love—loved—Robin. But she had no concept of money, except how to spend it."

"Why did you follow her down here?" Ian jotted in his notepad while observing Mr. Collins' face.

"She was running up my credit card. According to the divorce agreement, I had to pay alimony *and* cover her business debts. But now she was making new charges."

A brief glance passed between the detectives. Todd nodded for Ian to continue.

"You could've called the police."

Mr. Collins gazed into his lap. "I didn't want to get her in trouble."

"You could've sued her."

"What, and pay another lawyer? I'm still paying off *both* divorce lawyers." Mr. Collins scratched his locks. "I told her to cut it out or I would ask the judge to amend the divorce settlement."

Ian frowned and tilted his head toward Todd.

"What could the judge do?" Todd asked, scooting closer to the table. "You wanted to end the alimony?"

"And get rid of the life insurance policy."

Todd gawked, trying but failing to hide his surprise. "What life insurance?" Peripherally, he noticed Ian writing feverishly on a notepad.

"Under the divorce agreement, I had to maintain a life insurance policy on Robin for one year," Mr. Collins said. "After that, she would become responsible for the monthly payments."

Ian chuckled. "You paid for a life insurance policy on your ex-wife?"

"And who was the beneficiary?" Todd asked.

After taking a sip of orange juice, Mr. Collins said, "Her mom and René."

***

Twenty minutes later, Todd and Ian returned to their vehicle. While Ian made phone calls, Todd executed a U-turn and steered toward the station.

"Well, that was a surprise," Ian said, after ending the call. He stared out the front window while squeezing a muscle ball.

"Were you able to reach the mother?"

"No, but I left a message."

"Interesting. The sister hadn't mentioned a life insurance policy."

"She was in shock. Her twin died."

"Humph."

After parking in the employee lot, they ambled toward the police station. An officer propped open the door as they entered.

Ian asked, "Do you want to interview the sister first or Donald Evans?"

Todd's mouth opened to reply when he spied someone seated in a folding chair beside his desk.

A tall, slightly overweight woman with shining amber eyes glanced up and smiled as he approached. She stood, gripping a plastic container to her chest. A rich aroma of chocolate drifted toward him.

He walked forward and asked, "What brings you in, Dr. Douglas?"

Chapter 14

A dozen hungry eyes watched Myaisha's every move. Either she looked suspicious, or these police officers were starving. Perhaps she shouldn't have baked Todd a chocolate cake and brought it inside the police station.

His message read he'd call later but he hadn't. She had crucial information to discuss, and no one could resist her chocolate bundt cake with chocolate drizzle.

Todd and his partner—Ian was his name, she believed—entered. She stood, noticing Todd's grimace. *Was he upset to see her?* He must be busy.

She smiled as engagingly as possible. "Good afternoon, T—Detective Gamble."

A glint in his eye gave her pause. She considered it prudent to use his official title, although he had asked her to call him Todd when she'd helped him with Candace's murder case.

"I made you a cake," she said, offering it to him.

His solemn gaze fell on the plastic container, then he grinned.

"Thank you." He cleared his throat. "Dr. Douglas, you remember my partner, Detective de Jesus."

She shook hands with his partner, who appeared more muscular than she remembered. *What was Tina feeding him?*

Myaisha chastised herself. Detective de Jesus was a grown man. His mom didn't fix his meals anymore. *Or did she?*

Once introductions were completed, Myaisha lifted the lid's container and unleashed a cloud of chocolate goodness. If she thought everyone in the room was staring before, now they looked like a pack of orcas, and she was a seal.

"I remembered you liked cookies. This time, I baked a cake."

Again, he thanked her and invited her to be seated.

"This won't take long. Remember I told you about examining Robin the night before ..." She swallowed. "The night before she died."

He nodded.

While they spoke, Ian retrieved a long knife and carved up the cake. Like flies at a picnic, the desk was swarmed by police officers.

"Guys," Todd said, frowning, "we're discussing a case here."

"You're lucky we waited this long," someone said, stealing away with a slice.

By the time the horde dispersed, only an eighth of the cake remained. Although Todd acted disinterested, when a hand reached forward to snag the last piece of cake, his slender fingers shot forward and grabbed the tray.

"That's mine."

Myaisha chuckled. "Don't worry. I'll make you another one."

He side-glanced at an officer standing off to his right. "Don't bring it in here. Next time, I'll meet you outside."

She smiled and lowered her voice. "I ordered lab work the night Robin came into the clinic. You have to file a HIPPA request to officially obtain the records, but I wanted you to know the results were abnormal. I can't discuss what was said during her appointment, but—"

"We already know. Paramedics drew blood before she died. The medical examiner called about the results."

He handed her a thick paper with an official stamp. While she read the lab results, he nibbled at edges of the cake.

"This resembles the results I got. The PT and PTT were significantly elevated."

Ian licked icing from his lips. "What does it mean?"

"PT is prothrombin and PTT is partial thromboplastin time. Elevated levels indicate a problem with blood clotting."

"Did she have a bleeding disorder?" Ian asked, stabbing at the remaining slice of cake.

Todd smacked Ian's fork away with a spoon. "Hey. Watch it."

Ian glanced at Myaisha. "Next time bring coffee."

She smiled. "I drink tea."

"You can't talk about the medical appointment but were the lab results consistent with what you expected?"

"No."

Todd held her gaze. She paused, hoping to convey the importance of her words.

"I heard Robin died from pulmonary hemorrhage," she said.

The spoon dropped from Todd's lips. "How did you hear that?"

She shrugged. "I know someone who knows someone."

"Who someone?"

Myaisha had no intention of betraying Tina, a member of her writing group and mother to Detective Ian de Jesus. Poor Ian had no idea his mother snooped through police files when he stopped by for homemade meals.

"Is it true?"

Todd's chin thrust forward.

Her head tilted slightly, and she waited.

A minute passed. The detective caved. "Yes, that's how she died."

"Then it wasn't an assault?"

Todd jumped from his seat and assisted her up from the chair. "Let me escort you out, Dr. Douglas. And thank you again for the cake."

Before they stepped away from the desk, Todd glared at his partner. "Don't touch my slice."

Ian's fork retreated, and he sat back down.

Myaisha noticed other police officers in the station had returned to their different occupations. She permitted Todd to lead her outside and away from the building. Not until they reached the visitor parking lot across the street did he release her arm.

"What's the problem?" She curled up into her coat, sheltering from the biting winter breeze.

Todd rubbed his forehead and turned his back to the station. "Myaisha, I appreciate your help—and I'll file for the urgent care center notes—but I don't want you involved in this case."

"Why not?"

The veins along his neck stretched taut. "Because this isn't an accidental death. Not if those lab results mean what the medical examiner suspects."

"But if Robin had a bleeding disorder …" She thought about the different medical disorders to explain death by pulmonary hemorrhage. There weren't many. She frowned.

"She didn't have a bleeding disorder. Dr. Page—the medical examiner—spoke with Mrs. Jones-Collins' regular physician in Chicago. There's no family history of bleeding disorders or lung disease." Todd leaned forward and lowered his voice. "Did you forget what happened last time you became involved in a murder investigation?"

Her gaze narrowed. She wondered if he was concerned about her safety or bothered by her interference.

His back straightened. "I appreciate the information—and the cake—but I'll take it from here." He strode away.

"Why haven't you returned my calls?"

He grimaced. "Don't shout."

"What's wrong, Todd? I thought we were friends."

"We are. I apologize. Things got busy." He led her further away from the station. "But you need to stop investigating and stay out of the way." After a moment's hesitation, he said, "I'm up for a promotion and solving this case—"

"Oh, I get it. Independent, without outside influence."

"Something like that. Go home. Write one of your mystery stories and stay away from this case."

As he jogged back toward the station, Myaisha slipped on her sunglasses and hurried inside her car. Bright sunlight contrasted against the bitter cold.

On the drive home, she reviewed hematological conditions causing spontaneous pulmonary hemorrhage. Thinking systematically, Myaisha came up with lung abscess, tuberculosis, and aspergillosis. However, Robin didn't have any symptoms of fever or cough. Structural cardiac problems were possible, though on exam Myaisha hadn't detected any abnormal heart sounds, murmurs, or elevated blood pressure.

Bronchiectasis and cryptogenic hemoptysis occurred in smokers, but Robin denied smoking. Of course, idiopathic pulmonary hemorrhage could be responsible. Although, it generally manifested with hemoptysis, iron-deficiency anemia, and pulmonary infiltrates on chest x-ray. Robin's iron level and ferritin were normal. Myaisha hadn't ordered an x-ray at the urgent care clinic.

On the patient history form, Robin had denied any history of bleeding disorders and the medical examiner—according to Todd—had verified this with Robin's primary care doctor.

This was wrong. A spontaneous pulmonary hemorrhage, severe enough to cause death in a young woman, wouldn't explain Robin's lab results the night before her death.

Myaisha drove home, pondering the possibilities. *What would cause multiple bruises, elevated clotting studies, and spontaneous pulmonary hemorrhage?*

Five miles down the road, Myaisha reconsidered and executed a U-turn. She knew where to get answers.

Chapter 15

Once he returned inside the police station, Todd removed his suit coat and draped it over the chair. His piece of cake had dwindled by a third. He glowered across the desk at his partner.

"Not me." Ian grinned.

Todd shook his head, gathered a spoon, and savored the last pieces of cake. "We have an appointment with Mr. Evans this evening. He leaves the car dealership around six. I also want to speak with the twin sister again about when she arrived at the house."

"The staff at her daycare center corroborated the time she left."

"Yes, but," Todd wiped his mouth, "she could've slipped out a side door."

"They have surveillance cameras."

"Good. We'll ask Ms. Jones if we can view them, but also ask the DA about a warrant."

"We can reschedule Mr. Evans for tomorrow if the sister can speak with us tonight."

While checking phone messages, Todd considered Ian's comment. "I'll contact Mr. Evans for an earlier appointment."

"I'll call the Joneses."

Five minutes elapsed with Todd on hold. He glanced across the desk at Ian. "Any luck?"

Crunch, crunch. Ian licked salt off his fingers. "Mom and sister can speak with us at seven. You?"

Todd's head shook. "I haven't been able to reach Mr. Evans. He doesn't answer his phone."

Hearing a voice on the line, Todd returned to the call. The conversation was brief. "Thank you," he said before dropping the desk phone into its receptacle.

"What did you find out?" Ian asked.

"The company will fax a copy of the life insurance policy, but the representative confirmed what Mr. Collins said. He paid premiums on a million-dollar policy. The beneficiaries are the sister, who receives eighty percent, and the mom gets the rest."

Ian bounced a muscle ball on the desk. "Not bad."

"Is murdering your sister worth $800,000?"

"If you can get away with it." Ian smirked.

"Anything back from forensics?"

"Actually, yes." Ian tossed the ball into a side drawer. "They located an unknown blood sample on the deceased's hand."

Todd frowned. "The right hand with the scrapes and bruises?"

"Yep."

Minutes elapsed while Todd mulled over this new detail. "So, an unknown person could have assaulted Mrs. Jones-Collins and precipitated a pulmonary hemorrhage?"

"Remember, Dr. Page said a punch to the nose wouldn't cause her lungs to bleed."

Ignoring Ian's comment, Todd weighed the disparate facts while mumbling out loud. "A bloody nose. Scratches on her right hand. Bruises. Pulmonary bleed."

"What are you muttering about? Speak up."

"I'm trying to make sense of this crazy case."

Todd's desk phone rang. "Hello?" He mouthed the name *Dr. Page* to Ian. Over the next five minutes, he listened to the medical examiner. After he hung up the phone, he stared off to the side.

"Well, what did she say?" Ian asked, leaning across the desk.

"Brodifacoum," Todd said, slowly.

"What?"

"Rat poison."

Ian whistled.

"Now we have a definite homicide." Todd removed his service revolver from the desk drawer.

"Nothing we can do now but interview the Jones family and Mr. Evans," Ian said, powering off his computer and rising from the chair. "The medical examiner will compare the DNA from Mrs. Jones-Collins' hand against the ex-husband and boyfriend."

Todd slung his coat over his shoulders. "What about the sister? Oh, right. I forgot. They're identical twins."

"Geminis."

"They were born in—"

"No, I mean like Castor and Pollux." In answer to Todd's frown, Ian said, "Greek mythology. Twin sons of Zeus, I believe."

"Forget mythology. We deal in reality. If the DNA doesn't belong to the twin sister, ex-husband, or boyfriend, what are we left with?"

Neither spoke until they entered their vehicle. Todd climbed behind the steering wheel with a grimace.

"An unknown third party," Ian said, snapping his seatbelt in place.

With a long sigh, Todd started the ignition. From the moment Myaisha's name flashed on his caller id, he realized this case would be convoluted.

CHAPTER 16

Donald sat in his office chair searching his cell phone contact list. A minute later he made a call. While waiting for an answer, he walked over to the refrigerator. Mechanically, he reached inside for a thermos when he remembered there wouldn't be any more smoothies.

Robin was dead. All his planning and maneuvering—wasted. *What did it matter if Robin was gone?*

The call went to voicemail. He cursed and hung up.

For five minutes, he ambled aimlessly around the office. Certain things were already in motion. If he couldn't make the move with Robin, he'd do it alone.

A tightness in his chest persuaded him to sit down. He rubbed his breastbone and the pressure eased. Having a heart attack wouldn't help.

He gazed down at his desk. A round picture frame showing him and Robin seated at a picnic in Greensboro Country Park caught his eye. He caressed the frame with his fingers. He had finally found the woman of his dreams and … *How did Robin die? Why did Robin die?*

He slammed the desk with his fists and instantly regretted it. After replacing the frame, he searched inside the desk drawers.

"Where the hell did I place that splint?"

Once he secured the wrist splint, he turned on his computer to check the business accounts. He expected a large deposit once the auction house liquidated his remaining car inventory. A tiny wheel circled in the center of the computer screen while his bank website loaded. Thirty seconds later he logged into his account.

He gasped. "Where the hell is my money?"

Barely a second elapsed before he dialed the bank's customer service number. Minutes passed as a representative confirmed his identity.

"Thank you, sir, for answering your verification questions. How may I help you?"

"On Tuesday, someone made an unauthorized withdrawal from my account."

"Let me check for you."

Donald's fist tapped on the arm of his leather chair. "It must be some type of bank error."

"Yes, well, according to our records an online withdrawal was made by someone with the proper credentials."

"What do you mean? I didn't authorize a withdrawal."

"Have you shared your password with anyone?"

It took about ten seconds for Donald to realize what had happened. To the representative, he asked, "But if I didn't consent to the withdrawal can I get my money back?"

"If an authorized user on this account made a withdrawal, you would not be entitled to a refund."

Under his breath, Donald cursed, missing what the representative said. "Excuse me?"

"May I help you with anything else today?"

With a grunt, he ended the call. "She's not going to get away with this."

His stubby fingers held down the number two button on his cell phone. The call went through automatically, rang, but didn't go to voicemail. He dialed the number again. Still no answer or voicemail.

Uttering a torrent of curse words, he tossed the phone on the desk. On the computer, he checked each of his business accounts.

"I can't believe this." He rubbed his chin and stared at the open doorway. "Wait a minute?" Over the next half hour, he reviewed his overseas accounts.

"Damn her," he growled before snatching up the phone and dialing a different number. It rang once.

"Where are you?" he asked.

"Why are you calling me?"

"I know what you did."

"What are you talking about?"

"Did you kill Robin for the money?"

"Screw you." They hung up.

Donald stared at the phone. *What could he do?*

A horn beeped.

He glanced at his watch. It was ten 'til noon.

After two more beeps, he trudged down the hallway into the showroom. Out the glass double doors, he viewed a large car carrier trailer. From a wall adjacent to the door, Donald removed a circular metallic key ring off a hook and unlocked the double doors. One second outside and he wished he'd worn a jacket.

A dumpy man with bushy sideburns hopped down from the truck. "You the owner?"

"Yeah. Y'all the auction guys?"

"Yep."

Once Donald reviewed the paperwork, he signed the release. From inside the showroom, he watched two men load three cars on the carrier.

A half-hour later, the dumpy man entered the showroom. "We'll get the others tomorrow."

"Why can't y'all move them all today?"

"We have other deliveries scheduled," the guy said, stabbing a wooden clipboard with a pen. "Sign here."

With a grimace, Donald removed a pen from his shirt breast pocket and scribbled his signature.

"See yah tomorrow."

"Right."

After the man left, Donald locked both doors before returning the key to the hook. On the way back to his office, he pressed the number two button on his phone again.

"Hello?" asked a wavering voice.

"I need your help."

"Go to hell."

"Wait. Don't—"

The caller hung up.

"Damn."

Donald went to the refrigerator, again searching for Robin's smoothies. There were no more. *Dammit.* He slammed the door. It bounced back and hit him in the leg. He kicked the door repeatedly until it remained shut.

Robin was gone. Tears blurred his vision. A minute later, he collapsed into his desk chair.

He made another call. "Hello, baby girl."

"Daddy? What's wrong?"

"I need a place to crash for a few days. You heard about Robin."

"No. What happened? Did she leave you?"

"Of course not. She's dead."

"How?"

"Look, I don't want to discuss it right now. Can I stay with you tonight?"

"Sure. When do you think you'll get here?"

"I have a few calls to make—a couple people to see. I'll let you know when I head out. Probably late this evening. I don't want to sit in I-40 traffic all the way to Durham."

"Okay, Daddy. See you soon."

A tiny grin had formed on his lips as he spoke with his daughter. But once the call ended—and he remembered the missing money …

Donald was good at selling cars and hustling but computers confused him. He needed help if he was going to get his money back. His right hand throbbed. After removing the splint, he rubbed his wrist and considered what to do next.

Junior knew about computers but probably wouldn't help unless he got paid.

His list of helpful friends was short. In truth, he did have friends but not the kind to help with this type of problem. However, they could help him deal with the thief—once he recovered the money.

"This is ridiculous."

Bounding out the chair, Donald threw on a coat and hustled out of the office, exiting from the rear door.

"If I show up, she'll have to help me."

CHAPTER 17

Myaisha bypassed the circulation desk. Peace accentuated her steps. She climbed the stairwell up to the second floor.

Laughter wafted out a partially opened door. She entered, closed the door, and greeted her writing group.

In the conference room, women surrounded two small tables. Myaisha placed her book bag on a separate table near the door.

From the center of the room, Tina waved her over. "Dr. Douglas, come here."

"Tina, you can call me Myaisha." She glanced around at the animated faces. "What's up?"

Conspiratorially, Tina eased up beside her. "Did you find out anything at the police station?"

Her brow puckered. "How did you know?"

"Ian. I brought him lunch. He knows you're in my writing group." Tina grinned. "He wouldn't tell me anything, but I viewed the autopsy folder on his desk." Her eyes twinkled, awaiting confirmation.

A moment of doubt delayed Myaisha's response. She didn't want to be a gossip, but she'd like to know what Tina had discovered. Before she came to a decision, a bell chimed.

At the front of the room, near a peg board strewn with announcements, Mary stood with her tiny hands on her round hips.

"It's time to start. We can discuss real-life murders in," she checked a wristwatch, "exactly one hour. Begin."

Instead of editing her current mystery manuscript, Myaisha used the hour to jot down details regarding Robin's death. *Did she suspect murder, and if so, why?* Because the police did.

If Robin's demise had been an accident or an unfortunate medical occurrence, the authorities wouldn't have assigned homicide detectives to investigate. Besides, less than twenty-four hours before her death, Myaisha had examined Robin. Though she had a decent humility regarding her medical knowledge, she refused to believe the healthy woman she'd examined on Monday night died from idiopathic pulmonary hemorrhage the following day.

Monday night, Robin complained about bruising. Large bruises, especially on her back, developed over the past month. On the medical questionnaire, Robin answered negatively to prior bruising, sickle cell anemia, and hemophilia.

Despite a brief online search, Myaisha had failed to identify a bleeding disorder occurring in adulthood—but not affecting menstruation—potentially resulting in sudden severe pulmonary bleeding. Robin had reported regular menses, but she was on oral contraceptives. *Dammit. What was she missing?*

Time sped quickly away, and the hour ended without her reaching a conclusion.

Mary rang a silver bell, signaling the end of their *Think It, Ink It* session.

With her mind still on Robin's urgent care visit, Myaisha gathered her computer and notebook and prepared to depart. Her skin tingled. Someone stood beside her.

"What do you think?"

She frowned. "I'm sorry, Tina. I was thinking about something else."

"Robin's murder, right?"

Myaisha studied Tina a moment before reaching a decision. "We don't know it's murder—not yet."

"Sure, we do. Homicide doesn't investigate accidents or medical catastrophes."

Catastrophe. The word appropriately summed up Robin's death.

"Yes, but …" Myaisha's gaze circled the room. "I'm not sure we should discuss this here."

"Why not? Where better to conduct research than the library?"

Myaisha thought it a fair point.

While a half-dozen women streamed out of the room, Deniece entered. "Hi," she said, sauntering up to Myaisha and exchanging a hug. "Did I miss anything?"

Tina laughed. "This is a writing group, not a performance."

"Don't get snitty. I've had a bad day." Deniece perched on the edge of a square table. "What're y'all talking about?"

"Robin's murder," Tina said.

The room had emptied save them and Mary, who now joined their group.

"What's going on?"

"We're discussing Robin's murder," Tina said.

"We don't know for sure she *was* murdered," Myaisha said without conviction.

"It's not official. But we know better." Tina winked at Mary.

"Who do you think did it?" Deniece asked, reclining in a chair, and crossing her legs.

Simultaneously, Mary said, "The sister" as Tina said, "The ex."

Deniece laughed. "What do we know?"

With a glowing smile, Tina said, "I was going to suggest we pool our resources—information. This could be another great case for our group."

"You mean another true crime book for you." Deniece smirked.

"I don't mind sharing," Tina said. "Another member can write it up."

Myaisha's mouth puckered as if she tasted something sour. "This is serious and dangerous. I don't think we should approach it lightly."

Tina's face became sullen. "I'm sorry. I didn't mean to sound ghoulish. But let's be honest. We write mysteries because we find crime interesting. I know you're curious about the murder too, Dr. Douglas."

At the door, Myaisha pivoted around. "Tina, you don't have to call me Dr. Douglas outside of the hospital. We're friends."

In two brisk strides, Tina hustled to her side. "So, are you interested?"

Myaisha hesitated.

Deniece smacked her arm. "Of course, she is."

As Mary, Tina, and Deniece exited the room in whispered tones—planning how to investigate the case—a scene flashed into Myaisha's mind. She was tussling with a murderer, then a gun fired.

Sweat beaded on her forehead. Nausea churned in her rumbling stomach. She never wanted to experience that again. Déjà vu swept over her body as goosebumps erupted along her arms. Wiping her brow, she closed the door and exited behind her friends.

Earlier, when she had called René, Mrs. Jones had answered. The matriarch had stated René was asleep and hung up.

Instead of heading home, Myaisha decided it was time René woke up and addressed crucial questions. She hoped the answers would resolve the inconsistencies regarding Robin's death.

Chapter 18

At least half the townhomes in this residential community displayed Christmas decorations—more than Myaisha's cul de sac could boast. She recalled years past, driving around Greensboro with Josiah, admiring neighbors' holiday decorations.

It was a month before Christmas. She considered whether it was worth the effort to put up a tree. *How long would Josiah stay this year before returning to college?*

After parking, Myaisha sprinted for the front door. Freezing rain stung her face, pinging off her fedora. Because of the slick icy cement, she skated up to the house. Like a little drummer boy with ADHD, she rapped on the door.

Mrs. Jones's pinched face answered. "Yes? What do you want?"

"I'm sorry, Mrs. Jones," Myaisha said, shaking water off her shoes, "but it's important I speak with René—tonight."

Seconds passed, but Mrs. Jones refused to yield.

Raindrops pattered the back of Myaisha's coat. "I want to help figure out what happened to Robin. She was a beautiful person, and her death affected many people."

The last part was overreaching but apparently appealed to maternal instinct.

As Mrs. Jones retreated, Myaisha scurried inside the townhome. Her socks squished inside her soaked shoes.

"Chi," Mrs. Jones called up the narrow staircase, "it's your friend."

"Who?" René asked.

"The doctor. Get down here." Mrs. Jones glanced at Myaisha's shoes. "Don't mess up my floors." She skulked away.

Unsure where to go and not wet the floors, Myaisha waited near the front door. The stairs from the second floor ended four feet from the front door with no true foyer. When René descended the steps, she landed right in front of Myaisha.

They hugged. But even as Myaisha expressed sympathy, she sensed a chill in René's brief embrace.

"Thanks for coming by," René said and quickly turned aside, "but I need to be alone to process what happened."

Though René inched toward the front door, Myaisha remained by the stairs. "I'm not here to comfort you. I want answers."

René frowned. "What do you mean?"

"There's something wrong about Robin's death." Myaisha realized her comment was poorly articulated. She hastened to clarify. "I mean—"

Ding, dong.

Both women pivoted toward the door but neither responded. It rang again.

"Chi," Mrs. Jones yelled. "Where you at?" She stormed into the entryway. "Why are you standing there like a fool? Answer the door."

Because René still refused to move, Mrs. Jones pushed past her and answered the door.

"What?"

"Mrs. Jones, we'd like to speak with you and your daughter."

Though she couldn't see him, Myaisha recognized Todd's voice.

Despite being a police detective, he got no further than she had. Mrs. Jones left him and his partner outside in the rain.

"What questions could the police have at this time of night?"

"We called earlier. Ms. Jones agreed to speak with us."

"Humph." Mrs. Jones allowed Todd and Detective de Jesus to enter. She glanced down at their feet. "Don't mess up my floors." She stomped back into the kitchen.

Like a deer in headlights, René froze in place.

Todd unbuttoned his coat and glanced to the side. His face sagged when he noticed Myaisha.

She smiled. "Good evening, Detectives."

Detective de Jesus sighed, out loud. Todd's jaw clenched.

"Ms. Jones?" Detective de Jesus asked.

Not until Myaisha touched her arm did René respond.

"I'm sorry. Please come in," René said.

Both detectives, like Myaisha, considered their wet shoes.

"Don't worry about it," René said. "This is *my* house."

The slight venom in the last sentence wasn't missed by Myaisha—probably not by the detectives either.

In the living room, Myaisha took a chair near the fireplace. She wanted to get out of the way—and hoped her feet would dry.

The detectives sat together on a couch facing René, who sat in a chair with too many pillows. Clutching one of the pillows to her chest, René stared across the room.

"First," Detective de Jesus began, "we need to inform you that the medical examiner determined your sister was murdered."

"Murdered?" René leaped from the chair. Her eyes oscillated from side to side.

Myaisha rushed to her side, afraid René would faint. "Go get a glass of water and a damp rag." Her orders weren't directed to anyone in particular. As she reached René, Todd rushed into the kitchen.

"Sit down," she directed.

But René wouldn't bend. Her chest heaved and she clutched at Myaisha's forearm. "Robin, murdered."

Voices in the kitchen reached a crescendo as Mrs. Jones hollered, "Murdered!"

A minute later, Todd returned to the living room with water, a damp cloth, and a weeping mother.

"Who would kill my baby?" Mrs. Jones sobbed.

Detective de Jesus rose and assisted her into a chair next to the fireplace.

"She was an angel, such a beautiful child." While the detective retrieved tissues for the mom, Myaisha and Todd finally managed to deposit René into a chair.

While she checked René's vital signs, Todd asked questions.

"Now, you can understand why it's necessary to speak with you tonight. The sooner we get answers, the quicker we catch the person who killed your sister."

"But how did they kill her?" Mrs. Jones asked, drying her tear-stained face.

"Right now, we're keeping those details confidential," Todd said.

For a millisecond, René gawked. Then she glanced over at Myaisha and in a flash, looked away.

Did she imagine that? Myaisha wondered what had frightened René. Of course, hearing your sister was murdered would be upsetting. But fear sparked in René's eyes, not sorrow.

"I can't help you," René said, gazing into her lap.

Todd returned to the couch opposite René's chair. "What about your sister's friends? People she associated with."

"Robin didn't have any friends."

"That's ridiculous," Mrs. Jones interjected. "Of course, she did. Robin was popular. She went to parties. She'd be up all night talking to her girlfriends. How can you say she didn't have any friends?"

"Mama?"

"Don't be spiteful, Chi. Robin is dead, and we have to help the detectives find her killer. Forget about your childish jealousies."

Myaisha watched René's body recede into the seat. *Had Todd noticed?*

"Anything either of you could share with us would be helpful," Todd said.

"I don't know anything other than what I already told you." René became more diminutive as her voice shrank.

Mrs. Jones sat up straight. "Robin had been down here a few months, Detective, but she told me she had plans to start a new business. She was even looking at condos."

A brief glance passed between the detectives. Myaisha viewed the slight inclination of Todd's head before his partner spoke.

"Did she provide any specifics?" Detective de Jesus asked.

Mrs. Jones' large bosom rose and fell. "I know she was anxious to get her own place. This wasn't Robin's style." With a twitch of her nose, Mrs. Jones surveyed the living room.

Myaisha watched Todd observing René, who clutched the pillow tighter each time her mother spoke.

"Do you know any of her friends here in Greensboro, ma'am?" Detective de Jesus asked.

"No, but they should be in her phone. Which reminds me, when can I get her stuff back? I want to take her home. Bury her decent." Mrs. Jones cried into a wad of tissues.

While Detective de Jesus comforted her, Todd observed René.

Like a slow-moving storm, René glanced up and met his gaze. They locked eyes for a second until René pivoted toward her mom. She rose.

"Come on, Mama. I'll take you upstairs."

"I miss her so much. How could you let this happen? You're her big sister. She came down here for help and you let someone kill her."

Mrs. Jones elbowed René aside and bustled from the room.

Myaisha hurried to René's side. "She didn't mean that. She's upset."

René trembled. "No, she meant it."

The rain was audible in the intervening silence.

Searching for a proper sentiment, Myaisha scrutinized the charm around René's neck. Perhaps as a distraction from the uncomfortable silence, she asked, "Where did you get your necklace? I can't place the image. It looks—"

"It was a gift." René strode toward the front door. "If you'll excuse me, I need to be with my mom. I'm sure you understand."

Detective de Jesus marched toward the door first. Todd and Myaisha brought up the rear.

Spinning on his heel, Todd said, "We need to speak with you as soon as possible, Ms. Jones. Please call us when you're feeling better." With a flick, a card appeared between his fingers.

As if it were soiled, René held it by the edges.

Once the detectives left, Myaisha approached. "René, can I do anything for you?"

"No, thank you. I want to be alone."

"I understand."

Before crossing the threshold, Myaisha turned back. "If … if you can't tell the police, but you want to share—"

"What do you mean?"

"I think you know what I mean." She left.

The door slammed on her back.

***

Myaisha found the detectives talking beside her driver's side car door. On her approach, Detective de Jesus strode away—but not before shooting her a sharp glare.

"I don't think your partner likes me," she said, opening the car door and tossing her purse inside.

The rain had stopped but the temperature dipped. She shivered and slipped inside her car.

"Why are you here?" Todd asked as she rolled down the car window.

"René is my friend. I was worried about her."

"And?" His brow furrowed.

"What?"

"Myaisha."

"Okay. I suspected Robin was murdered. Most likely an assault or poison." She glanced up at Todd expectantly. He, however, didn't take the hint. "You're not going to tell me how she was killed?"

"No. Go home. Stop meddling in this murder."

"What have you uncovered?"

"Almost getting killed didn't sober you up? Homicide investigations are best left to the professionals. Go home. Live a happy life and stay away from my murder."

She bestowed a tiny grin. "Good night."

He shook his head as he ambled toward the idling car where his partner waited.

At the street corner, Myaisha turned left. A minute later, Todd did likewise. She wondered if he would follow her all the way home. He was insistent about her staying away from the investigation. *Was he concerned about her welfare, or irritated she would continue investigating?*

That evening, she received confirmation about one thing. René was scared.

CHAPTER 19

On Friday morning at the Evans Used Car dealership, Todd struggled sliding gloves over his cold, dry hands. The forensic technician's medium-sized gloves wouldn't accommodate his slender, piano-playing fingers. He peered down at what remained of the right side of Donald Evans' head. Todd mentally blocked out the technicians bustling about the square office space.

Blood, brain, and bone splatter covered the bulky wooden desk. Behind it, Mr. Evans slumped over the right side of a leather chair. A revolver dangled from his contorted fingers.

"Bag the splint," Todd said, pointing at Mr. Evan's wrist. "Make sure to swab his hand for gunpowder residue." He glanced around the room searching for Ian amongst a sea of law enforcement personnel processing the crime scene.

Beside the open office door, his partner interviewed the office manager. Todd strode over to the doorway while peeling off the gloves.

Puffy red eyes bulged from the office manager's face. Todd peeked over at Ian's notepad to obtain the woman's name.

Cynthia Howard sniffled. "I already told this to the other officer. When I arrived, the lobby doors were unlocked. The lights were on. It seemed wrong because Mr. Evans usually didn't come in before I did."

Ian offered her another tissue. "What time did you arrive?"

"Eight-thirty."

"And when did Mr. Evans usually get in?"

"Not before ten—unless he had something important scheduled."

"Did he have anything special scheduled for today?"

"Not that I knew about."

With a gentle touch, Todd guided Ms. Howard away from the door to make room for technicians wheeling a gurney.

She gawked as they removed Mr. Evan's body from the office.

Todd sent Ian a quick nod, signaling they should move the interview to another location.

"Where is your office, Ms. Howard?" Ian asked.

Her wobbly finger directed them left and across the hall.

Once there, Todd arranged three chairs in a semi-circle and invited her into the middle seat. In under a minute, he returned to the room with a cup of water, which he handed her.

"So, you found Mr. Evans in his office chair?" Ian asked.

She sipped water, then wiped her nose. "Yes. Well, no. I mean. Something wasn't right. The quiet …" Her eyes drifted past Ian and out the open door.

Leaning forward, Ian scooted his chair closer toward her. "Take your time. Tell us what happened."

"Well, I figured if Mr. Evans had come in early, it would be to meet with someone. But there weren't any voices, so, I headed for the back office."

A frown spread across his forehead as Todd bit back a question. *Why hadn't she called out?* Most people would. If you arrive at work and the office is unexpectedly unlocked, you call out, asking who's there. *Why hadn't she?*

Ian's pen was poised over a notepad. "What did you see?"

"Mr. Evans' door was cracked. I peeked inside and … He was …" Her body shook as she sobbed into a wad of tissues.

A minute elapsed before she reigned in her emotions.

"The first thing I saw was Mr. Evans' head. All that blood. I think that's when I noticed him."

"Who?" Ian jotted notes while observing her.

"Junior—Mr. Evans' son. Everyone calls him Junior."

Ian nodded. "Go on."

"That's it. Junior was standing beside the desk, near his dad. When he saw me, he turned—slow-like." She took another sip of water.

"I told him to call the police, but he didn't move. He looked strange. When he wouldn't answer, I ran across the hall—in here—and called 911."

"When you left the office was Mr. Evans still standing beside his dad—at the desk?"

She nodded. "Yes. He didn't move until I came back. I didn't go inside because then he was at the door."

For another ten minutes, Ian questioned her about the morning and preceding evening. After directing another officer to watch over her, Todd and Ian departed for the lobby. They conferred in a far corner of the showroom diagonal to the entrance.

"What do you think?" Todd asked, observing Donald Evans Jr. seated across the room, surrounded by two police officers.

Ian's pen drummed against a notepad. "This has to be related to Mrs. Jones-Collins' death. It can't be a coincidence her boyfriend is also dead."

"It looks like suicide."

"Looks like."

They exchanged poignant glances before Todd's chin motioned toward Junior Evans "What about what Ms. Howard said about the son?"

"Sounds suspicious."

"What was he doing in the office while she was on the phone with 911?"

Ian squared his shoulders. "One way to find out."

Maneuvering around the showroom cars, they advanced on Junior Evans, who rose upon their approach.

Todd displayed his badge. "I'm Detective Gamble. You've already met my partner. We have more questions. Would you like to sit?"

"No," Junior Evans said. His gaze drifted toward the hallway where forensics technicians stood around a stretcher carrying his dad's body.

"What time did you arrive at the office this morning, Mr. Evans?"

"Call me Junior, and I already answered these questions."

"We need to compare your statement against Ms. Howard's."

"Ms.—oh, you mean Cynthia? What did she say?" His gaze abandoned the horizon and landed on Todd.

"What do you think she's been saying?"

Crossing his arms over his chest, Junior Evans glared. "How would I know?"

"Why did you come in early this morning?"

"To see Dad."

"But I understood he didn't usually come in until ten."

Todd perceived a brief narrowing of the suspect's eyes. He also observed Ian documenting the incident.

Junior Evans' chin jutted forward. "I wanted to prepare, get things ready."

"For what? Was a meeting scheduled for this morning?"

"Not an official meeting. I … I wanted to speak with him privately."

"But you knew Ms. Howard came in at 8:30. You couldn't have expected to be alone."

As his jaw clenched, Junior Evans' eyes flitted from side to side.

Todd wondered how long it would take for the young man to think up another lie.

Leaned against the wall, Junior Evans said, "Fine. I didn't come in to speak with Dad. In fact, I came in early to avoid him."

Before Todd formed a question, Junior Evans drifted away from the wall and ambled around a small area in front of the picture window.

"I wanted to drop off a letter. Just place it on his desk and leave."

"And what happened?"

Wild eyed, he stopped circling. "Happened? What do you mean? Nothing *happened*. I found Dad …" His face paled.

Ian retrieved a chair and pushed him down onto it.

Todd signaled an officer to get some water.

Minutes passed as Junior Evans drank. Once his color returned, Todd pulled over another chair and resumed the interrogation.

"Start from when you came into the office."

Junior Evans sighed. "The front door was unlocked. I … It didn't make sense, but I thought maybe Cynthia came in early."

"What time was it again?"

"I'm not sure. Probably around 8:15. The office was quiet. I didn't hear Cynthia typing, and she wasn't in the break room."

Reclined against a nearby display car, Ian scribbled notes. Todd glanced up briefly to confirm with Ian. After his partner nodded, Todd's gaze returned to their suspect.

"Go on."

"I walked down the hallway and noticed the back door unlocked." The young man swallowed. "Then Dad's office door—it was slightly open. I pushed it aside and Dad was dead." He shivered. Tears pooled in his eyes without falling.

Todd believed Junior Evans mourned his dad's death but wavered on the young man's involvement. Killers cried over their victims. Sorrow didn't prove innocence. "What did you do?"

"I walked over to the desk." Junior Evans stretched his hand forward—as if reliving the event—then froze. "I had to be sure." Seconds passed as his outstretched hung in midair.

Slowly, Todd brought his arm down.

"Sorry." He blinked rapidly. "I touched Dad's wrist but didn't find a pulse."

"Did you touch the gun?"

The chair fell aside as Junior Evans leaped up. "No! I never touched a gun."

In concert, Todd rose. "Okay. Calm down. I had to ask."

Junior Evans' face twitched and he retreated. "You think I killed my dad. Why would I do that? I loved him."

"I heard you two recently had a fight."

"That was nothing." His lips shut tight.

"Tell us about it." Todd leaned in.

"It was about Robin. I told Dad she was making a fool of him."

"And he said?"

"F off." Junior Evans scratched his head. "Not in those words, but it amounted to that. He was selling his business, everything for that b—"

Todd's brow rose.

"Woman." Junior Evans' countenance cleared. "I didn't like Dad—not since my parents divorced. But I wouldn't kill him."

A uniformed officer hurried over to Ian, who in turn signaled Todd. The three officers sauntered into a far corner of the showroom, whispering.

"Make sure to inventory all cars on the lot outside and in the showroom," Todd said.

"You think it might've been a burglary?" Ian asked.

"Let's cover every possibility."

The uniformed officer started to walk away when Todd called him back. "And record the license plates."

"Yes, sir," the officer said before leaving.

Five minutes later, Todd and Ian returned to the deceased's office.

A member of the forensics team, wearing a white jumpsuit, waved them over.

"What've you got?" Ian asked.

"We're done here, but I wanted to give you a prelim before I headed out."

Carefully stepping over caution tape, Todd scanned the room. "Anything new?"

"Nope. Looks like suicide."

"Suicide," Todd and Ian said in unison, exchanging glances. They conferred with the lead forensics technician for another ten minutes before again exiting the office.

In the car showroom, an officer bustled over to them with a piece of paper in a clear plastic bag. Their wide gazes questioned him.

"Found this in the son's pocket," the officer said before handing Todd the baggie and sauntering away.

Todd observed Junior Evans brooding outside between two police officers standing like pillars at his sides. He read the note inside the clear baggie before passing it over to Ian.

Ian read and handed it back as Todd headed for the exit.

"You think it's suicide?" Ian asked.

"I don't know, but according to this note, Junior Evans had motive to kill his dad."

Chapter 20

A brief morning rain shower had left the ground outside the car dealership slick. Securing the coat firmly around his neck, Todd stepped outside. His lanky legs tread cautiously around icy gravel. He considered grabbing a thicker coat from the back of his vehicle but decided to speak with their suspect first. *It shouldn't take long.*

Together, he and Ian approached Junior Evans, who rested against the cement building.

"Give us a moment, guys," Todd said. Once the uniformed officers departed he handed Junior Evans the note, still inside the baggie. "Would you like to explain?"

Muscles around Junior Evans' mouth tensed. "It's none of your business. It was meant for my dad."

Ian leaned forward. "He's dead."

Junior Evans' shoulders slumped.

After a quarter minute of silence, Todd asked, "Do you believe your dad committed suicide?"

"Suicide?" His forehead receded.

"Answer the question." Ian's arms crossed over his chest.

"Dad wouldn't commit suicide." Junior Evans started to leave when Ian's palm directed him to remain.

"Not yet."

"Why? I need to call my mom."

A sharp wind had Todd reconsidering a thicker coat. "We've already contacted her. Your letter mentioned child support. Were you and your dad arguing about money?"

A quick dart of Junior Evans' eyes warned Todd of an impending lie. He waited, ready to challenge any false statements.

Instead, Junior Evans glowered. "You read the letter."

"Yes, and you mentioned alimony and child support."

"How old are you?" Ian asked.

"I'm twenty-one."

"Then what was the problem between you and your dad?" Ian asked.

During his pause, Junior Evans glanced over Ian's shoulder. "Mom." He bolted around Ian and up to an older, medium-sized woman wearing a long green coat.

At a more moderate pace, Todd and Ian followed.

Junior Evans gave her a bear-hug. His body shook as his head cuddled into her shoulder.

With a gesture, Todd signaled Ian to give them a moment. While Ian kept vigil over the pair, Todd retrieved a heavier coat from their vehicle. Five minutes later, he approached the son and mom.

After catching Todd's eye, Ian asked, "Mr. Evans are you ready to proceed?"

"What do you want from my son?" the woman asked, grimacing. "His daddy's dead. What can he tell you?"

Todd stepped forward. "I'm sorry about this … Mrs. Evans—correct?"

"Yes," she said. "I kept my married name."

"Mrs. Evans, we need to determine the cause of death," Todd said, burying his hands in warm coat pockets.

Ian tapped a pen against his notepad. "There's reason to believe your husband committed suicide, but your son disagrees."

A quick glance passed between mother and son.

Warm and more alert, Todd's gaze sharpened on the dead man's ex-wife.

"Ma'am?" Ian asked.

After a deep breath, she said, "Donald had money problems. Keeping a younger woman was expensive. He had to be reminded of his prior financial obligations."

"Did he owe you back alimony?" Ian asked.

"Yes. Not a lot, but enough."

"How long did he pay child support?"

"The court ordered child support until age 21 or college graduation."

"So, your son still received support?"

"And my daughter."

"A daughter?"

Her face pinched. "Yes, I have a daughter. Is there a problem with that?"

"No, of course not. We need to know—"

"What?" Junior Evans interjected. "Who had a motive to kill my dad?"

"Sir—"

"My daughter attends school in Chapel Hill," Mrs. Evans said, glaring at Todd. "She was nowhere near here."

"Chapel Hill isn't far."

A sudden thunderstorm grew across Mrs. Evans' face. "How dare you? My daughter had nothing to do with her daddy's death. Donald made a lot of enemies. In fact, the other day, someone threatened him about one of his rental properties."

Her large chunky arm reached around Junior Evans. "Now, if you don't mind. We have more urgent matters to see to—like burying my son's daddy."

Because Mrs. Evans bustled in front of him, Ian lurched backward.

Todd bounded forward. "One moment." He hustled after mother and son. "I have one more question. Why were you quitting?"

"What?" Mrs. Evans stopped suddenly and regarded her son.

Junior Evans stopped and wriggled from under his mom's arm.

"In the letter, you wrote you were quitting." Todd observed the dynamic between the pair. Mrs. Evans' scrutiny bore into her son's profile.

A sigh escaped Junior Evans' lips. "Does it matter now?"

"Why?" Todd insisted.

"Because I wanted to go back to school. I didn't want to work with Dad."

"If you returned to school, your dad had to continue paying alimony, right?"

Junior Evans started forward, but Mrs. Evans grabbed his arm, pulling him to her side. "No, baby. Don't."

The young man's body heaved, his hands clenching.

"Most divorce agreements have an age limit for completing college. We'll be checking with your dad's lawyer."

"I'm sure you will. But that's not why I wanted to return to college. I hated this place." Junior Evans gazed around the used car lot, frowning.

"Junior—"

"Forget it, Mom. They'll figure it out eventually." His head momentarily drooped. "Dad was a bastard in business. I hated the way he treated people."

A tense half-minute elapsed before he continued.

Todd observed Mrs. Evans' scowl.

"I didn't kill him." Tears gathered along his eyelids. "I loved him." His lips quivered and Junior Evans turned aside.

Mrs. Evans cradled his head on her shoulder. "You happy?" She glared at Todd. "Now go find out what happened to his daddy and leave us alone."

A waving forensic technician drew Todd's attention. He motioned to Ian, and they returned inside the car dealership. Before Todd could unbutton his coat, the technician gave a brief assessment.

"So, we've wrapped things up. The body is on the way to the medical examiner, but everything points toward suicide."

"You sure?" Ian asked, removing a candy bar from his coat pocket.

"Stipple marks on the forehead and a weapon near his hand are consistent with suicide. I ordered a paraffin test for the deceased, son, *and* Ms. Howard. They …"

Five minutes passed as the technician explained what had been completed and what was pending.

"Okay," Ian said, slapping the technician on the back. "Get us a prelim from the medical examiner asap."

"Dr. Page said she'd call you at the station," the technician said before departing.

Not until the entire forensics team and Ms. Howard had left the building did Todd and Ian discuss the case.

Munching on a candy bar, Ian asked, "You believe this was suicide?"

"For now," Todd said, searching in his pockets for gloves. "We'll wait for the paraffin test on Junior Evans. With Mrs. Jones-Collins' death officially a homicide—we could have two murders or a murder and a suicide."

Seconds passed as Todd considered what he had said. An idea teased at the back of his mind but slipped away. *Later.*

"We'll follow up with the son—and his mom. Mrs. Evans looks like she could've killed the dad with her bare hands."

"Momma bear."

"Exactly."

Although braced for the bitter, cold air, Todd found himself well-protected against the elements.

Mrs. Evans and her son were in their car, preparing to exit the lot but several vehicles blocked the driveway. A bottleneck created by numerous police vehicles and forensics vans.

Todd trotted up to their Cadillac. With his gloved hand, Todd knocked on the car's driver-side window.

"We still have questions, Mr. Evans."

"Really," Mrs. Evans spoke across her son from the passenger seat, "this is too much. We—"

"It's fine, Mom." Junior Evans placed the car in park. "What did you want to ask, officer?"

"Detective Gamble."

"Yes, detective."

"Could you repeat what happened when you arrived at the dealership?"

While the car idled, Junior Evans replayed what occurred when he'd arrived at the office.

"I planned to leave the note on Dad's desk. He usually didn't arrive before ten, so I knew no one would be in the office."

"What about the assistant?"

"Cynthia? She usually comes in after eight-thirty."

"What time did you arrive?"

With a deep sigh, Junior Evans glanced out the car's front window. "I'm not sure. What did I tell the officer?"

Neither Todd nor Ian answered. Less than a minute passed.

"I think it was eight ten or fifteen. Maybe later. I'm … I don't know."

"Umm hm. Did you check your watch?"

His bottom lip pouted. "I'm not sure. It was shortly after eight, though. I entered the lobby and found Dad in his office—"

"May I see your watch?"

With a grunt, Junior Evans stuck his right arm out the open window.

"Thank you." Flipping through several pages of his notepad, Ian asked, "You have a key to the front door."

"Yes, but …" Junior Evans stared straight ahead out the windshield. "The front door was open. I didn't have to unlock it. And the lights were on."

"What was your dad's usual procedure for opening the office?"

"Dad didn't open the office. Cynthia arrived before he did, or else I unlocked the lobby doors if Cynthia or Milton were busy."

"What's the meaning of these questions?" Mrs. Evan's asked, not receiving a reply.

"Who closed the office at night?"

Junior Evans shrugged. "Me or Dad. Cynthia leaves before five to avoid traffic."

"No other employees?"

Todd detected a slight hesitation. "Sir?"

"Dad let the last employee go yesterday. Things have been rough. You know, the credit crash, housing market."

Both Todd and Ian nodded. Junior Evans provided Ian with the name of the other employee.

"So, last night, who locked up?" Ian asked. "You or—"

"Dad," Junior Evans said before Ian could finish.

***

The Cadillac SUV exited the lot as Todd and Ian hurried inside their vehicle.

"Nice ride," Ian said as Junior Evans and his mom departed.

"Humph." Todd started the engine and joined a long line of vehicles waiting to leave.

"I think she caught on to the reason for my questions."

Ian scooped up a black muscle ball and squeezed. "Yeah, but the kid didn't."

"No, he didn't. Not too bright."

"Maybe he's upset about his dad."

Todd shrugged. "Maybe."

The signal light flashed red. Todd stopped before the crosswalk. "What about the watch?"

"I wanted to see if it had the correct time."

"Did it?"

"Ten minutes fast."

Todd peeked at Ian before observing the traffic light.

Ian tore open a bag of chips. "You don't believe it was suicide."

Before proceeding across the intersection, Todd glanced at his partner. "Why were the front doors to the showroom unlocked?"

Ian grinned. "And don't forget about the lights."

Once the signal light turned green, Todd proceeded forward. His mind reflected on an idea he had earlier. A thought he had regarding a murder and a suicide.

Chapter 21

Frosty evening mist glistened off the long rectangular church windows, sending rainbows of light throughout the sanctuary. A pianist exercised the organ, releasing a low melody of *Order My Steps in the Lord* crooned by a small contingent of choir members. Myaisha held a program for the memorial service while swaying to the music.

The number of church attendants dwarfed the number of mourners. Not surprising, given Robin had lived in Greensboro for such a short time. Most attendees were members of the Greensboro Women of Color Writing Group present to support René more than to mourn Robin.

Myaisha grimaced. Though Robin had accompanied René to writing group meetings, she hadn't spoken with the former often. Polite and personable, Robin didn't seem interested in writing. Once, Myaisha had inquired about her interests.

"I want to open a yoga studio," Robin had said.

"Oh, you do a lot of yoga?" she had asked.

"No, but it's really popular. You can make a lot of money from it." Robin listed several side projects she intended to launch related to her yoga business.

"Where are you getting the capital?" Myaisha remembered Robin's distorted grin.

"I have resources."

She never had an opportunity to follow up with Robin about the yoga business. *How did Robin plan to fund it during a recession? Who or what were those resources?*

Those bruises on Robin's body still bothered her. Although the radio announced the police had officially classified Robin's death a homicide, the manner of death had not been disclosed.

In front of the sanctuary, Pastor Matthew stood beside the podium and raised his hands. "Let's begin." He opened his Bible and led with prayer.

Music faded as Mary rose and recited a poem.

After Mary regained her seat in the front row, Myaisha came forward and shared a Bible verse provided by Mrs. Jones. On her way down from the stage, an angular, almost bony woman passed her. They hadn't met, but Myaisha had noticed this woman seated along the same pew as René and Mrs. Jones.

The entire memorial service lasted under an hour. Pastor Matthew closed with another prayer before leaving the podium to console the family.

With one eye on them, Myaisha thanked the choir.

Mourners lined up to pay their respects to the Jones family before exiting the sanctuary. A handful of her writing group members huddled around the last aisle, nearest the exit.

Unsure if they were waiting for her, Myaisha ambled down the center aisle and joined Pastor Matthew and Mrs. Jones. She rested a hand on René's shoulder. "Can I do anything for you?"

"Thank you," René said. "I appreciate you guys putting this together."

"Of course. You're our friend."

The two women hugged.

"If we can do anything for you and your family, Mrs. Jones," Pastor Matthew said, gathering her hands together warmly in his, "please ask."

He pivoted toward René. "Sister, you're welcome to join our fellowship anytime."

After expressing several kind sentiments, he returned to the front of the sanctuary where ushers cleared away Bibles, sheet music, and other miscellaneous items.

Myaisha accompanied René, Mrs. Jones, and the still-unknown woman out into the church lobby. She reached around René's mom and extended her hand toward the thin woman.

"Hello, my name's Myaisha Douglas. We haven't been introduced."

"I'm sorry," René said. "Myaisha, this is my cousin, Latrice."

"How long will you be staying in Greensboro?" she asked, shaking Latrice's hand.

"We'll be leaving as soon as they release Robin's body," Mrs. Jones said. "I can't wait to get out of this backward town."

Inhaling deeply, René said, "Mom, it's a city, *not* a town."

"Aunt Angela," Latrice said, "Chi needs us."

With a frown, Myaisha asked, "Chi?"

"A nickname." René bounded toward the exit.

"If you need a place to stay, I have an available room," Myaisha said to Latrice.

"Thank you. I might take you up on that," Latrice said, rolling her eyes toward the departing René.

They left adjacent to each other with Mrs. Jones bringing up the rear.

As they sauntered toward their respective cars, Myaisha observed a man approach Mrs. Jones. Tall with a medium skin tone, he paused and spoke with her.

Slowing her pace in order to overhear, Myaisha observed their conversation but was too far away to decipher what they said.

While René, her mom, and Latrice prepared to leave, the man retreated to his car.

Myaisha gasped. She recognized the white Camaro. For confirmation, she checked the car's license. The Illinois plate was the same one she saw at the urgent care center.

She dashed over to the Camaro before the man could depart.

"Hello. Excuse me," she shouted, waving the memorial service program, motioning for him to wait.

His craggy grimace turned in her direction. "Who are you?"

Leaning against the hood of the man's car, Myaisha took a second to catch her breath and adjust her hat. She extended a hand in greeting.

"I'm Myaisha, a friend of René—and Robin."

The man's features softened. "Terrence." A beat passed. "Robin was my ex-wife."

"I'm sorry for your loss. Is there anything I can do for you?"

His posture sagged. "No, thank you. It's … I'm still getting used to—to realizing she's gone."

Myaisha waited silently, giving him a moment to collect himself and judging the veracity of his sorrow.

She inched closer. "Did René explain what happened?"

Terrence hesitated. "She said something about bleeding in the chest. Have they completed the autopsy?"

His stumble over the last word gave her pause. *Was he disturbed by the idea of his ex-wife being cut open, or worried about what the medical examiner might find?*

"Yes. Robin's death has been ruled a homicide."

His gaze widened. "How?"

Seconds passed as Myaisha observed the metamorphism in his countenance. *Was he truly surprised or an excellent actor?*

"Angela didn't say anything," Terrence said, gazing across the parking lot where the women were speaking.

"No? Maybe she didn't feel it was the right time."

He nodded. "Perhaps."

"With her death ruled a homicide, you've become a suspect."

"What? You're crazy."

"Am I?"

His gaze narrowed. "They can't suspect me."

"Why not? You're the ex-husband. A spouse is always the prime suspect."

"But we were divorced."

"Yes, but you followed her here. Didn't you?"

"No, we—"

"I saw you grab her arm outside the clinic Monday night."

He glowered. "It wasn't like that."

"She had bruises on her body."

"Uh uhh. No way. I didn't lay a hand on her."

"What were you arguing about?"

"None of your business."

She shrugged. "It's police business though. I'm sure they'll be coming by to interrogate you about your whereabouts the morning of Robin's murder."

Terrence studied her face. Myaisha didn't waver.

Crunching sounded along the gravel. In her periphery, she watched Deniece and members of her writing group strolling across the parking lot.

"What do you want?" he sneered.

"I want to know what happened—to help René."

"You and Chi tight?"

"What does Chi stand for?"

"I don't know. Robin called her that, so I did too."

"We belong to a writing group and have done business together. She's a sharp businesswoman."

He reclined against the car. "She's proficient in business. Too bad Robin wasn't."

"Why did you divorce?"

"I loved Robin, but … She started businesses like other people changed underwear. She had brilliant ideas, but no follow-through." He scratched his short, curly locks. "And her hobby was running up credit cards."

"But she filed against you?" Myaisha was guessing, but Terrence didn't know that.

He chuckled. "Yeah. I loved her but couldn't afford her."

They talked for another five minutes before Myaisha watched him drive away. She settled inside her Honda, wondering how to verify what he'd said. As the car engine ignited, her gaze wandered across the graveled lot.

The Jones family was huddled near their vehicle now, speaking with two men.

Against the descending dusk, Myaisha recognized the men as Detectives Gamble and de Jesus.

She knew why the police would want to question the family. Myaisha had momentarily considered asking René if the police had notified them about the medical examiner's conclusions, but discussing Robin's murder before the memorial service seemed insensitive.

What was the cause of death? Until she had an answer—like treating a complicated patient—Myaisha wouldn't rest until she discovered the diagnosis. A puzzle needed a solution.

How to determine who committed this murder? If she hadn't been intent on speaking with Terrence, she could've asked René if the police told her the cause of death. *Maybe her friend already knew.*

CHAPTER 22

A sharp wind rattled the car windows. Despite the chilly temperature, Myaisha left her car and joined the Jones family as they spoke with the detectives.

On her approach, Myaisha made eye contact with René, who in turn diverted her gaze. Not detecting outright hostility, she listened from a distance of about five feet.

A shiny badge dangled from Detective de Jesus' belt as he spoke. "The medical examiner is sure, Mrs. Jones."

The matriarch gasped, slapping a hand around her mouth.

"But who could have *poisoned* her?" Latrice asked, moving slightly toward the detective.

René supported her mom's depressed shoulders. Myaisha moved closer to Mrs. Jones, prepared to assist if necessary.

"We don't know," Detective de Jesus said. "That's what we want to ask you about." He answered Latrice's question while observing René.

Perhaps detecting his scrutiny, René swallowed and gnawed her bottom lip. Her voice wobbled. "What would we know about poison?"

"How was she poisoned?" Myaisha asked, marching up to Detective de Jesus.

The pen in the detective's hand clicked. "Dr. Douglas, this doesn't concern you."

"Of course, it does. René is my friend. I didn't know Robin well, but … Why is her cause of death a secret?"

Four pairs of eyes studied Detective de Jesus.

Todd cleared his throat. "We're not releasing the actual name of the poison until we identify the killer. I'm sure you understand." With a pointed glare, he eyed Myaisha and flicked his head to the side.

If he intended for her to leave, he would be disappointed.

Aside to him, Myaisha asked, "Did you get a court order for the clinic lab work?"

"Dr. Douglas," Detective de Jesus interceded, "we're not here to answer your questions. Now step aside."

Myaisha noticed he'd been working out more. His suit coat barely contained his hulking biceps. Undeterred, she asked, "Is René a suspect?"

Her friend's body tensed.

"Surely, you don't suspect us," Mrs. Jones addressed Todd. "René and Robin had their problems, but they always stood by each other."

"Even when Robin started a sexual relationship with Donald Evans?" Detective de Jesus asked.

The sharp intake of air by Latrice and Mrs. Jones was not missed by anyone. René's head trembled. Her mouth moved but no words escaped.

Myaisha side-hugged René. "It's okay. You don't have to say anything if you don't want to."

Tears gathered along René's lashes. She shivered and remained silent.

Myaisha rubbed her shoulder. "Would you like to go home?"

As if scrutinizing the rocks beneath her shoes, René lowered her head and managed a brief nod.

With Latrice at the wheel, the Jones family piled into their car and departed.

Myaisha watched them exit the church parking lot.

Although they stood at least three feet apart, she sensed anger roiling off Detective de Jesus like heat on a Texas summer highway. Her shoulders stiffened as he glared in her direction.

"Dr. Douglas," he snarled, "don't you have anything better to do than interfering in our investigations?" Without awaiting a reply, he stomped off.

A light grin grew across her face as she faced Todd. "Are you mad at me too, or may I still call you Todd?"

Somber dark eyes regarded her. He rubbed his forehead. She admired the crisp sharp edges along his short, cropped afro.

"Not in front of people," he said in a low voice while glancing at his partner.

She smiled and ambled along with him as he approached the one car remaining in the lot except hers.

"So, what type of poison was used?"

He stopped abruptly, causing her to overshoot his stride. She retraced her steps.

"What?"

His teeth clenched. "That is confidential."

"No problem. I might be able to guess. Will you tell me if I'm right?"

"No."

"Hmm. Let's see. The lab report from the clinic showed Robin's PTT and PT were elevated." She gave him a side glance but detected no change in his demeanor. "What poisons cause prolonged bleeding and severe hemorrhage?"

Her gait slowed as her brain cogitated. "What about her nose?"

His gaze sharpened. "What about her nose?"

"I heard it was broken."

He touched the side of her arm. "And who told you that?"

"You have your sources and I have mine."

"It wasn't broken, only bruised. And it might have occurred when she fell. But it wasn't the cause of death."

"Rat poison." Myaisha heard her voice reflected in the surrounding silence. "Sorry. I didn't mean to shout, but rat poison can increase the PTT, PT, and INR."

"Are those labs—"

"I'm thinking out loud," she said, internally musing over possibilities. "Rat poison would also cause internal hemorrhage. Of course, I could be more certain if I reviewed the actual autopsy report."

Those last words clung in the air. She peered over at him and observed his nostrils flare.

"I'm not showing you the autopsy report."

"Fine."

From the car, Detective de Jesus yelled, "Gamble."

Todd turned to face her. "Look—"

"Myaisha."

A curl drew his lips upward, but he fought a burgeoning grin. She appreciated his tiny dimples. If he smiled, they would trail down his cheeks.

"Dr. Douglas," he said, peeking around her at his partner, "I will not share official police information with you. However, if you have information pertinent to the murder investigation—"

"Rat poison can cause internal bleeding, organ failure, paralysis, coma, and death. But it's not a reliable method of killing. Unless you can be sure your victim takes a dose high enough to cause death. Also, a murderer isn't likely to get away with the crime. It's easily detected."

"Really?"

"Look how easily your medical examiner uncovered the truth. It appeared to be murder due to a physical assault, but with the abnormal labs and significant bleeding—the truth was easily discovered."

Detective Gamble stared at her a second. "Dr. Douglas, if you have any more insights you'd like to share," he held out a card, "give me a call."

She declined the card and lowered her voice. "I already have your number. Come by the house. I might have more information for you—and I made a chocolate peanut butter tart."

Without acknowledging her comment, Todd entered his car and started the ignition.

She strolled away.

Because the detectives' car window was open, their conversation wafted on the December breeze.

"Where next?" Todd asked.

"Fire department," Detective de Jesus said, then gave an address.

"What's the guy's name?"

"Andrew James Thomas. His mom had a thing for disciples."

Myaisha heard laughter as they drove away. But she wasn't laughing.

What did AJ have to do with Robin's murder?

Chapter 23

Dusk settled across Greensboro as Myaisha drove home. As she turned into the cul de sac, she waved to Ms. Lula.

Wearing pink hair curlers under a head scarf, Ms. Lula—because she was carrying a crock pot—acknowledged Myaisha with a head nod.

Two cars were parked in front of Myaisha's house. One in the driveway and the other at the foot of the drive beside the mailbox.

As the garage door scrolled upward, she considered why homicide detectives wanted to speak with AJ. She would soon find out since his truck was parked beside her mailbox.

Dogs barked as she entered the house through the laundry room off the garage.

Boomer, her black Labrador retriever, greeted her with wet licks and kisses. Next to him, Zoey, AJ's brown Labrador, impatiently waited for hugs. Once the dogs were content, Myaisha entered the kitchen.

Seated at a glass table in the kitchen nook before a bay window, Deniece rose. "Hey, girl. Where've you been? The memorial ended an hour ago."

Tap water splashed over her hands as Myaisha washed up in the kitchen sink. "I had people to speak with."

"Like whom?"

Deniece handed her a glass of white wine before kissing her on the cheek. A man with a gray-peppered afro, slightly balding at the crown, reached around Deniece to peck Myaisha's other cheek.

"Hello, Mya," Barry said in a rich baritone. "We've been waiting. Ready to get whipped in spades?"

Deniece shoved her husband aside. "You wish. Mya and I are gonna crush you guys."

While the couple verbally sparred, AJ ambled over to Myaisha and gave her a light kiss on the lips.

"How're you doing?"

"Tired," she said. "How was your week?"

He shrugged, picked up her wine glass, and carried it over to the table. "I've had better."

Myaisha busied herself around the kitchen, providing snacks and other supplies she deemed appropriate for their monthly card game. A large bowl of pretzels tottered in her hand as she walked over to the table, where a stack of playing cards awaited.

"How's Carl?" Myaisha asked, remembering AJ's colleague she'd stitched up in the urgent care clinic the same night Robin came by. She placed the bowl of pretzels on the table and sat down.

"Better. Still working on the house." AJ sat and slid a wine glass in front of her.

Cards shuffled between Deniece's fingers. "Who's Carl?"

"A friend," AJ said, sipping wine. "He relocated here from Michigan last summer."

"He and his partner are renovating their house," Myaisha said, picking up her cards and arranging them according to suit.

AJ's forehead wrinkled as he studied the cards. "Not renovating. They're repairing defaults Evans neglected to mention when he sold them that dump."

Myaisha contemplated AJ's countenance. Not wanting to impede play, she dropped a card on the table.

Barry chuckled. "Don't speak ill of the dead."

"Dead?" Myaisha frowned.

"You haven't heard?" AJ said, discarding a card on the table.

"No, who—"

"Donald Evans was found dead in his office this morning."

That must be the reason the police wanted to speak with AJ. *But why?*

Thunk.

Deniece threw a card down on the table with emphasis. "Ha. I knew we'd win this hand." She gathered up the cards and gave them to Barry to shuffle and deal. "Y'all better focus on the game, or me and Mya are going to beat your behinds."

"I thought this was a friendly game," AJ said, retrieving the cards Barry dealt him."

"A game's not worth playing if it's not worth winning," Denice said, winking at Myaisha.

"Hey," Barry said, "no secret sistah communications."

Deniece laughed. "Just because you guys don't know how to talk without speaking doesn't mean we can't."

"AJ, pour Mya some more wine," Barry said.

Deniece smirked at her husband. "You think getting us drunk will help y'all win?"

"If you can send secret messages, AJ and I can use alcohol," he said.

Play proceeded in silence for the next twenty minutes, broken suddenly by Deniece's shout.

"Yes," she said, jumping up from the table and doing a brief dance.

The dogs scattered off the floor at her excitement, scurrying out the doggy door and into the backyard.

"Look," Barry said, "you've scared the dogs."

While Deniece tallied their points on a sheet of paper, Myaisha gathered the cards strewn across the table.

"Good game," she said, shuffling the deck.

"It's always a good game when y'all win," Barry said.

Reclined in a chair sipping from a soda bottle, Deniece asked AJ, "So what happened with your friend's house? Didn't they hire an inspector before closing?"

AJ folded his hands behind his head. "No. The market was crazy. People were scooping up homes left and right with outrageous bids. They didn't want to lose out."

"Then they can't complain if they find problems." Deniece slurped the remaining soda before carrying the empty bottle into the kitchen.

Myaisha's shoulders tensed as AJ's posture stiffen. The shimmer in his light brown eyes darkened.

"Of course, they can complain," she said. "Because someone doesn't get an inspection doesn't mean the seller can lie about the home's condition."

Sauntering back over to the table, Deniece plopped down on the chair. "True. But people shouldn't be surprised when they're cheated. There's no honor in business. A person's word is worthless."

"Remember when we bought our first home, D? Our realtor lied about everything from the flooring to the roof." Barry walked over to the sliding glass doors overlooking the yard.

"Yes, but we *got* an inspection," Deniece said. "And not from the person our realtor suggested."

AJ rubbed his forehead, inhaled, and exhaled deeply. "Not everyone has your experience. Carl's partner has multiple sclerosis. He wanted a ranch home without stairs or a lot of upkeep."

Curious, Myaisha placed a hand on AJ's shoulder and peered into his face. "Is his partner in a wheelchair?"

"Not yet, but he will be soon."

Conversation lapsed. Myaisha figured everyone—like herself—was considering the implications of losing their mobility. She rose from the table and refilled her wine glass.

"So, you've been helping with repairs?" she asked AJ between crunching on a pretzel.

"Yeah," he said. "Carl visits his mom every Sunday. She's in a nursing home in Asheboro. Between her, his partner, and work … Carl's overwhelmed."

"Poor guy," Deniece said. "He's got a lot on his plate." She drifted into the living room and sank onto a couch facing the entertaining center on the far wall at the other end of the great room.

Less than a minute passed before Barry joined her. Myaisha and AJ sat on the other couch, perpendicular to Deniece and Barry.

Everyone seemed lost in their own thoughts. For herself, Myaisha gazed out across the backyard, watching the dogs sniff stiff, cold grass.

The sun had set hours ago. Lights under the blue beadboard ceiling threw a somber, warm glow from the patio deck across the lawn.

Barry yawned. "Well, if you need help, my Sundays are free."

"Thanks, man," AJ said, rising and clapping Barry's shoulder. "We could always use another hammer."

"I can help," Deniece said. Her sinewy legs stretched forward across an oblong coffee table. "It might be fun."

Myaisha scooted along the couch closer to AJ. "I don't mind helping, but I'm not good with tools."

Deniece laughed. "You can say that again."

A pillow landed on Deniece's lap where Myaisha tossed it.

"Hey, don't get angry with me. You're the klutz."

"Actually," AJ said, extending his six-foot-ten-inch legs under the table. "I've been thinking about getting into real estate. Maybe purchase a couple properties, clean them up, and charge rent people can afford."

His gaze, which had been focused on the table, crept up to Myaisha's face. She held her emotions in check, unsure if he was searching for agreement in her expression.

Barry asked, "You have time for real estate with your job? Don't firemen work long hours?"

"I'm thinking about retiring."

No one spoke. The dogs trotted inside and curled up on the living room rug beside the coffee table. Using his foot, Boomer scratched behind his ears.

Myaisha knew the spot. She reached down and relieved his itch. The Labrador's rear leg danced. Her mind avoided exploring what AJ voiced. *He wanted to retire.*

She rose and locked the sliding glass doors. *Why was she bothered by the thought of AJ retiring?* He was a grown man. If he didn't want to work …

But that was it. She couldn't understand a grown man not working. Not a man AJ's age. He was barely fifty. What would he do, sit at home and—

"And do what?" Deniece asked.

Myaisha admired her friend's initiative. If Deniece had a question, she simply asked, no consternation about civility or improprieties.

"Start a real estate business. Rehab properties and make them available to low-income buyers."

"Why?" Deniece asked.

"D," Myaisha said, sitting on the couch but farther from AJ than before.

"What? I want to know why he wants to help people."

A smirk crossed AJ's lips. "You don't believe in goodwill toward our fellow humans?"

"Sure, but most people have ulterior motives." Deniece curled her legs along the couch underneath her torso.

"Truth," Barry said, extending his arm behind her neck. "So often people pretend to be helping when they simply want to make money. Suspect altruism until proven otherwise."

Myaisha peeked at AJ, weighing his expression to determine whether he'd taken offense. Deep dimples creased his grinning face. Her chest relaxed and she reclined into the pillows.

"Well," AJ said, "to be honest, I was thinking about retiring before this housing market nightmare started, but I didn't know what to do. When this occurred, I realized I could help."

Myaisha pivoted her body to face AJ. "Do you have a realtor's license?"

"Not yet," he said, "but I can rehab homes in the meantime."

She nodded, observing his face.

"You could make a difference if you do it right," Barry said.

As the two men conversed, Myaisha studied AJ, trying to understand the man she thought she'd known. Although they had only dated for six months, she'd believed she understood him rather well. But he hadn't mentioned wanting to retire. *What brought this about? Would AJ be able to afford retirement?*

"How much is your pension?" Denice blurted out.

"D," Myaisha and Barry said in unison.

"What?"

AJ laughed. "Enough to meet my needs."

Shooting Deniece a weighty grimace, Myaisha's stomach unclenched—because that was her worry.

She'd been raised by two old-school southern parents, who didn't tolerate foolishness. If you didn't work, you didn't need to eat was her retired military father's opinion. And that sensibility lay at the core of her understanding of adult work ethic.

After her husband Sammy's death, she could have retired and lived comfortably. But instead, she took on more work, accepting a part-time position at an urgent care center in addition to her private medical practice. She couldn't imagine dating a retired man in his early fifties. Work provided her with more than money. *Why retire?* But a second career sounded reasonable.

"You could retire and start a hobby," Barry offered, ignoring the silly glance from Deniece.

"No," AJ said, "I like working. I want to contribute, help people. This housing crisis is breaking up families."

Myaisha's thoughts returned to her college friend, Candace, murdered last summer. Candace had worked in real estate, but she hadn't been as beneficent as AJ proposed to be. Myaisha shivered, recalling her friend's brutal murder and the part she'd played in bringing the killer to justice.

AJ reached across the couch and squeezed her hand. *Did he perceive she was cold?* He couldn't understand that she was recalling Candace's murder. *Or did he?*

Cuddling underneath her husband, Deniece asked, "Do you think Donald Evans' murder had something to do with his real estate business?"

Deniece ignored Myaisha's glare, stuck out her tongue, and turned toward AJ.

"Don't know," AJ said, "but I wouldn't be surprised. Evans was a roach."

"Cockroaches and cats will survive the apocalypse," Barry chuckled.

"Hmm. I wonder if his real estate business or those cheap junk cars he sold were the reason behind his murder," Deniece said.

With his large palm, Barry brought Deniece's head near his face and kissed her on the temple. "Okay, Nancy Drew. Can you stop investigating for one night?"

"I'm thinking out loud," she said, planting a wet kiss on his lips.

"Sure. Soon you and Mya will be involved in another homicide if I know you two."

"You should be glad we investigate murders instead of committing them," Deniece said, smiling up into Barry's face.

AJ cleared his throat. "I agree with Barry." He slid along the couch closer to Myaisha. "You don't want to get involved in another homicide. The last time, you came close to—"

"Getting killed," Barry finished.

"We know what we're doing," Deniece said. "Don't we Mya?"

Myaisha addressed AJ. "I have no intention of confronting another murderer."

"Promise?" Deniece asked slyly.

"It's getting late." Myaisha stood.

"See, D," Barry said, "even Easy Rawlins over there doesn't want to tangle with a killer."

"I'm not Easy," Myaisha said.

"That's for sure," AJ said, grinning suggestively at her.

Her face flushed as Myaisha bustled into the kitchen, where she refilled the water and food bowls for the dogs.

Deniece and Barry ambled around the living room, gathering their coats and other items.

"Well, if Mya is Easy Rawlins, then I'm Raymond Alexander," Deniece said.

Helping Deniece into her coat, Barry said, "Mouse? You can't be Mouse."

"Why not?"

Making her way to the front door, Myaisha said, "Because he's a cold-hearted killer."

"Okay, he has some faults," Deniece said, "but he's Easy's best friend."

"Is he?" Barry asked. "Easy seems scared of him."

"Mouse considers Easy a good friend, and that's what matters." Deniece wriggled into her coat.

At the edge of the living room, AJ stood next to the hall leading into the foyer. "The point is to stay out of the police investigation." He glanced at Myaisha, and she held his gaze.

"Try telling Thelma and Louise here anything," Barry said, entering the foyer and opening the front door.

Both Labradors leaped to their feet. Tails wagging, they scampered to the front door.

Deniece smacked the side of Barry's arm. "We aren't Thelma and Louise. I'm Raymond Alexander and Mya is Easy Rawlins."

The couple sauntered outside, their voices audible from an open front door.

"Okay, Mouse. Whatever you say," Barry said.

"Really." Deniece giggled. "Are you willing to do whatever I say when we get home?"

"Yes, baby," Barry said, pulling her to his side.

"Good night," Myaisha said, quickly shutting the door before she heard more of their foreplay.

She returned to the living room where two pouty dogs glared at her.

"Wanna take a walk?" AJ asked Myaisha.

The yelping dogs answered before she could.

"I guess I do," she said, reaching into the coat closet.

"Good. We have a lot discuss."

Yes. Like why the police want to speak with you about Donald Evans' murder.

CHAPTER 24

Sunlight waned in the Friday evening sky as Todd and Ian approached the two-story brick home on a narrow street where five days prior, Robin Jones-Collins had died. However, this evening they needed to speak with the family of Donald Evans Sr. The medical examiner hadn't signed off on his death yet, but Dr. Page had hinted in her preliminary report suicide appeared unlikely.

In the car, before proceeding up the short walkway to the front door, Todd had agreed Ian would lead the interrogation. In his systematic mind, Todd struggled with reconciling the poisoning of Robin Jones-Collins with the death of Donald Evans Sr., whether from homicide or suicide. He pictured possible scenarios but failed to make them coincide with the facts. The order of their deaths seemed incongruous. *Were the two cases related?*

Plenty of people desired Mr. Evans' death, however, Mrs. Jones-Collins had been in Greensboro barely three months. She didn't even have friends here—not serious friends. The ex-husband stalked her down from Chicago.

Ian pounded on the door. *Boom, boom.*

Todd frowned. "Remember, they're family of the deceased, not suspects—yet. Go easy on the door."

Sending him a terse smirk, Ian swerved toward the opening door.

The deceased's son grimaced.

"Good evening, Mr. Evans," Ian said. "We have more questions. May we come in?"

Junior Evans' hand wavered above the doorknob. Half a minute elapsed before he invited them inside. "Call me Junior. It's easier."

Todd followed behind Ian. His gaze found the area on the carpet where Mrs. Jones-Collins had lain, her head doused in blood. Though it had been cleaned, Todd detected a faint outline of the bloody scene.

On the left, in the living room, Ian conversed with Junior Evans and his mother, the deceased's ex-wife. A different, younger woman sat in a window seat, peeking outside around heavily lined curtains.

"At least y'all didn't come in a police car," the young woman said.

"And you are?" Ian asked.

"That's my sister, Kamara," Junior Evans said.

After accepting a seat and declining coffee, Ian removed a notepad. "Since we haven't spoken before, I'll start with you, Ms. Evans." His body aligned with hers. "Can you tell me where you were Thursday evening?"

"So, Dad was killed Thursday night?" Junior Evans asked, popping up from the sofa beside the fireplace.

"The medical examiner hasn't determined the cause of death or the time yet. We want to establish where everyone was Thursday night *and* Friday morning."

"Dad called me," Kamara said.

Ian sat up straighter. "When? What did he say?"

Todd observed Mrs. Evans' gaze widen. He scrutinized Junior Evans, who brooded beside the fireplace.

"It was yesterday afternoon. He said he needed a place to stay."

"What time did he get to your place?"

"He didn't."

Frowning, Todd focused on Ms. Evans. "Why did he change his mind?"

She shrugged. "I don't know."

"Did you call him back?" Ian's pen tapped against the notepad.

"No." She shifted position in the window seat. "This wasn't the first time my dad failed to show up when he was expected."

Not much affection.

Over the next twenty minutes, each member of the Jones family related their whereabouts during the times in question. While Ian interviewed the family, Todd meandered around the living room and kitchen. Forensics had searched it the day Robin Jones-Collins died, and again after Donald Evans Sr. was discovered dead in his office.

Many items remained in forensics awaiting analysis. Chemical tests were conducted on food items, beverages, and hygiene products. Last time Todd had checked, results were still pending. The lab hadn't identified where the poison originated, but it was a substance called ... He couldn't remember the name. Bromadiolone or some such thing.

Myaisha had surprised him with her elucidation of the correct poison. But she was a medical doctor *and* wrote murder mysteries. *Should he be surprised?*

Actually, he was more concerned. Though he refused to admit it to anyone—especially her—he respected the doctor. Moreover, he liked her. Except ... *Dammit.* If she didn't remind him of his older sister, they could probably be good friends.

Concentrating on the crime scene, Todd scrutinized the house where Mr. Evans Sr. had married, raised his children, cheated on his wife then—

What? Did Donald Evans kill his lover?

Furnishings in the brick house were sparse. Large pieces of outdated furniture crowded the living room. *Did the ex-wife get the good stuff in the divorce? Was Mrs. Jones-Collins planning to dump him for her ex?*

One of Mrs. Jones-Collins girlfriends in Chicago said the dead woman hinted at the possibility. Mr. Evans *appeared* to be the big roller Mrs. Jones-Collins desired. And the girlfriend in Chicago had stated the dead woman had expensive tastes. In fact, she'd reiterated that fact three times. But Mr. Evans Sr. had been reticent about his finances. The friend stated Mrs. Jones-Collins recently voiced doubts about the relationship.

Nothing in the room suggested affluence or financial success. Todd made a mental note to have the accounting guys review Mr. Evans' personal *and* business finances. The department had made an official request for the will. It should be available by Monday—he hoped. Two people dead. This case had Todd puzzled.

On a bookshelf opposite a large picture window facing the front yard, Todd identified an absence of family photos. Three pictures of Mr. Evans' children rested on the shelf but none of the entire family together. However, a large red frame held a picture of Mrs. Jones-Collins.

Five pictures were of Mr. Evans Sr. and Mrs. Jones-Collins together, two in a restaurant, one in this house, and two at the used car dealership. In the dealership photo, Mr. Evans reclined in a large leather chair with Mrs. Jones-Collins on his lap. His right hand, covered with a black wrist splint, rested on her thigh.

Todd's brow wrinkled. He picked up the frame and removed the photo. On the back, he searched for a date stamp but didn't find one. He thought back over the scene in the office. *Had Mr. Evans worn a splint? When had Mr. Evans injured his wrist?*

Todd recalled the office crime scene and the bloody, gaping wound on the right side of Mr. Evans' head. *Would a wrist injury prevent Mr. Evans from shooting himself in the head?*

Knock, knock.

Conversation ceased as everyone pivoted toward the front door. Since he was closest, Todd answered the summons. To his surprise—and dismay—Mrs. Jones-Collins' mother stood on the doorstep.

Mrs. Jones' eyes boggled and her voice stuttered. "Oh, I … I didn't expect you. No one else has been killed, have they?"

"No, ma'am," Todd said, weighing her response.

"Oh, good." She waited, seemingly uncertain about how to proceed. Seconds passed.

Todd did nothing to assist her.

Junior Evans strode up behind him. "Can I help you?"

Perceiving the young man didn't recognize Mrs. Jones, Todd gave the introductions.

A gawking Junior Evans shook hands with Mrs. Jones, stumbling over his words. "I'm sorry about your daughter."

"Thank you," she said. "I heard you found your father— that he committed suicide."

"The police aren't sure," he said.

"They aren't?"

Both Mrs. Jones and Junior Evans eyeballed Todd. He retreated from the doorway without answering their inquisitive glances.

Turning back toward Mrs. Jones, Junior Evans asked, "Did you want to come in?"

"No, thank you," she said. "I wanted to pick up Robin's things—unless the police took them."

Again, they both regarded Todd. As he returned to the living room, they followed.

"Anything related to Mrs. Jones-Collins would be down at the station, ma'am. Was there anything in particular you wanted?"

He noticed Mrs. Jones scanning the room. Her gaze paused over Mrs. Evans. The latter bristled and her mouth pursed. Neither woman addressed the other or anyone else. Everyone waited and watched. Ian's pen hovered over the notepad.

"Mom, this is Mrs.—"

"I know who she is," Mrs. Evans said, approaching Mrs. Jones.

Todd's posture tensed. He started forward. In tandem, Ian rose and stood between the women.

"How dare you come here," Mrs. Evans said, her body shaking.

Raising her chin, Mrs. Jones said, "I didn't mean to interrupt your mourning." Her tongue lingered over the last word doubtfully.

Mrs. Evans veered forward but was no match for Ian, who prevented her from reaching Mrs. Jones.

"It wasn't enough that your daughters broke up my marriage," Mrs. Evans said, her chin trembling, "but you have the audacity to come here looking for something. Your daughters stole enough from this family."

"You can't steal what's freely given." Mrs. Jones placed her hands on her hips. "Besides, if you can't keep your husband, you don't deserve him."

Though she swung with a heavy fist, Mrs. Evans' punch barely made it past Ian's shoulders.

"That's enough," Ian said, blocking the assault and guiding Mrs. Evans back toward the fireplace.

"Let's go," Todd said, addressing Mrs. Jones. "There's nothing for you here."

"Get the hell out of my house, you skank," Mrs. Evans hollered, encircled by Ian and her son near the fireplace.

Pausing by the front door, Mrs. Jones lurched back into the room. "You sure it's your house? Better check the will."

Glass shattered against the wall adjacent to the front door where Mrs. Evans hurled a lamp.

Todd hustled Mrs. Jones outside. In that moment, he noticed René Jones sitting in an idling car at the foot of the driveway.

Chapter 25

It took Myaisha five minutes to lock the back door, then grab her hat and coat.

Deniece and Barry had already driven away. AJ stood at the door, waiting, and holding Zoey on a leash. Boomer whined and circled the foyer.

"Okay, I'm ready," she said.

With a short bark, Boomer expressed his doubts.

Myaisha skipped to the front door, locked it, and secured Boomer's leash.

"Oh, wait," she said, handing AJ the leash. "I need to zip up my coat."

AJ took the leash. "No problem. I got it."

A growl preceded Boomer's tugging and biting on the leash.

"Looks like someone doesn't want me walking him," AJ said, handing her back the leash.

"Stop it, Boomer. Mommy has to—"

Boomer barked and snorted.

"Fine." She accepted the lead from AJ, and they departed.

Night had swallowed the neighborhood. Besides her home, one other house in the cul-de-sac had its front house lights on. Myaisha could see barely ten yards ahead.

"Should we bring flashlights?" she asked.

"No, the night's beautiful."

A moment passed.

"Are you scared?"

She chuckled. "Not of being attacked." She glanced down the leash. "Boomer will protect his mommy."

The Labrador barked and snorted.

"I'm worried about tripping and falling."

"I'll catch you." AJ hugged her waist with his free hand.

Myaisha gazed up at him, admiring his strong chin but noticing for once he didn't smile.

Before they reached the street corner, a red glow flickered from the front porch of Ms. Lula's house.

Myaisha's gaze sharpened and she perceived a cigarette emitting a red light. Ms. Lula was rocking in a large chair, smoking on the darkened porch.

She waved. "Hello, Ms. Lula. Cold night."

"Sho is, child," Ms. Lula said. "Y'all better make it a short walk. Be frost on the ground tomorrah."

"Good evening," AJ said, saluting as they turned the corner onto a cross street leaving the cul-de-sac. His voice lowered. "Weird. Does she always sit in the dark like that?"

Myaisha shrugged. "I never noticed." Because she hadn't looked. She would from now on though because it was weird.

AJ and Zoey took the lead as Boomer dedicated personal attention to the hedges lining the sidewalk. Careful to clean up after her fur baby, Myaisha bounded after AJ and Zoey, not wanting too much distance between them.

Something about seeing Ms. Lula on the porch in the dark had unnerved her. *Or was it Robin's murder?* And now Donald Evans had supposedly committed suicide. *A coincidence?*

Evans could have murdered Robin out of jealousy. Terrence was an attractive man—and young. *Could Robin have intended to return to her ex?*

Doubtful. She remembered the argument between Robin and Terrence outside the urgent care clinic. But Evans didn't know that. He might have found Terrence hanging around and become jealous. A weak motive, but possible.

Though she didn't want to admit it, Myaisha realized René was the most likely person to murder Robin. She had access to Robin and a definite motive. *Could the introverted childcare owner murder her identical twin?* After the murder she'd investigated in June, Myaisha believed anyone could commit murder if sufficiently provoked.

There was a strange dynamic in the Jones family which eluded her. A tension—like a barrier—emotionally separated René from her mother. Myaisha detected it whenever they were together. And René was afraid. *Why?* Somehow, her friend was involved in Robin's death—or knew something about it.

Once the distance between her and AJ closed, she asked, "What happened between you and Donald Evans?"

"What?" AJ stopped and stared at her.

She touched his arm. "This is serious. The police want to speak with you about an interaction you had with Mr. Evans."

"How do you know?"

As they sauntered along the sidewalk again, she explained what she'd overhead in the church parking lot.

"Hmm." AJ stared straight ahead.

"Well?"

"It's not what you think. Or maybe it is."

"Tell me."

"I went to the car lot to speak with Evans about Carl's mortgage. It was bad enough Carl bought a piece of ..." He bit back his comment. "Sorry." He walked silently for a half-minute. "The mortgage payments in addition to the renovations were crippling Carl."

They paused at the corner while a car passed.

AJ glanced at her. "I asked Evans to lower the mortgage payments or pay for the repairs. He refused. Ass—" His jaw tensed. AJ breathed deeply, inching closer to her side. "Evans made threats, said if Carl missed another payment he would foreclose."

Myaisha sensed heat radiating off AJ, warming the small distance between them. He gazed forward, but she realized he was lost in the past.

"I grabbed him by the shirt." AJ's hands tightened around Zoey's leash. His narrow eyes stared distantly. A vein in his temple pulsed. "I caught a glimpse of my reflection in the showroom glass window and I … I released him and left the dealership."

Myaisha gave him a side glance. Despite the thick, dark night, she viewed a tiny grin flicker in the corner of his lips.

"Fine," he said. "I tossed him against the wall before I released him. But I didn't hit him."

"True."

They walked for a minute before AJ asked, "Do you think I could kill someone?"

"Anyone can kill with the right incentive."

His arm grazed her side, but he didn't speak.

"You care about Carl?" she asked, eyeing a car crawling down the street.

"He's a good kid with a lot of responsibilities for someone his age."

Myaisha used the moment to reflect on the two deaths. Donald Evans could have murdered Robin and committed suicide to avoid prosecution. But he hadn't left a note. Because he didn't confess to the murder didn't make him innocent. Nor did suicide make him guilty.

Who had a motive to kill both of them? René. Evans dumped René for Robin. And Robin betrayed her sister for a man. *How would Myaisha feel if her sister stole her boyfriend?* Since she couldn't imagine her sister doing anything of the sort, she—

"Do you have plans for Christmas?"

Myaisha squinted in the dark, viewing AJ's face.

"Not really. Josiah and I usually spend it alone."

"Your family doesn't come visit?"

She chuckled. "They aren't fond of North Carolina. If we want to see family, Josiah and I have to travel to California."

"My family always gets together on the holiday. Would you like to spend Christmas with us?"

"Thank you, but it's a special time for me and Josiah. We like to open our gifts on Christmas Eve and enjoy a big dinner."

"How about Christmas Day? Then you and Josiah can still share Christmas Eve together."

"Hmm, I'll think about it."

"Good." He smiled and drew her closer to his side.

They walked without speaking. She figured he was lost in his thoughts as was she. A shiver thrilled up her back before AJ wrapped an arm around her waist. She relaxed into his comforting embrace.

"You know they're performing *The Nutcracker* ballet in Charlotte. I'd love to see it with you. We can make a weekend of it. Go out to dinner after the show, reserve a hotel room."

Though she gazed forward, Myaisha perceived AJ's scrutiny. Her shoulders stiffened. "I have to think about it. I work alternate weekends in the office."

"We'll choose a weekend when you aren't working."

"I'll have to figure out something for Boomer."

"You can bring him over to my place. Carl can check on him and Zoey. We'll be away for two days and one night."

"Let me think about it."

"Myaisha," AJ halted mid-stride, causing Zoey to tug against the leash. "What's going on? Whenever I plan something special for us, you come up with an excuse not to go."

"Nothing's wrong."

He inhaled deeply. "Look, if you—if this isn't working, let me know. I don't want to pressure you."

"No, it's not that."

"Then what is it?"

She sputtered. "Nothing. I … I need to think about it. With my medical practice, writing club—"

"I understand." He shook his head and pivoted toward her house.

Myaisha silently swore and followed beside him. A gulf of emotions separated them. *How had she let things get to this point? Why couldn't she explain to him how she felt?*

When they turned the corner onto her street, Myaisha's head swiveled left, searching the porch deck of Ms. Lula's house. Apparently, the septuagenarian had retreated inside. Once they reached her house, Myaisha invited AJ inside.

"No, it's late," he said, clicking the truck's key fob.

Zoey hopped inside the cab. Boomer whined and started to follow. Myaisha pulled him back on the leash and directed him to sit.

She laid a hand on AJ's forearm. "You don't understand."

"How can I if you won't tell me?"

He peered into her soul like a spotlight scouring her heart for an explanation. She fidgeted. Words bubbled up in her throat, but she couldn't release them. *How could she share her fears with AJ when she couldn't address them herself?*

She swallowed. "I need more time. Please. It's not you—"

"It's me, right." He strode away, started to enter the cab, then turned back. "That's the same thing my wife said the night before she left me."

Tears welled in Myaisha's eyes. His comment shut down any reply. *What could she say to that?*

His truck pulled away from the curb.

With a trembling chin, Myaisha entered the house. She unleashed Boomer and collapsed on the couch. *How the hell had she messed this up?*

CHAPTER 26

Saturday mornings weren't a common time to interview suspects. But Todd couldn't rest, and he doubted the firefighter expected a police officer would approach him on the weekend. The element of surprise, he found, created uncertainty, making people more likely to reveal facts they wanted to suppress. Parked on the street across from the fire station, Todd absorbed the building and surroundings before exiting his car.

Inside the fire station, he explained his interest in speaking with Mr. Andrew James Thomas.

Three minutes passed before a towering man with short curly hair approached. Todd stood erect, self-conscious about the height and breadth of the man before him. *Maybe Ian was right, and he should exercise more.*

"Mr. Thomas?"

"Yes. Can I help you?" Though hard, the man's face wasn't unfriendly.

"I'm Detective Gamble."

They shook hands. Todd measured the firefighter's muscular grasp. *Note to self, get a gym membership.*

"If you have a moment, I'd like to ask some questions." Todd detected no change in Mr. Thomas' expression.

"Sure. Do you mind if we go outside? We can speak privately."

After alerting another fireman of his departure, Mr. Thomas preceded Todd outside, directing him to a sunny spot about fifty yards from the station.

"Hope you don't mind," Mr. Thomas said, "but I don't want this getting around."

Todd's gaze narrowed. "What to get around?"

With his back toward the station, Mr. Thomas said, "This is about Donald Evans, right?"

"Why do you presume that?" Unsure of its significance, Todd noted the grin on the fireman's face.

"I'm not an angel, but there's no other reason for a police detective to question me."

"Well, I'm glad you've led a blameless life." Folding his arms across his chest, Todd asked, "So what made a peaceful man assault a business owner?"

The corners of Mr. Thomas' eyes crinkled. "I didn't assault him."

Todd stared.

Mr. Thomas adjusted his stance wider. "I pushed him against a wall."

"It left a dent."

"I underestimated my own strength."

"Cute." Todd relaxed his arms. "What happened?"

"If you're investigating Evans, then you know what kind of parasite he was. My friend bought a property from him— a rent to own." Mr. Thomas stroked his chin.

"The place is a dump. It passed an inspection because Evans paid someone off. Now, my friend is stuck with a mortgage and a list of repairs he can't afford. I asked Evans to let up on the mortgage payments until my friend caught up on what he owed."

When the lapse in the story extended beyond a minute, Todd asked, "And?"

"And I didn't like his response."

"Who's the friend?"

While Mr. Thomas provided the details about his friend who'd purchased the home, a Mr. Carl Bryant, Todd considered when to interview him. Surely, Mr. Thomas would inform Mr. Bryant about his questions. A delay would give them an opportunity to fabricate a story. *Should he wait until Monday?*

Ian had a body-building event in the afternoon and wouldn't be back before six tonight. Todd had one more interview today—and it promised to be more rewarding. *Or would it?*

"Where were you last Thursday night and Friday morning?"

Motioning his head toward the fire station behind them, Mr. Thomas said, "There. I finished a three-day shift Friday morning."

"What time did you leave on Friday?"

His forehead puckered in thought a moment before Mr. Thomas said, "Probably sometime between eight and nine— at least that's when I usually leave. I didn't check my watch."

"Can anyone confirm the time?"

"No." Mr. Thomas stared at the ground. "Wait." His head raised. "My dog walker can confirm when I got to her place. She watches my Labrador when I work nights."

Once he obtained the dog walker's name and number, Todd verified Mr. Bryant's contact information, thanked Mr. Thomas, and left.

Inside his car, Todd checked the time. The doctor should be home by now. He hoped she still had some chocolate peanut butter tart and answers regarding Mrs. Jones-Collins' murder.

Chapter 27

Aromas from inside Green Pastures café enticed Myaisha's hunger. She salivated, peeking toward the back door, and wondering when the presentation would end. *Should've eaten breakfast.*

Since the Greensboro Women of Color Writing Group had begun meeting in the Green Pastures café conference room, Myaisha had discerned an increase in her girth. Previously, walking Boomer had helped maintain her weight. But now, she would need more substantial exercise. A café full of intoxicating foods was more than she could handle—or more than her waistline could.

The conference room erupted in applause. Attendees rose. Appreciative sounds reverberated around the room as people approached the speaker.

At the front of the conference room, group members conversed with Grace Jones. The private detective had become a quick friend of Myaisha's since their collaboration on the murder investigation of her college friend last summer.

Although Myaisha still didn't know the private detective's real name, she had discovered other interesting facts about her. Grace was a firearms expert and black belt in martial arts, which explained the private detective's presence in the café on a late Saturday morning.

"Thank you, Grace," Tina said, shaking her hand. "It was an awesome presentation. I didn't know about the kick from a gun."

The private detective's dark skin shimmered with sweat. She used a napkin to wipe her face. "Yeah, you don't see it in movies or on TV. Guns, especially large caliber weapons, have a recoil. If you've never fired a weapon before, it can surprise you."

"I think I can work it into my storyline," another member said, thanking Grace before slipping away.

Members circulated around the room, gradually ambling out the conference room and into the café.

Myaisha remained behind, waiting to thank Grace and pay the stipend the group offered to presenters. Since René was in mourning, and Mary was at a school event, it fell upon her to act as group treasurer. Once the crowd diminished, she approached.

"Thanks, Grace. Your presentation was educational. I took lots of notes. It'll help my manuscript sound more authentic."

A large smile beamed across Grace's mouth. "No problem. I loved it. It's nice to share my experiences with other women."

"We enjoyed it," Deniece said, patting Grace on the back. "You'll have to come back and teach us about martial arts."

"Oh, yes," Tina exclaimed. "I need help with writing fight scenes. What do you think, Myaisha?"

"I don't need help writing fight scenes," she chuckled. "I simply recall my last encounter with a toddler, wrestling to obtain a throat swab, or administering a vaccine, and I have all the imagery I need."

Their small group sauntered toward the exit, talking, and laughing. Before they could depart, a woman rushed inside and plowed into Deniece.

"Ow," Deniece cried as the woman slammed into her side.

"Sorry." The woman retreated a step but didn't look at Deniece. Instead, she searched their faces until her gaze landed on Myaisha. "Oh, there you are."

A second passed before Myaisha recognized her as René's cousin. "Hello, Latrice. What's wrong?"

"I'm sorry, but can we talk?" Latrice fumbled with her purse and moved closer.

"Of course." Myaisha re-entered the conference room, directing Latrice away from the exit. "Let's go over there."

Neither Tina, Deniece, or Grace made a move to leave. They watched Latrice and Myaisha walk over to a group of chairs in the center of the room. Piecemeal, they followed the pair, and soon they huddled less than ten feet away.

Aware of their presence, Latrice said, "I was hoping this would be private."

"Is it about Robin's murder?" Myaisha asked.

Nodding, Latrice said, "*Murders*."

"Murders," Deniece, Grace, and Tina said in unison.

"I think Donald was murdered too—at least that's what René believes."

Because everyone spoke at the same time, Myaisha couldn't follow the conversations.

Tina asked Latrice, "Why?"

Grace asked, "What evidence does she have?"

Deniece said, "Well, she better get a good lawyer."

With a whistle, Myaisha got everyone's attention. "Ladies, we can't do anything with everyone talking at the same time."

She directed Latrice to a chair. "Sit down. Tell us what's going on."

"I'm worried. René won't talk to me, but I know she's keeping something back. I asked her to speak with you, but she won't. When I asked her for your number, she refused to give it to me."

"Why?" Deniece and Tina asked in unison.

"I don't know." Latrice's wide gaze implored Myaisha, who frowned.

"What do you want from me?"

A folding chair scraped across the floor as Latrice inched closer to her. "I heard what you did last summer when your friend was murdered—how you solved the crime."

"I didn't—"

"Yes, you did," Deniece interjected.

"We can help too," Tina said.

With an arched brow, Deniece eyed Tina. "You looking to score another true crime book?"

Tina tittered. "I don't have to write the story; someone else can. Besides, I know a lot about crime. It'll be a good experience for my writing."

Myaisha glared. "This isn't a game—or an experience." She faced Latrice. "Someone's life is at stake here."

Latrice nodded and palmed Myaisha's hands. "Exactly. Will you speak with René? I know she'll listen to you. She respects you."

Her chest sank. Myaisha regarded Latrice's wide, tear-filled eyes. In her periphery, she viewed Deniece's slight nod.

She sighed. "I'll try."

"Thank you," Latrice said, popping out of the seat.

"I said, I'll try." Myaisha rose. Unsure what she'd committed to, she glanced around the room looking for she didn't know what. Maybe inspiration? If so, none came. She liked puzzles better when they were fictional. *Do I really want to try and solve another true crime?*

Deniece and Tina surrounded Latrice, peppering her with questions. After ten minutes, Latrice extracted herself from the circle. She grabbed Myaisha's forearm.

"René drove her mom to the airport, but she'll be home by six. Can you come over tonight?"

"Sure. Call me when she returns." Myaisha removed Latrice's hand and patted it.

"Give me your number." Latrice entered it into her cell phone.

A minute later, the group headed toward the exit. At a slower pace, Myaisha and Grace brought up the rear.

At the door, Grace pulled Myaisha aside.

"Can I ask you a question?"

Myaisha nodded. "Sure."

"No judging."

"Of course not."

Grace grinned. "Is she available?"

"I don't know. I only met Latrice—"

"Not her," Grace interrupted, "the dark one with the soft brown eyes and curvy legs."

Myaisha's forehead receded as she gawked. "Deniece?"

A thick finger flew to Grace's lips. "Shush."

"She's married."

"Is it solid?"

Myaisha smiled. "Yes, I'm afraid so."

Curses dripped from Grace's downturned lips. "Why are all the hot women married?"

"To a man."

Grace shrugged. "So. No big deal." She strode away.

Following after her, Myaisha wondered what she meant.

Outside in the parking lot, December had finally given Greensboro a respite from the premature winter with a calm breeze and sweater-temperature weather.

Before leaving, Grace whispered, "Let me know if her status changes." Eyes twinkling, she trotted to her car and drove off.

***

"Mya. Mya?" Deniece raised her voice. "Myaisha."

A third call broke the inertia, and she turned toward her friend.

"Close your mouth," Deniece said.

As commanded, Myaisha shut her lips, unaware she was standing in the parking lot, gaping after Grace's departing car.

"What's with you?" Deniece said, walking toward the car.

"Nothing. You wouldn't believe it."

"Tell me."

They climbed into Myaisha's Honda and exited the parking lot.

Executing a left turn, Myaisha asked, "Where're we going?"

"Barry texted me to meet him at his office. I told Latrice to also call me when René returned. We'll meet up at her place."

The Honda turned right, and Myaisha piloted it onto Interstate 85 toward High Point. "Is Tina coming?"

"No, she invited her son over for dinner. She's gonna search his work papers for information on the case."

With her eyes on traffic—while avoiding puddles from last night's downpour—Myaisha considered what evidence had led the police to determine Donald Evans was murdered. News outlets reported he'd been shot in the head. Sounded like suicide. It would be difficult to disguise a head shot as a suicide. *Too bad Todd was stingy with sharing details.*

"Did you hear me?" Deniece said.

"No," she said shamelessly.

"I asked what I wouldn't believe."

Myaisha couldn't decide whether to share what Grace had said when Deniece smacked her in the arm.

"Ouch," she said, rubbing her injured bicep.

"Don't think about whether to tell me, say it."

"Grace asked if you were available."

"Seriously?" Deniece grinned, her high cheek bones glistening with delight.

Frowning, Myaisha shot her a quick glance. "You're flattered?"

The visor flipped down as Deniece preened in the mirror. "Of course, I am."

Myaisha's head shook as she exited the expressway and turned onto a side street.

"You're jealous."

"No, I'm not."

"You should be." Deniece smiled like a Cheshire cat, applying lip gloss liberally to her pouting lips.

"You're crazy."

"I'm beautiful."

Deniece's laugh carried them down the road and to the office building where Barry worked.

The car idled as Deniece called Barry to open the office door.

Setting aside Deniece's vanity, Myaisha contemplated her meeting later with René. *What would her friend have to say?*

Before Deniece exited the car, Myaisha sent up a short prayer, hoping not to hear a confession to murder.

But she had more pressing matters to address. With a deep breath, she drove home. Perhaps she would find answers after resting—and maybe a way out of investigating another murder.

CHAPTER 28

Though not quite winter solstice, daylight had already begun a slow retreat across the evening sky when Myaisha steered into the cul-de-sac toward home.

A glance left showed a red glow at the end of Ms. Lula's cigarette. *How many nights had the seventy-one-year-old surveyed their neighborhood from her darkened porch? How had she never noticed before?*

She needed to be more observant. Queasy, whether from discovering Ms. Lula's nighttime habits or the upcoming appointment with René, Myaisha desired a simple relaxing bath and tea.

At the bottom of her driveway, she viewed a dark sedan. Her gaze strained and her neck tensed. The driver's head pivoted in her direction.

***

The garage door scrolled down as Myaisha preceded her guest inside the house through the laundry room.

As his foot hovered over the doorway, Todd asked, "Is your dog—"

Growls and barks raced in their direction.

Todd fled back into the garage.

Biting back a grin, Myaisha ordered Boomer to heel. With repeated reassurances, she persuaded Todd to enter the house.

Careful to remain behind her, he slunk inside, giving Boomer a wide berth.

She entered the kitchen. "Have a seat." Her finger directed him toward the living room, but Todd stayed beside her in the kitchen.

"I'm fine right here," he said, eyeing Boomer.

Her laugh followed her around the kitchen as she gathered glasses, dessert plates, and other utensils.

"I told you before, he won't bite."

"Humph. He has teeth, doesn't he?"

"Well, I can't argue with that. He does have teeth."

"I came by for a piece of tart."

A low rumble echoed from Boomer's abdomen. Todd inched closer to Myaisha.

She handed him a dessert plate and led him into the living room. "Good thing you came by." She sat on the large couch facing the backyard. "I was going to finish off the last piece tonight."

After sitting on the couch perpendicular to the one she sat on, Todd brought a forked piece of chocolate tart to his mouth.

A deep, heavy growl emanated from Boomer's belly.

"Aren't you going to give the dog a piece?"

"Uh un. It's chocolate." She glared at Boomer. "Not for dogs."

The Labrador snorted and continued to glower at Todd.

"Can you give him something to eat? I can't enjoy the tart with him staring at my throat."

"Good grief." She jumped up, retrieved a snack from the kitchen, and tossed it to Boomer.

The Lab glared once more at Todd before devoting lavish attention on his treat.

Having finished off half the tart, Todd washed it down with lemonade.

"I can make tea," Myaisha offered.

"No, I prefer lemonade."

"Good." She wiped her mouth and placed her plate on the coffee table. "So, what really brought you over?"

"I've been here for over an hour."

"Waiting for a piece of tart?" She smirked.

"A piece of *free* tart." He grinned.

"Why is your conversation less loquacious when your partner is around?" she asked, relaxing into the couch cushions.

Todd hurriedly chewed the piece of tart in his mouth. "I want to keep our collaboration secret."

"Are we collaborators?" Her eyes opened wide, feigning innocence.

"We have been in the past."

"I got the idea you preferred I ceased my investigations."

He wiped his mouth and gulped the remaining lemonade. "I do. But I know you won't, and I want to know what you've discovered."

His gangly legs crossed. He leaned back and exhaled, reclining against the couch.

"What makes you think I know anything?"

"We conducted a background check on Ms. René Jones and discovered you're an investor in her childcare business. She's also a member of your writing group."

"You've done your homework."

"I thoroughly investigate each suspect."

"So, René's a suspect in her sister's murder?"

His narrow head nodded. "Yes. The entire family."

"You suspect one of them killed Robin?"

"They had motive. Did your friend tell you about the will?"

Myaisha gaped as Todd informed her about the contents of Robin's will.

"That's a lot of money, but did you consider the ex-husband? His discussion with Robin the night before her murder wasn't innocent."

"We've looked into her ex. He has a motive, but also an alibi for Tuesday morning."

"Does it matter?"

Todd frowned. "What do you mean?"

"Poisoning precludes an alibi. A doctored substance could have been given to the victim at any time." Myaisha paused, believing she had said something significant. *But what?* Seconds passed but she couldn't discern what she'd missed.

"Did forensics discover how the poison was delivered?"

"I came here to get information."

She smiled. "Sharing is one of the first things taught in preschool. Besides, don't I get anything for the tart?"

He laughed and leaned forward. Boomer scampered off the floor in his direction. Todd receded back into the cushions.

"What's with your dog?"

"He loves his mom."

Todd's face flinched.

Had something she'd said upset him? She whistled and Boomer bounded to her side. They retired to the kitchen. She observed Todd's shoulders relax. He was not a dog lover.

She retrieved another piece of tart. While he devoured the dessert, Myaisha pet Boomer and observed the detective.

She wished to understand his attitude. In one moment, he seemed eager for help and friendship, and the next closed like a clam. *And men accused women of being fickle.*

Once he scraped crumbs from the saucer, Todd licked his lips and sighed.

Myaisha had already refilled his glass of lemonade. The detective's face softened, and he suddenly looked quite young. A minute elapsed as neither spoke. But the atmosphere wasn't tense. Quite the contrary. Myaisha perceived a sense of comfort in Todd's demeanor. *Would he trust her more?*

Massaging his neck, Todd said, "What I'm about to tell you can't leave this room."

She nodded her head eagerly and held her breath.

Seconds passed. Boomer rolled on his back and stretched out on the carpet near the coffee table.

Todd said, "There was an unidentified DNA sample on the victim's hand."

"Interesting."

"Yes. A third party is possibly involved, but we haven't located any other persons in Mrs. Jones-Collins life here in Greensboro. Someone in Chicago may have followed her down here—like Terrence Collins did. If so, we haven't located anyone with a significant grudge against her. Not enough to commit murder."

"Was she well-liked in Chicago?"

He threw up his hands. "From all accounts, she was a popular person. Had a large crowd of friends. A few close girlfriends. Several male admirers but nothing serious."

"Unfaithful?"

Todd frowned. "No. The marriage ended because her husband refused to pay her debts, which were substantial. Mr. Collins was right about that part. His ex-wife was a terrible businesswoman."

"Hmm. Interesting. René is sharp in business."

"Yes?"

"Oh, yes. I met her at a professional women's conference. We were at the same table. She introduced herself, and we talked for hours. A week after the conference, she came by my office and invited me to invest in her business."

"That's all it took?"

Myaisha recalled an incident where another friend had invited her to participate in an investment. It had not gone well.

"René presented a quality business plan with documentation supporting its viability. I consulted my lawyer and decided to join. I've not been disappointed. Her childcare business has been profitable from its opening. The business acquired debt to open its second location, but her last quarterly statements showed it should be profitable within another quarter."

"You like her," Todd said, sizing her up.

Raising her chin, Myaisha said, "I do. She's intelligent."

"So, she was the smart twin, and Mrs. Jones-Collins the—" Todd's mouth shut.

Myaisha grinned. "I don't think Robin was stupid, but she was ..." Now it was her turn to weigh her words. "Insincere. I think she took advantage of René."

"And Ms. Jones let her? Is she that kind of person?"

"No." Myaisha gazed into the backyard. Dusk settled, extending creeping shadows from the trees along the lawn. "No, she's not."

She reflected on the undercurrent in the relationship between René and her mom. Myaisha sensed an estrangement between them. *Did Mrs. Jones blame René for Robin's death? If so, why?*

Perhaps it was more basic than that. Mrs. Jones mourned the loss of the daughter she loved most. *How did it affect René?*

Could she kill Robin out of jealousy? Robin stole their mom's affection—and also René's boyfriend.

Silence enveloped the room, interrupted by Boomer's snoring.

Todd cleared his throat. "Well, twins aren't always alike. It's strange. The Jones sisters favor each other but have a big difference in skin color. One of the officers mentioned Ms. Jones could pass for White. But Mrs. Jones-Collins is dark-skinned."

"Hmm." Myaisha was thinking over an idea and devoting no attention to Todd.

"The answer might be in Chicago," Todd said. "Mrs. Jones-Collins hadn't been here long enough to make enemies. Tomorrow, I'll call my contact in Chicago. It could be the solution to the homicide."

"Chicago," Myaisha said, as if in a dream. Her gaze slowly took in Todd, who stared at her in concern.

"Doctor, everything okay?"

She smiled. "Todd, this might sound crazy, but have you heard the family call René, Chi?"

He shook his head. "No. What's—"

"There's this necklace René wears around her neck." Myaisha froze.

"I remember. Do you think Chi stands for Chicago?" Todd frowned. "I'll look into it. The murderer being from Chicago makes more sense. Mrs. Jones-Collins was more likely to make a mortal enemy there than in Greensboro."

A large envelope slipped from inside Todd's suit coat when he reached for the glass of lemonade. He picked it up off the floor where it fell.

Myaisha's gaze zeroed in on it.

"Crime scene photos from Mr. Evan's office. Have a look." He passed the envelope over. "There's something in these pictures but I can't grasp it. Maybe you can help."

Minutes ticked away.

She gave little attention to the photo of Donald's head, caved in from the right temple to the occiput. She glanced several times at the hand dangling at his side, covered in blood and a splint around his wrist and thumb. A wider photo displayed the office space. She viewed a desk, chairs, apartment-sized refrigerator, blender, and side table covered with assorted beverages and snacks.

"The forensic team's preliminary report stated suicide, but I asked the medical examiner to take another look."

"Why?"

He shrugged. "Don't know. It doesn't look like suicide to me. And from what I learned about Donald Evans, he didn't seem like the type of person to kill himself."

"You believe the person who killed Robin killed him?"

"That or Donald Evans killed Robin Jones and committed suicide out of guilt. Again, unlikely. All reports are Donald Evans was a selfish prick."

Her head tilted slightly right.

"Unofficially." Careful not to move quickly, Todd leaned forward. "What did you learn from the cousin?"

Not prepared to release confidences, Myaisha asked, "Did Mr. Evan have a scar on his right wrist?"

A frown creased Todd's brow. "I don't know. Why?"

She scooted across the couch, closer to Todd, and handed him a picture focused on the victim's hand.

"The hand splint," she said, directing his attention with her finger. "It's often used for patients with carpal tunnel syndrome."

"Possible. I can check the autopsy report." He removed a pad and scribbled a note. "Any particular reason it matters?"

"If he had carpal tunnel syndrome, it might affect his ability to use a firearm. It affects grip. Depending on its severity, carpal tunnel can cause a decreased range of motion in the wrist and fingers. The splint is for comfort and support."

She reflected upon the presentation Grace had given their writing group earlier in the café. "I understand a certain amount of pressure is required to squeeze a trigger. Certain guns need more force than others."

Todd squinted. "And?"

"Well, if Mr. Evans had carpal tunnel syndrome, could he generate enough pressure to squeeze the trigger?"

The question floated in the intervening space as they regarded each other.

"If he wanted to kill himself, and he knew he suffered from carpal tunnel syndrome, why didn't he use his left hand? Or choose a different method." She considered different options. "Carbon monoxide. Take a nap in the car." Again, Myaisha directed his attention to the photo. "I don't see a splint on his left hand."

Todd wiped his brow and glanced up at her a moment before accepting the photo from her outstretched fingers.

"I knew something didn't seem right. At his house, I viewed a picture of him wearing a similar splint." He rubbed his chin. "There was also a splint on his hand in the office photos."

She smiled. "You have good instincts but not enough confidence."

His gaze narrowed as if a tiny storm brewed behind his eyes.

Gathering their dishes, Myaisha returned to the kitchen. Boomer trotted behind her. She refilled his water and food bowl.

On the couch, Todd mumbled to himself. "A splint on his wrist—and in the pictures."

Two minutes later, she returned to the living room and found Todd looking at a small wallet photo.

She placed a fresh glass of lemonade in front of him.

He handed her the photo. "My sister. You remind me of her."

Delicately, Myaisha fingered the edges of the photo and admired a smiling woman with a giant afro and bright red lipstick flashing out against dark skin. The resemblance must be symbolic she thought, not seeing any similarity between herself and the woman in the photo.

"She looks happy." She returned the photo to his open palm.

Todd delicately inserted the picture into a clear plastic wallet container and rose. His Adam's apple bobbed as he cleared his throat. A heaviness descended between them. Even Boomer forgot his chew toy and watched Todd.

Myaisha said, "She's beautiful. You two look a lot alike."

"My older sister," he said, more to himself, "was like a mother to us."

The word *was* prickled Myaisha's consciousness.

Todd drifted toward the front door, apparently not interested in saying more. He started to exit.

Myaisha joined him in the foyer. She held the doorknob, not wanting to press for details.

After taking two steps outside, Todd swiveled around. "My sister used to help me with my studies. She died before I graduated from the police academy." He spoke from a distance, perhaps remembering the past. "You're a lot like her."

"Is that a good thing?"

He smiled. The first true smile she'd ever seen from him. His eyes shimmered and his cheeks puffed out. As he departed, his voice trailed behind him. "I'm not sure."

"Thank you," she said, speaking to his back. With a quick peek at Ms. Lula's house, Myaisha locked the door.

She reclined against the foyer wall. One piece of the puzzle about Detective Todd Gamble was now solved.

CHAPTER 29

Myaisha viewed a large empty lobby through glass doors. She expected to see a principal herding a group of students between classrooms.

Night had settled over High Point thirty minutes before she'd received a call from Latrice. René had returned from the airport but left for her childcare office. No, she had not agreed to speak with them, but Latrice implored Myaisha to try. After a brief stop to pick up Deniece, Myaisha drove to René's High Point office.

At the front entrance, a click sounded near the door. Uncertain whether to proceed inside or wait, Myaisha scrutinized the lobby while Deniece called Latrice on her cell phone.

From a speaker in the upper right corner of the porticoed entryway, a voice boomed, "Come in. The door's unlocked."

Myaisha recognized Latrice's voice across the grainy intercom. Once she and Deniece crossed the threshold, industrial lighting flipped on, overwhelming her vision with a bright, cheery palate of colors bouncing from walls and assemblages. A child's wonderland of toys, posters, and games representing anything and everything a child could desire. It made her medical office seem like a desert oasis in comparison. Myaisha made a mental note to update her office waiting room décor.

Long-faced with an ashen complexion, René came forward and shook hands with her and Deniece.

Lightly smacking the hand away, Deniece roped René tightly to her bosom for a deep hug. "What are you doing? We're friends."

René's body slumped, supported by Deniece's embrace. Minutes passed as René sobbed on her shoulder.

Standing beside them, Myaisha rubbed small circles of comfort into René's back. Several feet behind René, Latrice watched, concern scribbled in the wrinkles tattooing her brow.

Myaisha cleared her throat. "Let's sit down and talk this out."

Two minutes later, they were ensconced in René's private office. Myaisha and Deniece sat in chairs before a large steel desk. At the far-right corner of the desk, Latrice perched on the edge, a coffee mug squeezed between her fingers.

"Sure you don't want something to drink?" Latrice asked them.

Both Myaisha and Deniece declined.

Seated on the chair's edge, Myaisha asked, "René, what are you worried about?"

A moment of non-verbal communication between René and Latrice preceded a reply.

René folded her hands on the desktop. "I … I received a letter."

Latrice hopped off the desk and removed a long rectangular envelope from a bottom drawer. Her hand trembled as she handed it across to Deniece, who was closer to her than Myaisha.

After unfastening the envelope, Deniece briefly perused the single sheet of paper before passing it over to Myaisha.

Minutes elapsed as she studied the typed paragraph. Myaisha grimaced at the crude language and ominous threat. Once she studied it a second time, she read the words out loud.

I know what you did whore. Give me $10K or I call the cops and tell them about the will. Shouldve threw away the poison dummy. Now your ignorant ass gonna pay. Watch the mail for directions.

Audibly, the words sounded forced. The writing was indistinct. Blunt and simple, the language portended to be from an uneducated person, but Myaisha detected the simplicity was overdone. *What had the writer tried to convey?* Anger, anxiety. Neither rang true. The letter read as rehearsed and poorly drafted. It resembled something from a play or a prop. *But why?*

"When did the letter arrive?" Deniece asked, pulling it from between Myaisha's paralyzed grip.

The movement caused a thought to stir in Myaisha's mind. It didn't have time to mature as the conversation distracted her concentration.

"I found it on the doorstep," René said. "At my townhome," she added, in answer to Myaisha's raised brows.

"We should take it to the police," Myaisha said, hearing doubt in her ears.

Latrice landed back on the corner of the desk. "I'm sure the author used gloves."

"Besides prints, the police could develop a suspect from the letter writer's use of language," she said, reviewing the missive Deniece had placed on the desk.

For a moment, the women silently stared at it. Myaisha squirmed, desiring to free herself from the claustrophobic space.

"The question," she said, leaning back in the chair, "is why the letter was sent. What did it accomplish?"

A nervous titter escaped René's lips. "Besides scaring me?"

"But why?" Myaisha regarded her with knitted brows.

Three pairs of eyes gawked at her as if Myaisha had committed a serious faux pas.

She sat up straighter and took a deep breath. "What I mean is, the author isn't threatening physical harm. The implication is you had something to do with the murder, which you didn't."

Cognizant a slight question teased at the end of her sentence, Myaisha awaited René's reaction—or lack thereof.

But René did react. Her body trembled and her lips parted. "I … Do you—"

"No one's accusing you," Latrice said, placing a hand on her cousin's shoulder.

"What about the demand for money?" Latrice asked.

"Why would the author of the letter presume René would pay for a crime she didn't commit?"

"Unless they knew something you didn't want the police to discover," Deniece said.

René stood and circled the minuscule area behind her chair.

Deniece glanced at Myaisha and inclined her head toward the desk. Judging the intention of Deniece's hint, Myaisha approached René.

"We have to be brutal," she said, walking up behind her friend. "If you didn't kill Robin, you have nothing to fear from this letter. But you're keeping something back. If you want us to help you, we need to know *everything*."

A blubbering, crying René turned around to face her. Myaisha gave her a hug, then eased her into a seat. Latrice placed a fresh cup of coffee in her cousin's hand.

While she cleaned up René's face, Myaisha asked, "What happened the day Robin died?"

Mumbling, René said, "I told the police—"

"Don't waste our time lying," Deniece said. "We're here to help. We can't do anything until we know the truth."

Myaisha's shoulder tensed at Deniece's tone but couldn't argue with the result.

With a bowed head, René's words were directed at the desktop. "It was horrible."

None of the three women moved. Traffic on the nearby highway was audible in the quiet. Everyone stared at the childcare owner.

As if a spotlight shone on her, René raised her head toward her audience. "Robin called me at work. She wanted a ride to Donald's office."

Rocking her head, Latrice asked, "You were driving your sister to her boyfriend's office? The boyfriend she stole from you."

"I didn't want to drive her."

"Then why did you?"

"I told her it was the last time."

"There shouldn't have been a first time."

"Ladies," Deniece interjected, "priorities. You can discuss how to be a better sister after we leave."

"Continue," Myaisha said, leaning an elbow on the desk.

Sending a pointed glower at Latrice, René slid her chair forward then gazed at Myaisha.

"When I arrived at Donald's house …" René swallowed, her body trembling. She explained slamming the car door—mad because she hadn't refused Robin's request. That same ferocity propelled her across the doorway.

"I yelled for Robin."

Not awaiting a reply, she had trotted up the steps to the second floor. Jerked the master bedroom door open, hurling herself inside the room.

"So that's it? You're gonna go live with him?" she had said.

Robin's placid face gazed back at her. Beside the king bed, she tossed clothing into various open suitcases.

"Don't be dramatic," Robin had answered. "I didn't mean for this to happen."

A fisted hand hung at René's side. She beat it against her thigh, fighting the urge to lash out.

"You can choose who you sleep with."

"But you can't help who you love. Donald and I were meant to be together. He's wrong for you." Robin rose and reached forward to touch her shoulder.

René snatched her arm away. "And you know this because? You're not exactly the best judge of character. What about Terrence? Don't you think you should let the ink dry on your divorce papers before you shack up with another man?"

Robin's chest rose and fell like a deep swell. "It's over between me and Terrence. He understands."

"Then stop spending his money."

"He owes me alimony."

"He said he'll never give you a dime."

A smirk tugged at the corner of Robin's mouth. "He will."

"You think Donald will adopt your holistic lifestyle? Fund your yoga and smoothie businesses?"

Like a ballerina, Robin floated around René, smiling and humming. "He's changed. I've helped him become a better person."

René's jaw tightened as she flopped on the bed. "I've known him longer than you. He won't change."

"But he has."

"No, he hasn't." René tossed flimsy lingerie aside and off the bed onto the floor. "He's pretending. It's all about sex."

Robin's hands perched on her hips. "If he's such a low-life, then why did you stay with him?"

René spoke from a distance. "Because I loved him. Besides, with me, it was about business. I helped him with finances."

Robin leaned up against René. "You deserve someone who can love you. Donald never loved you."

Quiet tears slipped down René's cheeks. Her gaze refocused on Myaisha. "I smacked her in the face. She hit me back, then …"

When she realized René had become stuck, Myaisha said, "The two of you fought."

In a small voice, René said, "After I smacked her in the face, I ran from the room downstairs. She caught up with me and punched me in the head. I … It was a reflex. I didn't think about it. I spun around and kept hitting her."

Sobs prevented further speech. Latrice held René close, rocking her like a mother would a child.

"Her nose started bleeding," René said in halting speech. "She called me a bitch and I grabbed her head. Then—"

"What?" Latrice asked, gawking at her cousin.

"It happened so fast. She spit up blood. I thought it was from the nosebleed, but her body swooned. Before I could catch her, she fell down and started seizing."

"Why didn't you help her?" Latrice asked, retreating from René.

Eyes gaping, René said, "I was scared." She shuddered and glanced at Myaisha.

"I left but came right back," she nearly shouted. "I wiped away the blood—in case she was choking on it. Nothing helped. I called 911, started CPR, but her seizing increased until …"

Another flood of tears poured from René's eyes. Latrice handed her a handful of tissues but offered no compassion. Myaisha kneeled beside René's chair.

"It's all right," she said. "We're not judging you." She ignored the *tut-tut* sound from Latrice.

Two quivers from her shoulders ended René's torrent of grief—momentarily. "I tried CPR. She stopped seizing but her eyes rolled back and all I could do was hold her hand." She swallowed. "Ask her to forgive me and … I held her hand."

Myaisha rose. Massaging René's shoulders, she glanced across the room, considering what she'd heard.

"So," Latrice asked, glancing up at Myaisha, "did the nosebleed cause the hemorrhage?"

"No," Myaisha said, still staring into the ether, evaluating what she knew.

Deniece looked at Latrice. "The medical examiner discovered Robin was poisoned."

"How is that related to the nosebleed?" Latrice asked.

Lost in her thoughts, Myaisha ambled around the room. "It may not be."

She weighed her words, not wanting to cause René more grief than necessary. "The poison would have caused a hemorrhage eventually. The assault simply precipitated the inevitable."

Those words hung in the air, intermingling between the women as each absorbed them.

Settled against the wall adjacent to the door, Myaisha glanced across the room at René. "Have you told us everything? What else do you know about the murder?"

"You think I'm hiding something?" René asked, hysterically.

Probably. But today wasn't the time for confrontations.

Hunched forward in the chair, glaring at René, Deniece asked, "Then why did this letter distress you?"

"I assaulted my sister and then she died from a hemorrhage." Like vines, veins snaked down René's taut neck. "The police might suspect me. I didn't know about the poison. Besides, if I could assault Robin, they might believe I could also poison her."

"Hmm. Lord knows the police have charged innocent people with less evidence," Latrice said, rolling her eyes.

René whispered, "I didn't mean to."

"Of course, you didn't," Deniece said, standing and stretching her back.

"It still doesn't explain the purpose of the letter," Myaisha said, glancing down at the missive.

"What do you mean?" Deniece asked. "The letter writer wants money."

Her head shaking, Myaisha struggled to explain. "No, what I mean is, why would the writer of the letter believe René would pay them any money? Robin was poisoned, not beaten to death."

Deniece shrugged. "The author doesn't know that."

"Why not?"

Three women stared at Myaisha as if her mental capacity was in question.

"What I'm trying to reason out is who the author could be," Myaisha said, again circling the room. "The person is either someone in possession of information detrimental to René or a bluffing bounder."

"But what information could anyone have about René?" Latrice asked.

"Exactly," Myaisha said. "If what René said is true, unless someone stood at the window and watched the skirmish between her and Robin, what evidence could they possess to provide the police?"

Silence descended around the room.

"Nothing," René said, speaking like someone coming out of a fog.

Myaisha's gaze widened. "Then what was the purpose of the letter?"

Chapter 30

Heat had dissipated from his coffee mug an hour ago, but Todd still drank the inky fluid, desirous of a caffeine jolt. He had arrived at the police station at six Monday morning. Except for a quick coffee run and a trip to visit Dr. Page, he'd been at his desk, working out the significance of what the medical examiner had concluded.

Around noon, Ian sauntered into the office and sank into a chair across from him. Their desks abutted each other such that they faced one another. Todd waited a moment before bombarding Ian with questions.

"So, did you get a copy of the will?" he asked.

Paper crinkled as Ian peeled a candy bar wrapper apart and took a bite. "Yeah, I got it. But I didn't have time to read it."

Todd's fingers stretched forward, requesting the form. Ian handed it over and booted up his desktop computer.

"What did you find out?" Ian asked, licking chocolate off his fingers.

Head down reading the will, Todd responded absently. "The medical examiner officially classified Donald Evans' death as a homicide."

"What changed her mind?"

Todd's fingers drummed along the desk. Five minutes later, he sat up straight and slid the will across the desks back to Ian.

"I told her about Evans' wrist splint. On autopsy, she confirmed he'd had a prior carpal tunnel release but still had severe restriction in wrist movement—also bad degenerative disease," Todd said, glimpsing the official autopsy report summarized on his computer screen.

"So, no suicide."

"No suicide. Definitely murder." Reclining in the chair, Todd stretched his arms wide above his head.

Ian tossed the empty candy wrapper into the trash can. "Two murders and our suspect for the first homicide dead."

"You thought Evans murdered Jones-Collins?"

Ian's gaze squinted. "Didn't you?"

"He might've thought she had something on the side with her ex, but why murder her—and with poison?" Todd scratched his head. "If he was mad at her—jealous—he'd have shot her, strangled her, something more physically impulsive. Poisoning takes time. It's methodical, conniving. Besides, from what I've learned, Evans wasn't too bright."

"How smart do you have to be to poison someone?"

"Well, since we haven't discovered how the poisoning occurred, the murderer was clever in their delivery method if nothing else."

With a nod, Ian devoured his candy bar.

"It appears, Donald Evans left everything to his kids," Todd said, passing the will back to Ian.

"They definitely had a motive. And there wasn't much love lost between dad and son."

"Or the daughter," Todd said.

"Yeah, she didn't seem bothered when her dad didn't show up Thursday night."

"He was a serial philanderer. She might have considered he'd met up with another woman. Mr. Evans didn't take a break between his romance with the sisters."

"Good point."

"I wonder …" The words trailed off as Todd considered the dynamic between the Jones sisters. "Do you think Evans would reach out to Ms. Jones?"

Ian frowned. "Why? For comfort?"

"Or something else."

Both detectives stared at each other.

"Did we check Mrs. Jones-Collins' phone records?" Todd asked.

"Yep." Ian scrolled through the pages of his notepad. "Phone records confirm the call to her sister at the childcare center."

"What about Mr. Evans' phone records?"

"Requested. I'll check and see if they've arrived."

"Good."

Todd checked email messages. Occasionally, he paused to consider how Mrs. Jones-Collins had ingested the poison. Forensics checked all food and beverages in the home—even the dead woman's makeup. He concluded the murderer must have removed the poison on the day of the murder. And the only person they *knew* who entered Mr. Evans' home Tuesday morning besides the victim was the twin sister.

Identical twin sister. He pondered over his conversation with Myaisha. She had mentioned something—

"Who would hate Mrs. Jones-Collins enough to make her suffer and die a slow, miserable death?" Ian asked, eyeing Todd knowingly. "The twin sister."

"Most likely. She and the mom split the insurance."

"But the sister gets the majority of it—eighty percent I believe." Ian shuffled papers around the desk. "Where did I put those notes about the insurance policy?"

"Why kill Evans though?" Todd's head reclined against the chair's headrest as he stared up at the ceiling.

"Maybe he figured out who murdered Mrs. Jones-Collins. Or the sister killed him because he dumped her."

"Possible. The mom mentioned animosity between the sisters. Mrs. Jones clearly loved Mrs. Jones-Collins more."

"Yeah, it's pretty obvious the mom favored the dead sister." Ian read several entries from his notebook aloud.

Todd listened without responding, lost in his own thoughts. "Mr. Evans would also be in a position to know if a particular item had been removed from his house. Something containing the poison."

He considered what Ian had read, then returned to the computer to complete his report. "Amazing how identical twins can be so different."

"You mean one light-skinned and the other dark?"

"That too."

Fifteen minutes elapsed where each man was dedicated to their own thoughts and activities.

Ian's phone rang. Todd watched and listened to the one-sided conversation.

"Get forensic out there. Let me know what they find." Ian hung up.

"What?" Todd asked.

"An officer discovered evidence Evans crashed at one of his properties."

"Thursday night?"

Ian shrugged. "Don't know. The place hasn't been searched yet."

Todd picked up his desk phone. "I'll contact the DA and alert the chief."

Once Todd ended his call, Ian asked, still staring at the computer, "Did we get anything on the unknown DNA sample?"

"No, the medical examiner's office submitted samples from the Jones family, the ex-husband, Terrence Collins, Mr. Evans, and his son."

"What about Mrs. Evans?"

Todd frowned. "I believe so. We better check to be sure."

"Should we submit a sample from the cousin? She knew Mrs. Jones-Collins and could have had a motive we don't know about. She might also know more about Chicago than she told us."

Turning papers made a scratchy noise as Ian perused his notebook, the only sound in the large office space for an entire minute.

"There it is. Ms. Latrice—"

"What about the sister?" Todd interrupted. "The day of the murder, did we swab her hands for blood?"

"No, but aren't they identical?"

His fingers stiffened as Todd's hands hovered above the keyboard. "Wait a minute. How do we know they're identical twins?"

"Because they have the same DNA?"

"I have an idea." He searched among the papers on his desk and the folder he'd created for the Jones-Collins homicide case. "Do you have a picture of Ms. Jones?"

"The sister?"

"Yes," Todd sniped, "the sister."

A minute passed as Ian searched desk drawers.

"What's wrong with your arm?" Todd asked, noticing a splint on Ian's right shoulder.

"Oh, I pulled a muscle during the competition."

"How'd you do?"

"Not bad." Ian shrugged. "Which reminds me, I have to put in for a week off in May. I have a competition down in Florida."

Todd chuckled. "I can't imagine you in one of those skimpy swim trunks, greased up, flexing your biceps on stage in front of a crowd of people."

"Good. I don't want you to." Ian flicked a photo across the desks.

Picking up the photo, Todd reviewed the neckline of Ms. Jones. "No, you can't see it in this picture."

"See what?"

Todd began to put on his suit coat. "I have a hunch. If I'm right—"

"Right about what?"

"Come on."

In tandem, he and Ian exited the station.

"Where to for lunch?" Todd asked.

"Sandwiches," Ian said, buttoning his coat.

Not until they were belted into the car, did Todd return to discussing the case. "I got a copy of the Collins' divorce settlement from Mr. Collins."

"Spill."

"She took him to the cleaners. He had to pay her alimony for two years, all the marital debt, *and* maintain a life insurance policy on her when he wasn't even a beneficiary."

"Man," Ian said, squeezing a black muscle ball, "that sucks."

"He was contesting the judgment up until—"

"The day she died."

Todd side glanced at his partner before turning left into a deli parking lot. Terrence Collins had motive but not opportunity to poison his ex-wife. He might've killed Donald Evans, but why? *Did Terrence Collins suspect—or know—Donald Evans murdered Mrs. Jones-Collins?* He was reaching, but maybe the solution to this murder required imagination.

Right now, he needed nourishment. After lunch, he would get a picture of Ms. Jones' necklace.

***

Ten minutes later, Todd and Ian were cloistered in a far corner of a hipster diner munching on hoagies.

Mayonnaise dripped down Todd's chin. "I scanned Evans' will." He wiped away the condiment with a napkin.

Ian slurped ice water. "Yeah?"

"He left everything to the kids."

"Nothing unusual." Ian shrugged, crunching on ice.

"No, but …" Todd paused while chewing his sandwich. He swallowed. "But if he got with Mrs. Jones-Collins and their relationship became serious—"

"He might've changed his will," Ian said, finishing the sandwich and munching on a pickle.

"Knowing Mrs. Evans' attitude regarding her children, I'm sure it wouldn't have gone over well."

"Under their divorce agreement, could he disinherit his kids?" Ian asked, massaging his shoulder.

"Don't know. I'll ask … Who do we ask, finance or the DA?"

Ian grimaced and rotated his shoulder. "How about Evans' lawyer?"

"We can try. He might not answer." Todd frowned. "Is your shoulder bad?"

"Yeah. It aches something terrible."

"Did you go to the doctor?"

"I called but they didn't have any appointments available until next week. Maybe I'll go to the urgent care center off Friendly."

"Dr.—" Todd stopped. He was about to mention the urgent care clinic where Myaisha worked in Kernersville, but he didn't want to give Ian reason to suspect he'd established a rapport with the doctor. It didn't matter, but Todd still hadn't decided if the doctor was a friend or not. She reminded him so much of his sister it hurt. But it also felt good—*and* the doctor was an excellent baker.

Ian wrapped the splint around his shoulder.

"Are you supposed to wear it over your clothing?" Todd asked, eyeing the splint squeezed on top of Ian's suit coat.

"I don't think so, but it helps the pain—for now."

"You need to see a doctor."

"So, what's next?"

Ian's snappy rejoinder persuaded Todd to change topics.

"I asked the finance guys to review the Evans company books for the real estate and used car lot businesses. They were supposed to call me this—"

His pocket vibrated. Todd removed his cell phone. "Detective Gamble."

Two minutes elapsed before he said, "Thanks. Can you get a copy of your report to me tonight? Tomorrow's fine. Right."

He dropped the phone into his suit coat pocket, removed his wallet, and laid several tens on the table beside the bill. "Let's go."

Throwing back his head, Ian guzzled the rest of his beverage, grabbed an unopened bag of chips, and trotted behind Todd.

"What you got?"

"The guys in finance found discrepancies in Evans' business accounts."

"Someone was stealing from him?" Ian hopped in the passenger seat and buckled in.

"Apparently."

"A motive for murder?"

Todd peered across the seat at Ian. "Maybe a motive for two murders."

"Who first?"

"The office manager."

Ian grabbed his notebook. "Ouch."

"What?"

"Nothing, man." At a slower pace, Ian turned pages of the notebook. "Cynthia Howard. Want me to call her and make an appointment?"

"Can you call without crying in pain?" Todd smirked.

"Screw you, dude. I'd like to see your skinny behind bench press even a hundred pounds." Ian dialed the number he'd recorded for Cynthia Howard.

"Why would I do that? I don't see the point of these weightlifting contests."

"Exercising is relaxing. Everyone needs something outside of work. Otherwise, the job eats away at you. When was the last time you picked up your fiddle?"

"It's a violin."

"Or played piano?"

"None of your business," Todd huffed. "Do you win any money in these contests?"

"You can at some—" Ian broke off.

Todd presumed the person at the other end of the phone answered. While he drove toward the downtown police station, his partner scheduled appointments.

"Okay," Ian said into his cell phone, "we'll see you in twenty minutes."

Eyeing, Ian, Todd pulled off the road and into the parking lot of the McGirt-Horton library. Remembering that the facility was named after two African American poets made him think about Myaisha and her writing group. He frowned.

"Where are we going?"

"Ms. Howard said she could meet us at her place." Ian gave Todd the address.

"Fine." He exited the parking lot and headed toward Ms. Howard's house. "And after that, I'm dropping you off at an urgent care center."

"I knew you cared." Ian grinned, glancing over at him.

"I'm just tired of your moaning," Todd said and proceeded across the intersection. He hoped Ms. Howard had information about Evans' business finances—and a clue to the murderer. If not, he would follow up on the necklace. It could be the clue to both crimes.

CHAPTER 31

Monday morning, in the small bungalow home she'd converted into a medical office, Myaisha wiped the drum of her stethoscope and exited the exam room.

"Mrs. Doctor," Dina called out, bustling down the hallway from the front office, "you have a phone call." Dina's voice lowered. "It's personal."

Myaisha frowned, entered her personal office, and closed the door. After hanging her medical coat on the back of her chair, she picked up the desk phone.

"Hello?"

The voice said hurriedly, "Myaisha, I wanted to tell you something before I forget."

She recognized Mary's voice among squeals of laughter in the background. "Where are you?"

"The mall. Have you finished your Christmas shopping?"

For two minutes, they discussed upcoming holiday festivities.

"Anyway," Mary said, "I know you're busy, but I heard something about Junior. It might be significant."

Seconds passed as Mary conversed with someone off the phone.

While waiting, Myaisha brought up the EHR, electronic health record, and charted on her morning patients.

"Sorry about that," Mary said.

"No problem. Is this about Robin?"

"Kind of. Greg told me Donald Evans' son—they call him Junior by the way—takes night classes at the college."

While her fingers tapped away at the keyboard, Myaisha barely registered Mary's words. "Um hmm."

"Don't you get it? Junior was supposed to be in class Thursday night—but he wasn't."

The emphasis Mary placed on the last word caught her attention. She stopped typing and weighed her friend's comment. If Junior hadn't been at the college Thursday night, he could've been at the car dealership killing his father.

Did Todd tell her the time of death? He hadn't. She needed to find out when Donald Sr. was murdered. Maybe Tina could find out from her son.

"Myaisha? Myaisha, you there?"

Raising her voice above noisy shoppers in the background, Myaisha asked, "Is Greg sure he wasn't in class Thursday night?"

"As sure as he can be. You know Greg. He's blind to most things not involving numbers or equations. But Junior is one of the younger students in his evening class. He's pretty sure."

"Well, we need to keep him in mind."

Five minutes later, Myaisha ended the call and tramped to her next patient exam room.

***

Later that evening, Myaisha collapsed in an office chair, slipped off her Birkenstocks, and reclined her head along the edge of the chair back.

Yvette slipped inside the cracked office door. "Mrs. Doctor …"

Minutes passed as Yvette discussed supplies, patient schedules, and holiday office hours. Myaisha gave monosyllabic responses, her attention divided between Robin's murder and what to eat for dinner. Whether it was the growling from her stomach or the ringing of her phone, she glanced up at her office manager and excused herself.

"I have to get this."

Yvette nodded and exited the room and closed the door.

"Hello," Myaisha said before quickly pulling the phone away from her ear as a loud voice blared across the line.

"Myaisha," a woman's voice said, "you have to help us."

Searching her memory, Myaisha recognized the voice but couldn't identify the caller. "I'm sorry. Who is this?"

The person inhaled and ripped ahead with another torrent of speech. "Latrice. René's cousin. I met you—"

"Yes, I remember," she said, sitting up straighter in the chair. "What's wrong? What's happened?"

"The police arrested René."

Chapter 32

Myaisha and Deniece headed down dark rainy streets toward the police station. After she managed to calm Latrice down—with a promise to come right away—Myaisha phoned Deniece. Because Deniece was still at work in Winston-Salem, she had managed to complete her notes and patient scheduling before they drove downtown.

"But why arrest her now?" Deniece asked, swirling through radio stations. "I can't find any holiday music."

She ignored her friend's frustration with the radio and dexterously avoided a deep water-filled pothole. The last thing she needed was to hydroplane and crash.

"I'm not sure, but Latrice was frantic."

"What do you propose to do?" Deniece leaned back into the seat as *8 Days of Christmas* by Destiny's Child chimed throughout the car.

"I don't know. We'll hear what Latrice has to say. Maybe she'll give us a clue about what to do next." Fictional puzzles didn't have real world consequences. What if she couldn't solve these murders? What if the authorities arrested René and she was convicted? *Could I deal with that?* Myaisha reconsidered her decision to pursue these mysteries.

Ten minutes elapsed before they strode up to the downtown Greensboro police station entrance.

Because she'd forgotten her umbrella in the car, rain drizzled on her hat, bringing uncomfortable memories of her first visit to the police station in June. It felt like years ago when Todd had questioned her about the death of her college friend. Myaisha shivered, recalling the tiny, boxy interrogation room.

Before she could open the glass door to the station, a woman popped out and bumped into her face.

Myaisha stepped back, apologized, and rubbed her forehead. The other woman recovered before she had.

"There you are." Latrice embraced her, slipping aside to allow other people to exit.

"What's going on?" Deniece addressed Latrice before turning aside to address the two other people. "Hey. What happened? I thought you were arrested."

René's arms wrapped around her trembling body. "They didn't arrest me, but—"

"Why don't we step away from the station and get out of this rain," said a tall, heavy-set woman who Myaisha didn't recognize. The woman led René away from the police station entrance by the elbow.

Everyone hurried across the street.

Once in the parking lot, Myaisha addressed René. "Tell us what's going on."

"Who are you?" asked the unknown woman, scrunching her face as if she'd tasted something foul.

"And who are you?" Deniece asked, craning her neck around Latrice to view the woman.

Clearing her throat, the woman said, "I'm Ms. Jones' lawyer." After rolling her eyes at Deniece, the lawyer addressed René. "I advise you not to speak with anyone." With her nose in the air, she surveyed Myaisha and Deniece.

"*Anyone* about this case. This isn't over. The police will seek a court order, and witnesses can be compelled to give evidence. Do we understand each other?"

Like a mouse, René squeaked, "Yes."

No one spoke until the lawyer climbed into her SUV and drove away.

A beat after the lawyer departed, Latrice said, "Okay, René, tell Myaisha what's going on."

If she'd harbored doubts, René's slight hesitation quickly dissolved. "I don't know where to begin."

Myaisha studied René's countenance, appreciating the haggard lines framing a generous mouth.

René shivered as light from the streetlamp glistened off a gold charm around her neck. Rain spattered the circular emblem with a large C suspended inside.

"Let's talk in the car," Myaisha said. *What happened to the gold-winged lion?*

Once everyone settled into her Honda, Myaisha turned up the car's heater, pivoted around in the seat, and questioned René.

"Better?"

With a slight tilt of her head, René signaled "yes."

"Why did they bring you downtown?" Deniece asked.

A huge shrug proceeded René's reply. "They requested another DNA sample. They mentioned a new piece of evidence." René stared distantly out a side window.

A frown creased Myaisha's brow. She glanced at Latrice. "This afternoon you said she was arrested."

"I thought she was. René's office manager called me and said the police took her downtown. René didn't call me. When I arrived I found out she wasn't arrested. Why would they want to run another DNA test?"

"I called my lawyer." René glowered at her cousin.

"Smart," Deniece said.

"I don't like your lawyer," Latrice pouted.

"You don't have to like her. It's not a popularity contest," Deniece said. "Is she competent?"

"Yes," René and Latrice said simultaneously.

Leaning into the back seat, Myaisha asked, "Did the police say *why* they wanted another DNA test now?"

Though René's mouth opened, Latrice interrupted.

"Yeah," Latrice said, "they've decided Donald was also murdered and want to frame René for both crimes."

"And René had a motive for wanting them both dead," Deniece said.

"I didn't," René exclaimed.

"Of course, you did," Latrice said.

A dispute erupted between the cousins. It took Myaisha five minutes to restore calm.

"Look," Deniece said, "we don't have time for arguing." She scrutinized René. "You didn't learn anything from the police?"

"They weren't sharing information," René said, her lips downturned. "They kept questioning me about Donald—and where I was Thursday and Friday."

Myaisha listened to the emotion in René's voice, but it didn't sound like sorrow. *Was it anger, disappointment?* No, it still sounded like anxiety. *Why?*

"Did the police tell you when they believe Donald was murdered?"

"There must be some reason they doubt your alibi," Deniece said, eyeing René.

Defiantly silent, René held their gazes.

"Or they have proof your alibi is false," Latrice said, duplicating Deniece's glare at René.

Raindrops pinged off the car's roof. A minute passed.

"You asked for our help," Myaisha said, glancing slowly over Latrice and René.

With a large sigh, René's chest sank. Under lowered lids, she side-glanced at her cousin.

Latrice said, "If you want their help—"

"No one can help me," René said.

"Let's dispense with decorum," Myaisha said, swiveling around as completely as possible to face René. "You're scared. Why?"

"She's suspected of murder," Latrice said. "Of course, she's scared."

"Don't interrupt," Myaisha said, shooting Latrice a silencing glare. "You've been scared from the moment Robin died. We already know about the fight between the two of you. What else don't the police know?"

Like a defiant child, René shut her lips.

"This is ridiculous," Deniece said. "Why are we here?" She glanced at Myaisha. "It's cold and wet. Let's go home."

"No, wait." Latrice grabbed René's arm. "Tell them, Chi. I can't help you."

"That's it, isn't it." Myaisha watched alarm flash across René's face. "I noticed you aren't wearing your winged lion necklace tonight."

René's body stiffened.

"I thought your family called you Chi for Chicago. But Chi is short for chimera. Correct?"

Although René remained silent, Latrice chimed in.

"Of course, it is. So what?"

Deniece frowned. "What the hell is a chimera?"

"René?" Myaisha paused to see if her friend would provide details but again Latrice answered.

"One of our cousins needed a bone marrow transplant. We all signed up as donors. When Chi—René—went to the lab, they discovered she had two different sets of DNA."

"Exactly," Myaisha said. "In mythology, a chimera is a lion with a goat's head and snakes for a tail. And chimeras are female."

In a halting voice, René said, "I designed the necklace myself as a reminder I was special—and had something Robin would never have."

How deeply did the animosity between the twin sisters go?

Myaisha continued. "A natural-occurring chimera occurs when a twin absorbs cells from a dead embryo, incorporating some of that DNA into its own. A chimera has two different sets of DNA. A type of micro-chimerism."

"I went to the hospital where I was born," René said, "and found out my mom had triplets, but one died in utero. Our parents hadn't told us."

"So cool," Latrice said.

Although inappropriate, Myaisha understood what she meant. "The unknown DNA on Robin's hand—"

"Is mine." With a sigh, René sank back into the car seat.

"If they discover the blood belongs to René, then they'll realize there was a fight," Latrice said, her eyes enlarging as she spoke.

"The case against René will be stronger."

"This is bad," Deniece said. "Especially since you hid information about the fight from the police."

Myaisha snuck a peek at Deniece before returning to René. "You don't have to tell us if you don't want to, but are you hiding anything else?"

A moment passed. René stayed silent.

"Any more messages?" she asked.

"No," René said.

"What about Donald's son?" Myaisha asked. "He would have a motive, right? What do you know about him?"

René's brows furrowed as she seemed to ponder the question. "I can't imagine Junior killing his dad."

"Why not?" Latrice asked. "You said he lied and stole money."

Jumping forward in her seat, René said, "I didn't say he stole."

"He took money from the office without telling his dad," Latrice said. "That's stealing."

"No," René said, "not really. Junior would consider it belonged to him, as Donald's son. He … he wouldn't hurt his dad."

"Why not?" Deniece asked. "René, tell us what you know."

"Okay." René's shoulders collapsed. "Junior gambled. He blew his entire salary at the casinos. When his debts got out of control—"

"How bad did they get?" Myaisha asked, reading the answer in René's startled eyes. "He borrowed."

"From people who don't wait for their money." René wiped her eyes.

Latrice gave her a tissue.

"Thank you." She blew her nose. "Junior took money when things became desperate. A few times, I loaned him money."

"You what?" Latrice asked, staring at René as if for the first time. "Are you the world's biggest fool, or what?"

"Latrice, please," Myaisha said, observing René's downturned gaze.

"Hmm." Deniece glanced at Myaisha. "One vice leads to another."

Together, Myaisha and Deniece regarded René.

"Fine," René said. "Junior liked to go to strip clubs. He was dating a dancer for a while—still might be. After Donald … I dated Donald for about two years—not consecutively. When I found out he was married and wouldn't divorce his wife, we broke up. After his divorce, we started dating again. It lasted for about six months, then Robin came to visit. I introduced them. I had no idea they would—"

"Hook up," Latrice said.

"Have you communicated with Junior since you and Donald broke up?" Myaisha asked.

"Yes—but not in about two weeks. He needed money. The people he borrowed from threatened to beat him up if he didn't pay them back by the end of the week."

Latrice sniffed. "And you gave it to him?"

"I couldn't let him get hurt." René frowned.

"Why not? It would serve him right. It's not like he needed money for a kidney." Latrice crossed her arms over her heaving bosom. "He could buy a girlie magazine if he had a—"

"What strip club did he—" —Myaisha searched for the correct terminology—, "frequent."

"Why?" René asked, her forehead wrinkling.

"The people at the club could provide him with an alibi, or—"

"Or not," Deniece interjected.

Myaisha glared at her.

Before exiting the car, René provided Myaisha with the strip club address.

Myaisha watched René and Latrice enter their car and exit the lot before she belted into her seat and drove off.

Half a mile away from the police station, Deniece turned up the radio as *Christmas All Over Again* by Tom Petty played.

"I guess we're going to a strip club," Deniece said. "Doesn't it feel like Christmas. Ho, ho, ho."

After sending her friend a side glare, Myaisha focused on the road. "René is still hiding something."

"Why are we helping her?" Deniece asked.

"Because she didn't kill her sister," Myaisha said, stopping at the signal light. "By the way, this was your idea."

"What?"

"Helping René, remember?"

"Oh, right." Deniece drummed on the dashboard along to the musical rhythms. "What about Donald?"

"It depends on the time of death, whether he was killed Thursday night or Friday morning."

"You can ask your cop friend."

"Todd won't tell me. He's more a taker than a giver during an investigation." Unless it could also benefit him.

Deniece gazed out the side window. "Do we think René killed Donald?"

"She could have—psychologically speaking."

"But."

Myaisha inhaled deeply and blew it out through her mouth. "If she wanted revenge, why make it appear to be a suicide?"

"To get away with it."

"Then why make the mistake with the hand?" Myaisha glimpsed at Deniece for a second before returning her attention to the road. "René knew about Donald's carpal tunnel release surgery. She knew he couldn't grip a gun in his right hand."

"Maybe she didn't think the police would figure it out," Deniece said.

"No, René would be an emotional killer. She would commit a hurried brutal crime, but not a detached prolonged murder."

"If she killed Robin, she would have beat her to death." Deniece paused a moment before saying, "Doesn't Robin's death seem like overkill? Why would René poison her, then smack her around? The police must think she got impatient and decided to eliminate Robin at once."

"Hmm. That's a good point." Myaisha peered into the dark night. "We have to travel into the mind of a killer. Someone who's calculating and has murdered twice."

"Brr. I'm cold." Deniece turned up the heater.

CHAPTER 33

Thirty minutes north of Greensboro off Interstate 85, Myaisha and Deniece parked in a muddy lot among a dozen other vehicles. Music vibrated off a ramshackle building. Along the building's façade, flashing lights encircled life-sized pictures of scantily dressed women.

Myaisha placed the car in park but left the engine running. She glanced across the seat at Deniece. "Maybe this isn't a good idea."

"Don't wimp out now." Deniece opened the passenger side car door and bustled up to the heavy steel front door.

One deep breath later, Myaisha walked up to the establishment behind Deniece, securing her fedora as they approached the entrance. The door looked to be the sole solid part of the entire building.

As Deniece reached for the knob, the door sprang open, and a man staggered out.

An odor of cigarettes and alcohol wafted up Myaisha's nostrils. She skirted away from the drunk man and followed Deniece inside. Through the hazy air, she searched for someone in charge. Myaisha covered her mouth, choking back a staccato cough. She bent toward Deniece's ear.

"D, who should we—"

"Come on," Deniece said, grabbing Myaisha's arm. "Let's ask her."

Myaisha allowed herself to be directed toward a stage lit by a half dozen spotlights. In the center on the stage were two poles. A scraggly woman with blond extensions strode off the platform. She wore flimsy silver lingerie with high-heeled plastic pumps.

Men ogled the dancer. Before Myaisha could protest, Deniece deposited them in front of the woman.

"Excuse me," Deniece said, releasing Myaisha's arm and greeting the woman. "May I speak with you a moment?"

The woman's bedazzled eyes with inch long eyelashes flared. "I'm on break. In thirty minutes, I have my next routine."

"I promise," Deniece said, "it'll be quick."

With obvious exaggeration, the woman sashayed over to a long wooden bar on the left side of the building not ten feet from the stage.

Motioning with her finger, Deniece alerted the bartender. "Hi. I'd like a Cuba libre. And my friend ..." Deniece left the sentence open for the dancer.

"Hey, Harry," the dancer said, "I'd like a cola." In an aside to Deniece, the dancer said, "I like to be sober when I dance."

"I bet," Deniece said, paying the bartender in cash.

Myaisha stood behind Deniece, observing her friend while sneaking a peek at the dancers on the stage.

In under two minutes, Deniece and the dancer were sipping their drinks.

"Thanks for speaking with me," Deniece said. "Do you know Junior Evans?"

For a split second the dancer gawked. She swallowed half her cola, then eyed Deniece. "You a cop?"

"Please. Do I look like a cop?" Deniece chuckled. "No, I'm a grandmother looking for the bum who knocked up my daughter. I already have two jobs and can't afford to feed another mouth."

The dancer's body loosened. "Junior did that?" She drank her cola. "Hmm. Not surprised. He's been acting pretty stupid lately."

Confidentially, Deniece slid closer to the dancer. "I know. That stuff with his dad." She shook her head. "I'm gonna get my money before Junior splits."

"You think Junior's involved?"

"What do you think?" Deniece prompted.

Long press-on nails tapped along the counter as the dancer seemed to consider the question. "Possible. I know my baby daddy would clear out if he came into money."

"Yeah, but Junior has to split his with his mom and sister."

"Does he? I heard the momma got her cut in the divorce. But his mom … She could kill her baby dad easily."

"I haven't met her. Guess we'll be family now."

"Forget it. That woman only cares about her own kids. She don't respect blood. She'll let your grandbaby starve rather than give up a dime of her money."

"Well, Junior still has to share with his sister. And my daughter needs money now. Diapers don't grow on trees."

"Girl, tell me about it." The dancer slurped the remaining cola. "My youngest finally got out of diapers."

"I tried calling Junior on Thursday night, but he skipped class at the college. I bet he was here spending the rent money."

The dancer frowned. "Thursday night?" A half-minute elapsed. "No, I'm sure he wasn't here that night. I dance on Mondays, Thursdays, and Saturdays. I didn't see him if he did slip in."

Over the next five minutes, the dancer shared what she knew about Junior before glancing at her watch.

"Well, maybe he was paying off the loan shark," Deniece said, gazing innocently.

The dancer's eyes flashed. She grimaced and inched away from Deniece. "Oh, crap. I need to prepare for my next show. I hope your daughter gets what she's owed."

Deniece started to move away from the bar, then doubled back. "If you're ever interested in dancing in a classier joint, let me know." She scribbled a number on a cocktail napkin.

"Thanks, but this place isn't bad. Harry lets me work whenever my mom can watch the kids. I make enough to cover rent." With a princess wave, the dancer trotted behind a dark velvet curtain beside the stage.

Myaisha gazed a Deniece, her mouth curled at the edge.

"What?" Deniece asked, watching the performance on stage.

"You're a good liar," Myaisha said.

"I'm a nurse. I hear a lot of lies." Deniece chuckled.

"Let's go." Myaisha headed for the exit but detected Deniece lagging behind. "What's wrong?"

"Nothing. I wanted to see the end of her show." Deniece's gaze directed Myaisha back to the stage, where a dark-skinned dancer snaked down a pool using her legs. "Wow. Can you imagine how strong her legs must be?"

Scowling, Myaisha said, "You seem impressed."

"I am. It's hard twirling around a pole. Besides the chafing, you need strength and agility."

Myaisha gasped. "You've pole danced?"

Deniece threw her head back and cackled. "Don't look surprised. There's nothing wrong with it."

A man missing several front teeth eyed Myaisha. She retreated toward the door, pulling Deniece with her.

"When did you pole dance?"

"Not for money, silly. A gym in Greensboro offered a class. It was fun."

"Why?"

"Why not? It's exercise. And if you do it right—it's sexy." The last word slithered off Deniece's tongue. "Speaking about sexy, what's up with you and AJ?"

Myaisha's face slackened as she headed for the large steel front door with a dull orange exit sign above. Outside in the evening air, she inhaled deeply, appreciating the cool freshness. As she ambled toward her car, Deniece's arm entwined around hers.

"Talk to me," Deniece said, pulling lightly on her arm.

Abruptly, Myaisha stopped a yard outside the strip club and regarded her friend. "I'm not sure I want an intimate relationship with AJ."

Boggle eyed, Deniece stammered. "What? Are you crazy? I thought you were hot for him."

She smacked Deniece's arm, hauling her friend further away from the door. "Quiet."

"What's wrong? Is he a bad kisser? I've dumped men who were bad kissers."

"No," Myaisha whispered. "It's not that."

"Well, it can't be you." Deniece smiled. "A woman in her forties has more sex drive than a twenty-year-old computer nerd."

"I can't talk about this if you're going to joke about it." Myaisha bolted away.

"I'm not joking," Deniece said bounding after her. "Seriously, what's wrong."

"Promise. No teasing."

Like a Girl Scout, Deniece held up her fingers in pledge. "On my honor."

"Okay." Myaisha squared her shoulders. "I'm worried the sex might not be good."

Deniece blinked rapidly five times but didn't speak. "Why wouldn't it be good? A woman could get turned on simply looking at AJ. Imagine with his clothes off—"

"Okay, let's keep it clean."

"I thought you wanted to get dirty." With a smirk, Deniece elbowed Myaisha's side.

"See. I knew you couldn't be serious." Myaisha huffed and stormed off.

By the crook of Myaisha's arm, Deniece pulled her back. "I'm sorry. Please, tell me."

After a pouty moment, Myaisha relaxed. "Because a man looks good doesn't mean he's …" She searched for a proper term but couldn't find one. "An attractive man can be a disappointment in bed."

"Speak." Deniece giggled.

Myaisha bit her lip. "I can't believe I'm saying this, but it's the truth. I loved my husband, but Sammy wasn't good in bed."

"No?" Deniece raised her brows.

With a nod, Myaisha said, "It's true. I loved him, but he had performance problems, premature ejaculation. Then, once he gained weight … I didn't enjoy sex."

"Did you guys seek help?"

Her brow wrinkled in a question. "Help?"

"You know. Sex therapy."

"No, we didn't try therapy. I asked Sammy to see a urologist, but he refused. Did you and Barry consider sex therapy?"

Deniece nodded. "Not because Barry couldn't perform. He's dynamite in bed." She lifted her brow suggestively.

"No details, please."

"The gynecologist recommended it during our fertility treatments. Sometimes couples are hyper focused on conceiving and sex becomes a means to an end instead of being mutually satisfying."

"Did it help?"

"No, because we didn't need it."

Seconds passed as Deniece gazed into the starry night sky.

"After Barry and I divorced, we both did our own thing. I dated other people, but it was simply physical—the same for him. Once we met up again, and he asked me out, we started over from the beginning. Things simply fell in place. We loved each other. Trying to create a baby got in the way."

Myaisha nodded but didn't reply. The saga that ended Deniece and Barry's marriage had been more tumultuous than her friend had described, but she understood.

"Sex wasn't your problem."

"A Black man isn't going to admit to a doctor he can't perform sexually," Deniece said.

Arm in arm, they sauntered toward Myaisha's car.

"I know," Myaisha said. "I put up with it, but it wasn't satisfying. What if sex with AJ is bad? I'd rather have no sex, than bad sex."

"Preach," Deniece said, raising her left hand toward the sky.

Myaisha laughed. "Seriously, I like AJ, *a lot*. And I want to take things to a more intimate level. But I couldn't deal with another bad sexual relationship."

Deniece shook her head. "That's the problem with you married virgins. You've never experienced sex with a different partner. It limits your vision."

"Okay, you tramp," Myaisha said, grinning. "What would you suggest?"

"Try it and see if you like it."

"And if he's unable to perform?"

"Y'all aren't married. You can get something on the side." Laughing, Deniece danced toward the car singing.

"Thank you, Lady Marmalade." Using the key fob, Myaisha unlocked the car and slid under the steering wheel.

The seat belt clicked into place as Deniece sang, "Voulez vous—"

"Enough Mrs. LaBelle."

Deniece clicked on the radio. The broadcaster discussed the ongoing police investigations in Greensboro. Neither woman spoke during the program. When it ended, Myaisha switched off the radio.

Ten minutes down the road, she asked, "What did we learn?" She peeked at Deniece before observing the late evening traffic.

"Junior gambled and had money problems."

Myaisha nodded. "Yes, and he wasn't at the club when his dad was murdered."

"Nope. Where was he?" Deniece snuck a glance at Myaisha before clicking on the radio.

As Christmas carols played, Myaisha wondered if Junior had shot his father in the right temple to protect his inheritance. And what about René—who was still hiding something? If it wasn't the DNA …

What could be worse than the police finding out René had assaulted Robin right before the latter seized and died? Myaisha wasn't sure she wanted to know, but if she was going to help René—

"Why do people make things difficult?"

"What?" Deniece asked.

"Oh, sorry," she said. "I didn't realize I was thinking out loud."

After dropping Deniece off, Myaisha intended to confront René, but she had to do it away from Latrice. The childcare owner would be inhibited in the presence of her more dominant cousin.

Could the intelligent, introverted René be a double murderer? Maybe I should consider another hobby besides murder mysteries, like Sudoko.

Myaisha had seen more bizarre things in her life, and she had no doubt she would see more.

CHAPTER 34

Inside the police station, the interview room door clanged shut after Todd entered behind Junior Evans. Mother and son had arrived at the station to sign their witness statements. However, the detectives had more behind their invitation. Facts had to be clarified and statements amended.

Already seated at the small square table, Mrs. Evans glared at Ian. Her lips pursed into a bitter scowl. Despite her age, Todd realized Mrs. Evans was an attractive woman. *Why had she wasted time on Donald Evans?*

On the wobbly table, Ian placed a manila folder in front of Mrs. Evans. Junior Evans, seated beside his mom, reached for it.

"Before you open that," Ian cautioned, "is there anything you'd like to tell us? Maybe correct your statement about your whereabouts on the day Mrs. Jones-Collins was murdered."

As his hand retreated, Junior Evans' posture stiffened.

"There's nothing to change. I had nothing to do with Robin—before, during, or after her death." He sniffed. "She was nothing to me."

"No, but she was something to your dad," Ian said, tapping the folder with his index finger. "If he'd lived, your dad would've married her. What would happen to you and your sister?"

Mrs. Evans' wagging finger darted in Ian's face. "How dare you accuse my son? He had nothing to do with that nasty woman's death."

"No?" Ian's head pivoted toward her. "What about your whereabouts, ma'am? You certainly had a motive for killing Mrs. Jones-Collins."

"Hmm." Mrs. Evans reclined into the seat, eyeing Ian. "I would've snatched those extensions off her head and strangled her with those braids if she hurt one of my children. But she was poisoned by her sister, according to the news."

Todd observed a slight movement in Ian's shoulder. With a slight grimace his partner repositioned himself on the stool.

"What do you know about René Jones?" Ian asked. "I understand she was dating your husband before Mrs. Jones-Collins."

Mrs. Evans' glare smacked onto Ian, who inched back from the table.

"Donald Evans was a serial philanderer," she said through gritted teeth. "That … woman wasn't the first to turn his head. She soon found out she wasn't the last. My husband may have divorced *me*, but he always took care of his children." Under the table, Mrs. Evans squeezed her son's hand.

Having stood in the corner during the interview thus far, Todd now sat parallel to Ian but at the far end of the table.

"Were you aware of the contents of your ex-husband's will, Mrs. Evans?" he asked.

She regarded him suspiciously, then turned back toward Ian. "Yes, I was. He consulted me about everything affecting the children."

"Did you know he intended to change it?" Todd asked.

Time slowed as Mrs. Evans' neck incrementally swiveled toward him. Her grimace summed up her opinion of his question.

"No, he did not." She glared at him, daring him to refute her statement.

With a peek at Ian, Todd signaled his partner to continue.

"Mr. Evans, where were you the evening before Mrs. Jones-Collins' murder?" Ian asked.

"I told you, I had a class."

"Your math class meets every Tuesday and Thursday evenings."

Gaping, Junior Evans squirmed. "Oh, right. I forgot. You mean Monday night. I was with a friend."

"Who?" Ian removed a pen from his coat pocket.

"My girlfriend? Her name is—"

"We already know her name," Ian interrupted, "and she denied seeing you Monday evening."

Sweat beaded on Junior Evans' forehead. Todd noticed the young man release his grip on his mom's hand. The matriarch turned toward her son, worry scribbled along the wrinkles in her face.

"I … uh. I don't remember."

"He was home with me," Mrs. Evans asserted, her frame rod-straight.

"Ma'am," Ian said, barely glancing in her direction, "please."

"Prove me wrong."

Ian glanced at Mrs. Evans then at Todd.

"Lying will not help your son." Todd rested his hands on the table in front of her.

"I am not a liar." Mrs. Evans' body trembled with indignation.

"Isn't it true you play bingo every Monday night?" Todd asked.

"That night I was tired and stayed home."

"Mrs.—"

"No, Mom," Junior Evans said, placing a hand on her shoulder. "I don't want you to get in trouble." Glancing from Todd to Ian and back, Junior Evans said, "I was at the casino, gambling."

Todd exchanged a look with Ian before he rose. "Fine. We'll need both of you to sign a statement to that effect. Mr. Evans, if you'll come with me, I'll prepare your statement first."

***

Once he settled Junior Evans into a chair beside the desk, Todd booted up his computer. While the machine hummed to life, he regarded the young man.

"Where were you *Thursday* night? And no crap this time—your mom's not here."

Junior Evans swallowed. "I was at a strip club."

"Which one?" Todd collected the information. "Did you ask your mom to lie—"

"No, I didn't tell her to lie about where I was on Monday night."

"I wasn't going to ask about Monday night." Todd stared at his suspect. He watched the young man squirm in the plastic chair.

Minutes passed. Todd surveyed the station. Most of his fellow police officers had left. It was late Tuesday night. A week since Robin Jones-Collins' murder. Now a second murder had occurred, and he was no closer to solving either homicide.

Although the chief had ordered Todd to bring René Jones in for lying in her statement to police, they weren't prepared to charge her with murder. The unknown blood sample had been compared against their suspects, but Todd had requested another sample from Ms. Jones.

He'd deduced she was the likely source of the unknown blood sample. He'd found a picture of the necklace Myaisha had mentioned. The picture was of a mythological creature. A chimera. If Ms. Jones was a chimera, she possessed two different DNA profiles. One of those profiles could match their unknown sample. *But how did blood get on Mrs. Jones-Collins' hands?*

Todd recalled the scratches on Ms. Jones' knuckles on the day of the murder. Both he and Ian had documented them. Forensics had taken photos of Ms. Jones' hands when they'd obtained her blood sample the following day. The sisters could have fought. Ms. Jones struck her sister in the nose and Mrs. Jones-Collins fell, seized, and …

She died from poisoning though. Perhaps, Ms. Jones had planned to poison her sister, but their fight precipitated Mrs. Jones-Collins' death. It didn't sound right, but he would work on it. Either way, Ms. Jones was hiding secrets. And Todd intended to discover what they were.

On the surface, Ms. René Collins, Junior Evans, and Mrs. Evans had the strongest motives for murder. But all three of them couldn't have committed the crime. *Or could they?* Maybe he needed to look for two different murderers.

"Look, I only asked my mom to lie about my whereabouts the night my dad was murdered."

Todd leaned forward. "Why?"

Half-laughing, almost hysterical, Junior Evans' voice broke. "Why? Because I knew I had a motive. He was wasting our money on that b—his girlfriend."

"Did you know your dad was going to change his will?" Todd scrutinized him.

"No, I swear. I didn't know."

Not detecting any movement in the young man's countenance, Todd's gaze lightened. "Where were you?"

"I had to meet a guy." His lips quivered. "A man who loaned me money."

"How much are you into the loan sharks?"

"Fifty thousand."

"That's a lot of money."

"I got it down to twenty."

"How?"

A gulf opened between them. Todd sensed a lie. He started to speak when—

"I stole it. From Dad's business account." Junior Evans' gaze drifted onto his lap.

Todd gave him a moment before asking, "Did your dad know?"

"No. At least, I hope he didn't."

"You were seen in the vicinity of your dad's home the morning Mrs. Jones-Collins died."

"I… I …" Sweat trickled down Junior Evans' face like a swollen stream.

Todd handed him a box of tissues. He felt sorry for the young man. Almost. But Junior Evans was a gambler and thief. Worse yet, he'd stolen from his own dad. Another spoiled child who couldn't accept no. *Had his dad found out?*

There was no evidence he had. But if Mr. Evans Sr. did … *How far would Junior Evans go to prevent his dad from finding out about his embezzlement?*

Mrs. Jones-Collins might have discovered the missing funds. Unlikely. Terrence Collins stated his ex-wife was terrible with finances—proven by her many failed business ventures. The people most likely to discover Junior Evans' defalcations would be his mom or the bookkeeper. *What time was their meeting with Ms. Cynthia Howard again?* Todd consulted the computer calendar.

"Go on," Todd said after Junior Evans regained his composure.

"I was at Dad's place Tuesday morning. But I didn't see Robin."

The smirk on Todd's face needed no comment.

"Fine." Junior Evans wiped his face, tossed a handful of napkins in the trash, and sat up straight. "I wanted to speak with Dad outside the office. Cynthia's always sneaking around, listening at doors. I was going to ask him for a loan."

"You didn't expect your dad to bail you out of debt to a bookie."

"He hadn't before, but this was different. They were threatening to break my legs." Junior Evans slid his chair closer to the desk. "I figured Dad wouldn't want to see me hurt. I had to try."

"And Mrs. Jones-Collins answered."

He nodded. "She was standing in the doorway, sipping on one of those stupid smoothies. I asked if Dad was home, and she said no. So, I left."

"Like that, you simply left."

"I hated her. Acting as if she owned everything—owned my dad. Making a fool of him."

Todd scrutinized the snarling expression evolving across Junior Evans' immature face. *Was it the face of a killer?*

Perhaps sensing Todd's survey, Junior Evans tried to laugh off his prior comment, but it sounded hollow.

"No big deal. She wasn't the first woman my dad screwed around with. He would've tired of her like he did the others. The one person who ever truly cared about him was René."

"Really? The woman who broke up your parents' marriage."

"I've told you the truth. I went to my dad's place. Robin said he was at work, and I left. If you have a witness, they can tell you I never entered the house."

Though he knew it to be true, Todd didn't reply.

"Tell me about Ms. Jones."

"I'm not talking about René."

"Why not? Your dad cheated on your mom with her."

"That's their business."

Todd grinned. "You like Ms. Jones. Is it friendly or intimate?"

Like a rocket, Junior Evans shot up out of the chair.

Todd mimicked his actions. Several police officers rose and approached Todd's desk. With a wave of his hand, Todd signaled things were fine.

"You've got quite a temper."

"Where's my statement? I need to leave."

"Why did you go into the office early on Friday morning?"

"To drop off the letter—"

"Don't lie." Todd was shaking his head with a dour face. "You were looking for money to pay your bookie. You didn't get up early to send a 'Dear, Dad' letter."

Junior Evans lips trembled as he glanced at the floor.

"I don't want to type up your statement and then have to revise it a minute later when you decide to tell the truth."

"I thought dad might have money hidden around the office."

Todd's brows rose. "Did he usually keep large sums around the place?"

"Not that I knew about."

Because Junior Evans diverted his gaze immediately after speaking, Todd detected a lie. "What made you think he did then?"

"Desperate times, right?" He attempted a grin, but his face refused to participate.

Todd eyed him.

"I'm ready to sign my statement," Junior Evans mumbled, surveying the desk.

Fifteen minutes later, Todd escorted him out of the police station.

***

When Todd returned to his desk, Ian was typing. Todd handed his partner a soda and resumed his seat.

Without looking up from the computer, Ian asked, "How did it go?"

"Interesting. He admitted to asking his mom for an alibi."

"Was he at the strip club?"

"No, he said he was paying off a debt."

The two shared a glance. Ian resumed typing, while Todd gazed into the distance.

"He also admitted to coming by his dad's home on the morning Mrs. Jones-Collins died."

"We already knew about that from the next-door neighbor."

"Yes, but he didn't know that." While sipping soda, Todd filled Ian in on the entire interview.

"I would've loved to see him leap at you."

"Mr. Evans has a short temper."

"Not ideal for a poisoner."

"But a precipitous killer who shot his dad in the head to protect his inheritance?"

Fifteen minutes later, Ian powered down his computer.

Todd reflected on the case, observing his computer without reading the screen.

"Do you think we'll get a subpoena for another DNA sample from the twin sister?" Ian asked.

Speaking from a distance, Todd said, "I don't know. It doesn't matter though. Whether or not the DNA belongs to her, she's obviously afraid it might."

"She's hiding something."

Todd shrugged. "Everyone is. They always do."

"Who do?"

"Suspects."

"Speaking of suspects …" Ian swallowed the rest of his drink before chucking the can into the trash. "Are we any closer to narrowing down the murderer?"

"No. They all have weak alibis. We haven't completely eliminated anyone."

"Except the ex-husband, Terrence Collins."

"True. He can't figure in on the poisoning. The medical examiner concluded that a cumulative dose of rat poisoning led to Mrs. Jones-Collins' death."

"So why are we chasing the sister? She might have punched her twin in the face, but it didn't cause her death."

"Yes, but the fight might have been a precipitous event, and she had planned to murder her sister with poison. Can you imagine a better defense? Your honor, my client had a fight with her sister. Why would she slap Mrs. Jones-Collins around when she knew she'd be dead in a few days?"

Ian exhaled. "Do you believe Ms. Jones is smart enough to think up a false alibi of assaulting her sister?"

"It's not false. She got mad and hit her. Doesn't mean she didn't already plan to poison her to death."

"True."

Todd sank into an abstracted abyss, reviewing certain items he'd heard.

"What next?"

Lost in thought, he missed Ian's question.

Ian whistled. "Did you hear me?"

"No."

"Who should we interview next?"

"I remembered something Mr. Evans said."

"Would you like to share it, or should I try and guess?"

Todd glared at his partner then removed his coat from the back of his chair. Likewise, Ian grabbed his coat and rose.

As they exited the station, Todd said, "Mr. Evans said he was paying off the loan shark the night his dad was killed."

A second passed before Ian's arm shot out and stopped Todd.

"Wait a minute. Donald Evans wasn't murdered Thursday night."

"No, he wasn't." Todd grinned.

"He was killed Friday morning."

"Mr. Evans didn't know that."

"Then he isn't the murderer," Ian said, ambling toward his personal car.

While his partner drove away, Todd reviewed the interviews over the past week. If Mr. Evans thought his dad was killed Thursday night, it suggested he wasn't the murderer. But a sociopath could tell a convincing lie.

Did Junior Evans fit the profile?

If not, why did Junior Evans believe his dad died the night before?

CHAPTER 35

Due to the limited space between the track homes, Cynthia hid behind a large oak tree until traffic in the neighborhood quieted. The night was cold, and she estimated the hike was about a quarter of a mile to René's townhome.

She'd intended to leave an hour earlier, but those homicide detectives had insisted on speaking with her about Junior. *Idiot.*

Donald's son had been a disappointment—to everyone. Mrs. Evans protected him like a newborn baby, but even she had to admit Junior was a wastrel.

Cynthia didn't regret what she'd told the detectives. If they had any intelligence, they'd eventually discover Junior's theft. *Why not save them the trouble?* Her contribution to civic engagement.

The bum had even asked her for a loan. Like she would waste her hard-earned money on him. *Why?* So he could slip it into the G-string of a stripper or toss it away at the local casino? Even Mrs. Evans threw away good money at a bingo hall. A family of morons. But when Donald hooked up with that heifer, they realized *this* time the party was over for real.

Cynthia couldn't understand her boss' attraction to the slutty girl from Chicago. At least his fling with René made sense. The one thing Donald liked better than sex was money—actually lots of both.

She peeked around a tree trunk. Smoke from fireplaces filled the air, the white gases rising into the chilly sky. Once the family next door finished loading groceries inside their house, Cynthia tiptoed from behind a tree and slipped up to René's porch.

Barely a second passed after she inserted the paper into the Christmas wreath when a car's headlights slammed onto the townhome's front façade.

Like a squirrel, Cynthia darted for a tree. She paused a second before scampering between townhomes and behind those manicured yards. Without looking back, she raced past a small grove of trees until she reached a sidewalk outside the housing development. Her pulse raced. A minute later, she slowed her pace to a brisk trot.

The cold night air stimulated her increased gait. Not a time for dawdling.

Once inside her car, she reclined against the headrest and considered what she'd done. It was risky. There was a chance the letter would have a negative effect, but Cynthia didn't think it would.

She had no loyalty to the Evans family. Not simply because Donald had fired her, but because his wife and kids had never been kind. Junior treated her like dirt—after all the hard work she'd done for them. And the daughter ... Cynthia wondered about Kamara. Donald adored his daughter, but the latter rarely came by the office. Perhaps the daughter had sense.

For years—decades—Cynthia had toiled daily to keep Evans' car dealership and realty company solvent. *And what did she get for her efforts?* No retirement, respect, or remuneration for overtime.

Did they give her an ounce of appreciation for her dedication? Simply two measly weeks of severance pay.

At age fifty-eight, it wouldn't be easy for her to find another job—and definitely not as a bookkeeper. Not with this economy. In addition, most businesses now hired accountants with degrees and alphabet after their names. She'd have to go back to living with her parents. Already, she could hear her dad's condescending words *"Back again."*

Cynthia pounded on the car's dashboard. "Damn him."

As she started the engine, curses flew from her mouth. It took another minute before she became calm enough to drive. With a glance in both directions, Cynthia eased her car out of the shopping center parking lot. As she entered the main road, she spied another car easing onto the road behind her.

Could someone be following me? Police?

She chuckled. Of course not. She hadn't done anything wrong. But she knew things. Information the Evans family wouldn't like the police to know. A glance into the rearview mirror showed the car had disappeared. Her shoulders relaxed.

Cynthia was glad she'd warned René. She—

Electricity shot up her arm. A car barreled toward the driver's side of her car. A second before they made contact, Cynthia slammed on her car brakes and swerved toward the road's graveled shoulder.

The driver who had nearly hit her blared their horn before speeding away.

Like a jackhammer, Cynthia's heart reverberated in her ears. Her body spasmed. Though her hands clenched the steering wheel, her body temporarily disconnected. In the rearview mirror, she noticed a police car approaching. *Had the officer seen what had occurred? Would he stop her?* There was no plausible reason for Cynthia to be in this part of Greensboro.

If the cop asked, she could claim she was Christmas shopping, but Cynthia didn't even know the names of any stores in the shopping center.

She bit her lip and eased back onto the roadway. Careful not to attract attention, she drove five miles under the speed limit. Her shoulders ached from gripping the steering wheel. Once the police car passed, she exhaled.

At the next intersection, she pulled into a parking lot, turned around, and headed in the direction she had intended before being forced off the road. With her right hand, she eased a cell phone from her purse. Without ceasing, her eyes jockeyed between the car mirrors.

She hit send and the phone rang.

"Hello," a groggy voice said.

"Ma," Cynthia said, "I'm coming by."

"What's wrong, baby?"

"Nothing, I ..." Cynthia paused. "I miss y'all."

"Oh, baby, that's sweet."

That wasn't Cynthia's sentiment as she hung up. Once she was confident no one followed her, she steered onto Interstate 40. She wasn't sure how long it would take her to reach Cary, but on the way, she would consider her next steps.

"He messed with the wrong woman this time," she said, scrutinizing any vehicles lingering in her periphery.

The incident with the car might be unrelated to Donald's murder, but she didn't believe it. There were two people Cynthia thought could've come at her like that. Only two with a reason.

At the next freeway exit, she stopped at a gas station. After a quick purchase, she jumped in her car and re-entered the freeway. A mile down the road, she placed a call with the disposable phone she'd bought in the gas station market.

She would have to take better precautions. *Dad has plenty of guns.*

The car lurched forward as she stepped on the gas. On the ninety-minute drive, she reviewed everything she knew about who might want her dead.

Chapter 36

The childcare center parking lot was crammed full of cars. Myaisha managed to squeeze her Honda between two SUVs but getting out of the car was difficult. She sucked in her gut and wriggled out the door without scratching the other car, barely keeping her Irish walking hat intact. *Need to lose weight.*

She had no idea how she would get back inside her car and exit the parking space, but she'd worry about it after speaking with René.

Dropping in at the Greensboro childcare center in the middle of a Wednesday was risky. More than likely, René would be preoccupied. However, Myaisha was determined to get answers. *Why was René being obstinate about this case?* She'd learned how foolish people acted when involved in a homicide investigation.

A melodic tune belted out from the buzzer. Myaisha waited at the door to be escorted inside.

"Who are you here to pick up?" a woman wearing a multicolored smock asked.

Myaisha smiled. "I'm here to meet with Ms. Jones about a business investment."

The woman's face lightened and her smile enlarged,

displaying a mouth full of braces. "Of course, please come in." She stepped back allowing Myaisha inside.

This facility's lobby dwarfed the High Point office in appearance and size. Another fantasy land for children. *I really must discuss our office décor with Yvette. Later.* Right now, she needed to speak with René.

Small, segregated rooms lined an expansive hallway. Laughter drifted through plexiglass windows positioned inside the doors. Myaisha viewed children engaged in playing, eating, and reading. René's childcare business was a success.

More than two years had passed since René had approached her about a business investment. As an internist and pediatrician, Myaisha understood the value of good, affordable childcare for working families. Because she had her own medical practice, she didn't place her son, Josiah, in childcare when he was an infant. But many of her families depended upon it to maintain jobs and feed their families.

In a short time, she came to value René's business acumen. Myaisha had been impressed with René's organizational outline and eventually invested. She'd not been disappointed. The modest childcare business René had started blossomed into two facilities. One in High Point, and this one, the flagship office, in Greensboro.

After René joined the Greensboro Women of Color Writing Group, Myaisha socialized with her informally, but they hadn't become close. Until Robin moved to Greensboro, Myaisha had no idea René was a twin.

Five minutes passed before the guide opened a large wooden door and directed Myaisha inside. Having been in the office before, Myaisha entered and walked up to the receptionist's desk.

A short, round woman with designer glasses rose. "Come in. Please be seated."

Myaisha obeyed.

"I'll call and let her assistant know you're here. What's your name?"

Once she provided her name, the assistant escorted Myaisha into a separate smaller room. Ten minutes elapsed as she rested in the waiting room outside René's private office. Occasionally, the assistant snuck a glance at her. Curious about her interest, Myaisha sauntered over to the desk.

"I should have made an appointment. Ms. Jones is a busy woman."

"Yes, she's been busy this week," the assistant said, returning immediately to her computer screen.

Because it was tilted at an angle, Myaisha peeked at the screen and noticed the assistant had a calendar pulled up. She needed a way to get the woman to open up. If she had to wait, Myaisha would investigate. She smiled at the assistant.

"I've heard good things about this company. How long have you worked for Ms. Jones?"

"Oh, I've been here since the childcare center opened, but I used to work with the kids—toddlers. When the opportunity came to work in the office, I jumped at it."

"Good for you. Move up the ranks, right?"

"Exactly. I want to have my own business one day. I've learned a lot already from working with Ms. Jones."

"She's a smart businesswoman. That's why I'm thinking about investing."

"It's a solid business—and Ms. Jones has a great head for finance."

Myaisha leaned over the desk and lowered her voice. "But I heard ... Well, people have been talking about the murder." She paused, hoping the assistant would expand on the topic.

"Don't listen to that nonsense. Ms. Jones can't help it if her sister was murdered by her boyfriend."

"Oh, the boyfriend did it?" Myaisha gaped in feigned surprise.

The assistant leaned across her desk. "Yes. Then he killed himself in remorse."

"How sad. I saw a picture of her sister in the paper. Such a beautiful woman."

"Humph." The assistant sniffed. "She was nasty. Always strutting in here like she owned the place. She'd talk to Ms. Jones like she knew about finance and childcare. Ms. Jones told her to mind her own business."

Myaisha nodded. "That's the problem with family, always giving unwanted advice."

"I know it. Ms. Jones told the front staff not to let her sister into the back office anymore without her permission."

"Umm um." Myaisha shook her head sympathetically. "It takes a lot of focus not to let personal problems interfere with business."

"Not Ms. Jones. She's a hard-working woman. Nothing stops her from taking care of business."

"Oh?" Myaisha perched on the corner of the desk. "I heard—"

Suddenly, the door leading to René's private office opened. A stout man wearing a pin-striped suit exited, conversing rapidly with René.

"Yes, Ms. Jones," he said. "Wonderful speaking with you. The bank will get those forms over to you by the end of the week."

When the door opened, the assistant had popped off the seat like a jack-in-the-box and scrambled to René's side.

René conversed with the man for another minute. She handed her assistant a small business card while giving directions about entering the banker's information into the computer. During this time, Myaisha observed their interactions, noticing René peeking at her between conversations. In under two minutes, the assistant left to escort the banker from the building.

With an open hand, René stood aside and invited Myaisha into her private office.

Unlike the small room in High Point, this office was enormous. Centered before a large picture window was a gun-metal gray desk over eight feet long. A small bar on a side wall held an assortment of crystal glasses and a wine refrigerator. On the opposite side of the room was a large leather couch flanked by overstuffed club chairs.

How long had it been since she'd visited René's offices? Probably not since …

René generally came to her place. They completed business paperwork at the lawyer's office. Other than reviewing the monthly corporate statements, Myaisha hadn't been interested in seeing the childcare centers where René conducted her affairs. *How could someone who lacked general curiosity in life be interested in writing mysteries—and solving homicides? Murders weren't like medical puzzles.*

"How can I help you?" René closed the door behind Myaisha, marched to her desk, and sat down, without a greeting, hug, or prelude.

Myaisha's brow rose. "I see. Straight to business."

René stared at her.

"What are you nervous about?"

René's mouth started to open.

"And don't tell me nothing. You want to dispense with decencies? Fine. You roped Deniece and I into helping you, now answer my questions."

Straightening her posture, René individually enunciated each word. "I. Don't. Need. Help."

"Tell yourself that enough and you'll believe it." Myaisha plunked down in a chair in front of René's desk. It was warm, most likely from the banker. She popped out of the chair and into one beside it. "The police know about the DNA. They're going to discover your fight with Robin."

"How?" René said, leaning forward with a slight pinch in her top lip. "Are you going to tell them?"

Myaisha shook her head. "It amazes me how women can be intelligent in business and have no common sense." She paused, measuring René. *Could she be wrong about this woman?* "The police are not stupid. Detective Gamble is persistent. It's only a matter of time."

In the silence, Myaisha heard children's laughter in the playground behind the center. But she kept her gaze on René, whose jaw trembled. *She's gauging how much I know and whether to trust me. Maybe I can help her.*

"There's a lot of money involved." She watched René for a reaction. "I see you're meeting with bankers. You've already scheduled to meet with a builder for a third location. How did you know ahead of time you'd come into eight hundred thousand dollars?"

"You think I killed Robin for money?" René cried, leaping from her chair.

"So why did you kill her?" Myaisha said, also rising.

René's façade fell, tears teetered. "You …" She sniffed. "You believe I killed her?"

Circling the desk, Myaisha rushed over and hugged her. René collapsed into her arms sobbing.

"No, I know you didn't. But I wanted to force you to speak."

Seconds passed while René cried lightly in Myaisha's embrace. Then she wiped her face and sank into her chair. Myaisha sat on the edge of the desk.

"You're right. I am stupid."

"René—"

"Please. I—" She blew her nose loudly, wiped her face, and sat up straight. "I was stupid, but I'm not anymore. Donald messed me up. I lost myself to our relationship."

René stood and paced around the room, speaking without looking at Myaisha. "I was the smart one. In school, it was fun. Teachers liked me. Other students asked for my help. Everyone knew I was going to be the successful sister, and it felt good."

Myaisha sat quietly in a chair watching René.

"It was compensation for not being the pretty one."

"You're beautiful."

"Huh." René grimaced. "Not to my parents." She strode over to her desk and removed a picture frame. The photo showed a younger René and Robin with their parents in the background. With a finger, René pointed at her dad.

"My dad is light-skinned like me. That's why he married a dark-skinned woman. He hates his skin color. He hates my skin color."

"You're exaggerating."

"No, I'm not. He told me I would've been the perfect daughter if I wasn't white."

"You know how some Black people can be about skin color."

"Sure, but when it's your parents … Mom is color-conscious too. It was constant."

René inhaled deeply and exhaled, shaking her shoulders. "Anyway, I left that behind in Chicago. Came here and created a successful business—until Robin arrived. She was supposed to visit for a week but stayed for three months." René stared out the window.

Myaisha didn't want to discuss skin color or family drama. "Donald and money. That's what I need to understand."

"What's to understand?"

With a tilt of her head, Myaisha signaled to stop the crap.

René crossed her arm over her chest. "Okay. I helped Donald with his business."

"How? What did you do?"

"I advised him to invest. Showed him how to diversify his capital."

Because René averted her gaze with the last statement, Myaisha sensed a partial truth. "The police will investigate his financial investments. Donald Evans scammed people. He had a young girlfriend to maintain. His prior girlfriend—the twin sister of his murdered girlfriend—managed his money."

"I didn't manage it."

"But you were familiar with his accounts."

"To help him—" René snapped her jaw closed.

"What?" Myaisha strode up to René. "Tell me."

"If you had to testify—"

"We are trying to discover who killed Robin—and Donald—so no one will have to testify for or against you." Myaisha gripped her arm. "You helped Donald hide money." Although it was a guess, the expression on René's face confirmed its accuracy.

"How much?"

"I don't know."

"Stop—"

"Seriously, I don't know," René shouted. Her words reverberated around the room.

Myaisha retreated a few steps to give them both space. René's eyes were aflame. At that moment, Myaisha could see her friend beating up Robin. But since the cause of death was poisoning … However, Donald had been shot. It could have been an impulse murder. René could absolutely be an impulsive killer.

"I helped Donald establish accounts overseas. I moved a couple hundred thousand dollars for him—but it wasn't illegal. It was his money."

"And his wife, and family … I presume this was while he was still married."

"Don't judge me."

"I'm not. Truly. If it doesn't involve his murder, I don't care what you did."

René blinked back tears and retreated behind her desk. "After we broke up, I don't know what happened to the money."

"You set up those accounts. Do you remember the access codes?"

A tiny smile formed in the corner of René's mouth. "You're quick." She sat down. "I never considered touching that money. Donald is—was—a bastard. If I stole from him, he would've come after me. But when Junior told me loan sharks were after him—"

"You went into the accounts."

"I tried but couldn't. Donald must've changed the codes. He was a crook, not a fool."

Myaisha observed René searching for signs of deception.

"Did you tell Junior about the money?"

Why is she hesitating?

"René?"

"I don't want Junior to get into trouble."

"I'm not the police. Did you?"

"Yes. I told him about his dad's overseas accounts. When I realized they'd been changed, I loaned Junior money from my personal account."

Loaned. She'll never see that money again.

"So, Junior could've gone to his dad for money."

"Junior wouldn't hurt his dad."

"Why, because he loved him?"

René chuckled. "Because he was scared of him. Junior's weak and stupid."

"Please don't tell me you're in love with him."

"What? No. I feel sorry for him. My mom treated me like crap, but I have brains—another trait I share with my dad. And I can take care of myself. Junior can't."

She had a point.

Seconds passed as René and Myaisha sized each other up, but their gazes gradually drifted apart.

"While we were together, I helped Donald stash money overseas. He said it was for us. He wanted to leave his wife and start a new life with me."

"But he lied."

The pulse in René's temple throbbed. "Apparently, he used that line with all his women." Slamming her hands on the desk, René choked back a cry. "I discovered he changed the passwords to the accounts after he dumped me."

Pain etched across her friend's face. Myaisha empathized but needed to push for more information.

"Did he tell Robin about the accounts?"

René shook her head. "Not that Robin admitted to."

"Would Robin have lied to you about that?"

"Why would she? Robin was upfront about her relationship with Donald. It made her feel superior. She always had to compete with me."

Myaisha frowned. "Why?"

"Who knows. I did better academically, but Robin was socially popular. Dad thought she was beautiful, but he could talk to me about business and finance. Mom loved her more but relied on my judgment for money matters."

"Stop saying she was more attractive than you."

"Men thought so."

"We know what they were thinking with, but let's set that aside for now. Did anyone else know about Donald's secret accounts?"

René started to shake her head, but Myaisha interrupted.

"Think. This could be the difference between you going to jail or identifying the real killer."

Her face frozen in thought, René stared into the distance. A minute later she shook her head.

"No one I can think of."

With a large sigh, Myaisha leaned back into the chair.

"Oh, wait. Cynthia might."

"Who?"

"Cynthia. Donald's office manager. I always thought there was more between them, but …"

Myaisha surged forward. "But what?"

"Well, she was always nice to me. If she had been involved with Donald, then she wouldn't have been kind to me. Would she?"

"Maybe." *Perhaps the office manager was playing the long game.* "Anything else, René? Even if it seems insignificant. I can't help you if I can't trust you."

"That's it."

"And the plans to build a third location? It was scheduled prior to Robin's death."

René smirked. "I didn't need anything from Robin. I make my own money. Check the business' profit and loss statements. The High Point office had been profitable for an entire quarter. I plan to borrow half the money from the bank and the rest from business profits."

"I'm impressed."

"I believe you mean that."

Myaisha smiled. "I do."

After another five minutes, Myaisha left. She now had to consider whether Junior—or his mother—murdered Donald for money hidden overseas.

This case was becoming a space odyssey with murdering Geminis. It would've made more sense if Donald had been murdered before Robin. But Myaisha couldn't have crimes the way she wanted like in her manuscripts.

Donald could've been the intended victim—and Robin's death an accident. With poison, an unknown person could be affected. *How was Robin poisoned?*

She would have to ask Todd. News reports hadn't identified the source. Tina could search her son's work papers.

That night in the clinic, Robin had complained of bruising for over a week, which proved the murder—whether Donald was the intended victim or Robin—had been planned in advance. Unless someone from Chicago traveled down here to kill Robin—unlikely as poisoning required time—that meant Donald was the intended victim.

Junior or his mom may have wanted to eliminate Robin to end her relationship with Donald. *What were the terms of Donald's will?* More questions for Todd. Until she got more information, she wouldn't be able to solve these homicides.

After wiggling her Honda out of the parking lot, Myaisha drove to the nearest grocery store. If she was going to speak with Todd, she would need chocolate.

CHAPTER 37

Myaisha startled awake. Boomer scurried off the floor and out of the master bedroom. The book she'd been reading now rested on her lap. With the back of her hand, she wiped sleep from her eyes. Lilac from her candle scented the air. *What woke her up?*

A knock sounded on the front door in the middle of her yawning.

As she threw on a robe and trudged down the hall, Boomer barked and circled the foyer. On the way to the front door, she glimpsed the time brightly shining from the microwave. It read 10:48. *Who would come by this late without calling first?*

The Lab skidded out of the way as she advanced toward the door. His barking increased. She reached into the foyer closet and removed a bat as Boomer growled and woofed. Myaisha peeked through the peephole. Todd.

Her legs slid Boomer aside as she creaked open the door.

"What's wrong?" she asked, stepping back to allow him inside.

Once he entered, Todd's gaze beamed on Boomer. "I'm sorry to get you out of bed, but this is important."

"Of course." After shutting the door, she invited him into the living room. "Can I get you some tea? Lemonade?"

He collapsed on the couch facing the backyard. "Lemonade, please."

Neither spoke as Myaisha gathered refreshments. She heated water for tea then placed cookies on a plate.

She entered the living room, handed him a tall glass of lemonade, and set the plate on the center coffee table.

"They're oatmeal and cranberries," she said, helping herself to two cookies—one she tossed to Boomer.

Todd swallowed half the lemonade then placed the glass on the table. "Thank you. I've been busy—haven't eaten anything since breakfast."

Myaisha rose. "I can whip you up some eggs, toast—"

"No, no. Thank you. I'm fine." He grabbed three cookies. "These are great."

She waited, stifling a yawn.

After Todd wolfed down the second cookie, he drank more lemonade and reclined into the couch cushions.

"You know about Ms. Jones coming down to the station."

"That sounded more like a statement than a question." She grinned.

He did not. "I noticed you speaking with her and the cousin."

Myaisha nodded.

"Did she tell you what we wanted?"

She wondered what *he* wanted, and whether to give it to him. "Todd—"

"We asked her to provide another DNA sample. This time we requested blood, a skin scraping, and hair."

His black eyes bored into her. She responded with equal intensity.

"René's a friend."

"She's a murder suspect."

"I don't believe she murdered anyone."

"Oh. How was your judgment in June, when your college friend was murdered?"

Her jaw clenched. *How could he throw that in her face?* "Don't be cruel."

He slid to the edge of the couch.

Boomer lurched in his direction, but Todd didn't budge.

"I'm being honest. You see the good in people but ignore the evil."

"I give everyone a chance."

"To lie to you. To kill you."

Myaisha's body tensed. She glared at him.

A low growl rumbled as Boomer's hair stood up on end. The Lab displayed his canines.

This time, Todd retreated into the couch. He peeked at Boomer and then looked at Myaisha. "Why didn't you tell me about her being a chimera?"

"You figured it out."

"When you mentioned Chicago and her necklace—I put it together eventually. You knew on Saturday but didn't tell me. Why?"

"I didn't want to mislead you."

"You didn't want me to have more evidence against her."

For a minute, they engaged in the staring game.

Todd exhaled deeply. "How did blood get on Mrs. Jones-Collins' hand?"

"I won't betray a confidence."

"I believe Ms. Jones assaulted her sister," he said, seemingly oblivious to her comment.

"She's a friend."

"And what am I?"

Myaisha diverted her gaze. *What was he?* Though she considered him a friend, their relationship had been fluid from the first day they met during a homicide investigation. Once the case was closed, their association ended—until Robin's death.

Perhaps he was right. Maybe she was too trusting. Though she considered him a friend, he only wanted her for information—and desserts.

"You're my friend."

He leaned toward her. "Did Ms. Jones assault her sister?"

"I'm not going to answer that."

"Do you know anything about the day Mrs. Robin Jones-Collins was brutally murdered? Choking on her own blood, seizing—"

"Stop." She stood up and ambled around the living room.

Todd also stood but moved in the opposite direction when Boomer charged up off the floor.

Myaisha grimaced. "Your behavior is grotesque."

"Murder is ugly." He snuck a step closer to her, with a side-eye on Boomer. "Tell me."

"No."

His temples clenched. "Time to choose sides, doctor."

"Doctor?" Her eyebrow arched. "When you entered, it was Myaisha."

"I came to speak with a friend."

"And I invited Todd—my friend—inside."

His face slackened. "I'm also a cop."

"You're a person with feelings and emotions."

"Sentimentality clouds professionalism. I'm a cop first and always."

She chuckled. "Now, that's immaturity speaking." *He'll discover the truth soon enough.*

His dark eyes flared, and he darted in her direction.

Boomer bolted between him and Myaisha. With a command, she directed the Lab to sit.

Todd removed his sister's picture from his wallet. He held it where Myaisha could see but not touch the photo.

"You see her. My sister was a Marine. She served two tours overseas." He swallowed. His chest heaved while he paused. "While on leave, she visited a high school friend. The friend was being assaulted by her boyfriend. My sister intervened and broke up the fight. She stayed the night with the friend—to keep her safe." His body trembled.

Myaisha knew how it would end. The word *sorry* was already forming on her lips.

He nodded. "Exactly. The bastard came back to kill his girlfriend, but my sister shielded her friend's body."

She opened her mouth but closed it after viewing the angry ripples creasing his forehead.

"Not a month after I buried my sister, that damn fool married another abusive bastard." His lips trembled.

Todd took another step toward Myaisha. She had to grab Boomer's collar to prevent the snarling Labrador from attacking.

"What purpose did my sister's death serve?"

Struggling to hold Boomer, Myaisha said, "We act according to who we are, not because of what other people do. Would your sister have been able to live with the guilt of not protecting her friend?"

His neck muscles taunt, Todd opened his mouth briefly then seemed to reconsider. He stormed over to the bookcase.

Boomer howled, growling to be freed.

"Down, Boomer. Sit." Once the Lab heeled, Myaisha petted his head.

Todd spun around as his chest rose and fell deeply. "I … You're a nice person. I'd hate to see anything happen to you."

Myaisha took a step toward him, then hesitated. "I don't plan to risk my life to prove anyone's innocence."

"You did for your college friend."

Though her shoulders stiffened, Myaisha detected no malice in Todd's demeanor. Besides, he was right. She had risked her life and nearly lost it. *Why do this again? Is René that important to me?*

"I have a lot to live for."

He swallowed. "So did my sister."

As he headed for the door, Todd came within a foot of her. He paused for a second and glared into her eyes. "One day, I hope you'll trust me." He departed without looking back.

"I already do," she said to his back.

Myaisha stood on the threshold and watched his car turn right out the cul-de-sac. Before she closed the door, she observed a tiny red dot hovering over Ms. Lula's porch. The old lady was outside again. *Hope you enjoyed the show.*

She slammed the door, careful to lock it and attach the chain. Myaisha secured the bat under the doorknob, feeling a need for extra protection from evil.

In her bedroom, she marked the last page she remembered reading with an engraved reflex hammer. It had been a gift to her husband, Sammy, when he completed his neurology residency.

Reclined against the headboard, she considered what Todd had said. She was trusting but not in a foolish, reckless way. Not credulous, but prudent. She didn't give money to scammers or believe unsubstantiated internet conspiracy theories.

From the moment René approached her about an investment in a childcare business, Myaisha did her due diligence. She consulted experts and researched the market—or the accountant she'd hired did. Over the past two years, she'd grown to trust René's acumen.

When the Greensboro Women of Color Writing Group expanded into their new location, she had invited René to join. Their friendship became more personal and blossomed from a simple business transaction.

Myaisha enjoyed René's reserve and wit. Though not voluble, René had opened up about her interests, a desire to write self-help books, and encourage other women in business. With her expertise, René had valuable insight to share.

However, their friendship hadn't been intimate. They didn't confide secrets. René had never even mentioned being an identical twin—or a chimera. *Did she trust René?*

Todd would be surprised to learn she did not trust her friend. But Myaisha knew people. As a physician, knowing people, reading their emotions, understanding their foibles … It wasn't an inherent quality, but that and being a military dependent who moved all over the United States gave Myaisha an ability to relate to others. She liked people, even those who sometimes lied to her.

Twins. They shared physical characteristics, but the Jones sisters differed a lot. René was not an honest person—and she was a terrible liar. However, she hadn't committed this murder.

For a brief moment, Myaisha considered writing down the list of suspects on a notepad she kept on the bedside table in case she thought of a good idea for a mystery while in bed. But she was tired.

After extinguishing the light, she lay in bed, staring at the ceiling. Time passed. Boomer snored. But Myaisha couldn't sleep.

Too tired to write, but too awake to sleep. Mentally, she reviewed the suspects. Donald Evans Jr, his mom, Terrence. Mrs. Jones, and for Todd she included René.

Robin had been poisoned. Donald Evans Sr. was shot in the head. René and Mrs. Jones received money from Robin's life insurance. Junior and his mom ... Wait, wasn't there a daughter? *Damn.*

Because of Todd's snit, Myaisha forgot to ask him about Evans' will. She also wanted to ask him about Donald's time of death. While she contemplated calling Todd, sleep finally came.

CHAPTER 38

"Now you rinse those greens until the water runs clear," Ms. Lula said, leaning against Myaisha's kitchen countertop, drinking iced tea. "Next time I come over, I'll help yah make iced tea."

Myaisha turned off the faucet and placed the greens in a salad spinner to remove excess water.

"What're yah doing?"

"Drying them off."

"Sugah, you book smart but not cooking smart." Ms. Lula stepped in front of Myaisha and dumped the greens back into the sink. She filled it with water and a tiny drop of liquid dish soap, then began cleaning the greens. "We gonna cook the greens in boiling water. No need to dry them off."

Although chastened by the septuagenarian's comment, Myaisha agreed it was valid.

"Look here." Ms. Lula held up a limp, dead grasshopper. "I could tell you hadn't cleaned them greens right. I don't think your boyfriend would appreciate biting into a bug."

Another valid point. To ease her ego and nerves, Myaisha filled the tea kettle from the tap.

"I tole yah—"

"But I like hot tea," Myaisha said, interrupting her kind but bossy neighbor.

When she discovered AJ liked greens, Myaisha called her mom about how to prepare them. Although she ate greens often as a child, Myaisha hadn't prepared them in years. Her husband and son had preferred cabbage.

The directions her mom gave sounded too simple to be correct. Myaisha had skipped over to Ms. Lula's with a simple question—not expecting her neighbor to volunteer a free cooking lesson. Incrementally, she regretted her decision.

Once Ms. Lula cleaned the greens to her satisfaction, she directed Myaisha to remove a large metal pot from the bottom kitchen drawer. While the greens cooked, they chatted.

"So, when's your boy coming home?"

"Josiah? Probably not until Christmas week. Maybe not until the day before."

"Hmm. He's independent."

"That's a good thing, right?"

Ms. Lula's gaze trailed off into the distance. "Not usually for boys. They need more time to mature. They should stay close to home longer."

Ding dong.

Boomer barked and scampered to his feet. At a slower pace, Myaisha headed for the door. Before she reached it, the knob turned and Deniece entered. Peering around her friend, Myaisha spied Tina and Mary trailing behind.

A whining, crying Boomer scampered around their legs as the women exchanged hugs.

Myaisha led everyone into the kitchen and made introductions.

"This is my neighbor, Ms. Lula." She turned to her neighbor. "Ms. Lula, this is Tina. She's a nurse and member of our writing group."

"Hello," Tina said.

Ms. Lula returned the sentiment.

"And you met Mary before."

Mary circled around Myaisha and hugged Ms. Lula.

"Hello, Ms. Lula. How you been? Have you stopped smoking yet?"

The old woman chuckled. "Never. They haven't stopped me from living this long. Why should I give them up now?"

"And you remember Deniece."

After a short, stiff sniff, Ms. Lula returned to the pot of greens on the stove, ignoring Deniece.

"Hello, Ms. Lula," Deniece said loudly. "Nice seeing you."

Ms. Lula nodded but didn't turn to face her.

In an aside to Myaisha, Deniece whispered, "Old bat. She'll never die."

Myaisha smacked Deniece on the arm and led the group toward the kitchen table in front of the bay window.

"Let's get down to business. So, what have we learned?" Tina asked, taking a seat against the wall before opening a bound notebook.

Mary sat right in front of the window with her back toward the yard. "Not much from me. I told Myaisha about Junior not attending class on Thursday night."

"Check. Got that," Tina said, making a quick notation.

A loud clanging rang out as Ms. Lula slammed the lid on the simmering pot. "If y'all gonna talk crime, I'm going home."

"Good riddance," Deniece said, not low enough to not be heard.

Myaisha shot her a glare before rising from the seat. "Thanks for helping with the greens, Ms. Lula. If I have any questions, I'll stop by."

"Now don't you rush. Greens take time. Be patient and your gentleman friend will love those greens."

"I wrote down everything you told me."

"Don't worry, Mya, I know how to cook greens," Deniece said.

"No man wanna eat your greens," Ms. Lula said, headed toward the foyer.

Deniece raised her voice. "My husband loves my greens."

"That's not what keeps him coming back to you."

"Old crow," Deniece murmured.

Before Ms. Lula exited, Myaisha heard the sassy senior mumble, "Hussy."

Once in the kitchen, Myaisha glared at Deniece. "Really, arguing with a senior citizen."

Deniece sauntered over to the pot of greens, lifted the lid, and sniffed. "If old people want to be respected, they should act nice."

"She is nice. She helps out around the neighborhood. Cooks for shut-ins."

"Hmm. She's probably casing their houses to steal stuff."

Myaisha frowned. "Now, that's just wrong."

Laughing, Deniece settled in a seat at the table. "Okay, who first?"

Over the next hour, they discussed different aspects of the murder cases. Tina and Mary proposed Junior as the murderer, Deniece believed the crimes weren't connected, and Myaisha reserved judgment.

"Everyone thinks the crimes are connected," Deniece said, rising from her chair and walking toward the pantry, "but plenty of people had motive to kill Donald Evans. He was a creep, a crook, and a philanderer." She returned to the table with a bag of chips.

"Yes, but that wouldn't explain Robin's death. A disgruntled customer wouldn't want to kill her," Mary said.

Deniece shrugged. "Her murder could be unrelated. Poisoning is a distant murder. It takes time. Someone from Chicago—"

"And how would they gain access to her food and drink?" Tina asked before crunching on a handful of chips.

"They broke into the house."

"But Robin stayed with Donald and René," Mary said. "She was bed-hopping."

Myaisha grinned. "I think you mean couch surfing."

"Not necessarily." Deniece winked.

A potato chip hovered before Tina's gaping mouth. "You think—"

"Let's not start rumors," Myaisha said, closing the bag of chips. "Robin was dating Donald and no one else."

"That we know about." Deniece gazed weightily at Myaisha. "Maybe she was still hooking up with the ex-husband."

"And he killed her?" Myaisha asked with knitted brows.

"He didn't get anything in the will," Tina said.

"But he no longer had to pay alimony," Deniece said.

For a full minute, no one spoke.

"Why did he kill Donald?" Mary asked, breaking the silence.

"There might be two murderers," Deniece huffed, snatching up the bag of chips. She circled around the kitchen munching, liberally from the bag.

"No, I agree with Tina. One killer is simpler, makes more sense," Mary said.

Tina pulled out her cell phone. "I snapped pictures of the police report when Ian wasn't looking." She passed the phone around.

"Tina," Myaisha gasped, "you could get him in trouble."

"Oh, no one cares. It'll be public record eventually."

Doubtful of Tina's assessment, Myaisha scrutinized the photos.

"Is this Evans' house?" Mary asked.

"Yep," Tina said. "I even have a picture of the carpet before they cleaned up the blood."

Her nose crinkled as Myaisha considered what the scene must have looked like when Robin was still on the ground. Another vision sprang into her mind. A picture from last June of her college friend sprawled along an office floor. She shook the images from her mind. *Focus on these murders.*

Deniece accepted the phone from Mary's outstretched hand. "Look at those pictures of him. In his bedroom, living room."

"I know," Tina said. "Most of them were of him and Robin."

"Robin?" Myaisha asked.

"Yeah. The guy was like obsessed or something," Tina said, retrieving her phone and placing it in her purse.

Deniece peeked at her watch. "Well, I guess that's it for tonight. Who's leading *Think It, Ink It* tonight?"

"I am," Tina said.

"A friend of mine is dropping by," Mary said, "so I have to get home."

Mary and Tina gathered their personal items and headed for the foyer. Myaisha, however, remained seated. Her thoughts returned to René's office. She recalled seeing photos of Donald Evans with René.

"Are you guys coming?" Tina asked.

From the recesses of her mind, Myaisha heard conversations, but she was engrossed in recalling the photos in the High Point childcare office. One, in particular, had a grinning Donald Evans with his arm draped over René's shoulder.

"Bye, Myaisha," Mary called from the front door.

"Huh? Bye. See you Thursday," Myaisha said.

"It is Thursday."

"What? Oh, right. Sorry." Myaisha stood and followed her guests to the front door. "I can't make it. I've got to finish cooking these greens."

Mary smiled. "For AJ." Her eyes twinkled mischievously.

"Bye," Myaisha said, pushing her lightly across the threshold before her blush fully bloomed.

After locking the front door, Myaisha gravitated toward the kitchen. Ideas bombarded her mind, slowing her gait. A thought germinated in the back of her mind, but she couldn't grasp it. She sauntered over to the stove and peeked at the greens.

Deniece collapsed on the couch, scratching Boomer's neck as he rested against her legs. "You can't think of anything to help René?"

"No." Myaisha set the lid on the pot and stared down at the stove.

"Mya," Deniece shouted. "Did you hear me?"

"Don't you think it's strange Donald Evans took so many pictures of his girlfriends?" Myaisha asked, entering the living room and plopping on the couch next to Deniece.

"Kind of—but he was obsessed with Robin, even René said so. It would be different if the pictures were of him alone. He had many women. Maybe that was how he kept track of them."

Stretching her legs out along the coffee table, Myaisha grimaced. "He didn't seem like the sentimental type. He didn't keep a lot of photos of his kids."

"Maybe he didn't get along with them."

"But his son worked with him at the used car lot."

"They argued, remember."

Myaisha frowned, trying to recall a detail. "Not with his daughter though."

Deniece shrugged. "The daughter doesn't seem to be involved with the family at all."

"But he had the same pictures of himself with Robin at his house as the ones in the office. Doesn't it seem weird?"

"Dude was a freak."

"I don't think so. Those pictures mean something."

Reclining into the couch cushions, Deniece stretched her arms. "Like what?"

"I'll mention it to Todd. Ask him to check it out—if he's still talking to me."

Deniece frowned. "What do you mean?"

Over the next five minutes, Myaisha detailed the exchange between her and Todd.

"So, he's mad at mother."

Myaisha grimaced. "I'm not his mother."

"Then why are your always baking desserts for him?"

"Because he likes sweets and I like baking. This way he's satisfied, and I don't get fatter."

Deniece laughed. "Liar. You like him."

For several seconds Myaisha thought about it. "I do like him. And …" She didn't want to voice her opinion. It felt pejorative, but she was sorry for Todd. Instead, she said, "He's lonely."

"Why? He's a nice-looking man with a good job. If he's alone, it's because he wants to be."

"Yes, that's it. He wants to be alone." *But why?*

The sky darkened as Myaisha's thoughts wandered.

"Maybe he wants you to be more than his momma."

Myaisha frowned. "I doubt it."

"He could have a mommy complex. Attracted to maternal figures. Isn't that Freudian?"

"Whatever."

Deniece rose and stepped outside onto the back porch with Boomer. When she returned inside, Myaisha was busy scribbling notes on a legal pad.

"Those your notes on the homicides?" Deniece asked, settling on the couch.

"Yes. I'm listing questions to ask Todd. I want him to check out those photos. Maybe he can have the police lab blow them up, find a detail we can't."

"Why wait to speak with Todd?" Deniece sat up. "We can check it out ourselves."

"How? The photos are in Donald's office and home."

"We can look at the ones in his office."

"We don't have a key."

A grin lit up Deniece's face.

Myaisha's head shook. "No."

"It'll be easy. No one will be there. The showroom is empty because the cars were moved out on Monday."

"That doesn't mean it wouldn't be considered breaking and entering."

"Chicken."

"How old are you?"

"What would Easy do?"

"The last time I did what Easy Rawlins would do, I ended up wrestling with a murderer."

Deniece stood up and yanked Myaisha to her feet. "Yes, but this time Raymond Alexander will be with you." She grinned.

"Mouse is a cold-blooded killer," Myaisha said, peeling Deniece's fingers from around her arm.

"Who better to escort us on our investigations." Deniece dashed around the living room, retrieving their purses and cell phones.

"Maybe we should call Barry and AJ. Tell them where we're going."

"If you do, we might as well stay home."

Good. Myaisha's stomach flip-flopped recalling her last murder investigation. An experience she did not wish to revisit. "There's no rush. We can wait 'til tomorrow." *Puzzles should be solved on a couch, safely ensconced at home.*

"What if the killer gets to the evidence before us? It could be lost forever."

"Then we should call the police."

Deniece pouted and crossed her arms over her chest. "Fine. Call them." She plopped on the couch. "Why were we wasting our time if we weren't going to do any investigating?"

Observing her truculent child of a friend, Myaisha's face softened. "And after we see the pictures, we leave immediately."

"Sure," Deniece said, hopping off the couch and planting a fedora on Myaisha's head.

Once Myaisha turned off the stove and secured the house, they drove away in Deniece's car.

Her friend glanced across the seat at her. "You know you're the biggest sucker."

Myaisha sighed. "I know I'm going to regret this."

They drove down Lawndale, headed for Evans Used Cars lot, engulfed in their individual thoughts.

Five minutes later, Deniece asked, "Why're you making greens? Josiah coming home this weekend?"

"No, they're for AJ." Myaisha stared out the window.

"You guys spending the weekend together?" Deniece grinned.

"I wanted to talk with him about sex like you recommended."

"Good. A healthy relationship is built on communication. Nothing hidden. Make your feelings clear and keep no secrets."

Secrets. Clear. Myaisha bolted upright in the car seat. "D."

The car swerved and momentarily deviated off the road and onto the median.

"What's wrong? You scared the—"

"Make things clear."

Deniece side-eyed her. "Mya, what are you talking about?"

"It would've been clear." She glanced at her friend, then realized she wasn't making sense. "Listen. Robin's death was immediately suspicious, right?"

"Right."

"Why?"

"What?" Deniece asked.

"Why? Because a young, healthy woman doesn't simply seize and die from pulmonary hemorrhage. Her sudden death would be suspicious, and an autopsy would be ordered—"

"Was ordered," Deniece interjected.

"Exactly. How could the killer expect to get away with killing her by poison?"

With her eyes on the road, Deniece shrugged. "I don't know."

"Think about a mystery novel. The killer tries to make poisoning look like an accidental death caused by another idiopathic condition. Gastritis, medication overdose—get it?"

A minute elapsed before Deniece replied. "You mean the killer couldn't have expected to get away with poisoning Robin."

"Exactly."

"Then why kill her? If they didn't expect to get away with it—"

"But they did." Myaisha smiled. "The killer expected to get away with murder but hadn't planned on killing Robin."

Chapter 39

In the large office space of the downtown Greensboro police station, most desk lamps had been extinguished. Todd and Ian sat at their respective desks, facing each other, shrouded in dusky lighting.

"They need to do something about this place," Todd grumbled. "I can barely read."

"That's an educational deficiency." Ian chuckled.

"It's a lighting problem."

"We're supposed to be home. They do it on purpose to prevent over-achievers from burning out." Ian reached into a side drawer and groaned.

"What now?"

"My damn shoulder." Ian rubbed his triceps.

"Where's your brace?"

"It doesn't fit over my shirt."

"Why don't you go to physical therapy like the doctor ordered?"

"Because I have a meet this weekend."

Todd's phone rang. He scooped up the receiver. "Detective Gamble." His head nodded at different intervals preceded by "Yes," or "Okay." Another five minutes passed with him scribbling notes.

"Thank you. I appreciate it. If you could get the official report …" More writing. "Thanks." He hung up.

"Well?"

Before answering, Todd spent another minute jotting down information from the caller. "It was the medical examiner. Remember when we were discussing Mrs. Jones-Collins' poisoning?"

"Yeah?" Ian rose and ambled over to a table against the wall behind his desk. "Want some coffee?"

Todd grimaced. "Not that crap."

"Go on."

"I told you, she might not have been the intended victim. She was at Evans' place when she died. What if she accidentally ingested the rat poison?"

"And the coroner proved it was accidental?"

"Dr. Page proved Mr. Evans also had a large amount of—what is that stuff called?" Todd rechecked his notes. "Brodifacoum in his system."

"The same stuff that killed the girlfriend."

"Right. And Mr. Evans suffered from atrial fibrillation. The medical examiner said if he had died from a sudden bleed, it might have been associated with his pre-existing heart condition, or maybe an accidental prescription medication overdose. He took blood thinners. She spoke with Mr. Evans' regular doctor, who said the deceased hadn't been compliant with getting his blood levels checked. He could've bled out and everyone attributed it to his regular medication."

"Does Dr. Page think so?"

"She said it's conceivable. He wasn't in the best health and had a prior bleeding ulcer that required a blood transfusion."

Ian sat at his desk and removed a container from his side drawer with another groan.

Speaking to himself, Todd reviewed the notes he took during the phone call. "The doctor said second-generation anticoagulants have a half-life of up to thirty days. Someone could've been poisoning him for a month or more." He frowned, staring over Ian's shoulder.

"That makes more sense," Ian said, pouring powder from a small plastic container into his coffee mug. "Evans had a lot of enemies. The Jones-Collins lady could've been an unfortunate victim."

Todd glanced at his partner. "What's that?"

"My protein powder." Ian gulped from the cup.

"I thought that stuff was bad for your kidneys."

"Anything in moderation."

"That's not ..." Todd's body stiffened, and his gaze enlarged.

"Man, what's wrong with you?"

"Did we confiscate *all* food and beverages from the office?" Todd asked, scanning his desk.

Ian swallowed the remaining coffee. "What beverages?"

Drawers opened and slammed shut as Todd searched around his desk. "Where are the forensic reports documenting the office contents?"

Without speaking, Ian slid a folder across to Todd. The latter perused the file.

"It's time to go. You're starting to hallucinate," Ian said, rising and gingerly inserting his arm into his coat jacket. "You coming?"

"No. Yes." Todd clambered out of his chair and into his coat. "But we're not going home."

"What? Man, I'm—"

"Forensics didn't check the office break room."

"Of course, they didn't. Dude was shot in the head. They took everything from his personal office though."

"Yes, but there's a chance the murderer left the poison somewhere else." A large grin grew across Todd's face.

"Whatever. You're driving. My shoulder's killing me."

"I always drive your princess behind around."

Ian punched Todd in the shoulder. Both men winced.

Todd's hand hovered above the exit door when a voice called him back.

"Detectives," a uniformed officer called, jogging up to them.

They both pivoted around.

"Yes?" Ian asked.

Panting, the uniformed officer said, "The desk sergeant wanted to let you know they haven't located Ms. Howard. She left home Tuesday night and hasn't been seen since."

"Did they try calling her family?"

The officer nodded. "Her parents said they expected her Tuesday evening, but she never arrived."

After thanking the officer, Todd and Ian glanced at each other before racing out of the station.

Chapter 40

A cold mist had fallen across Greensboro as Deniece drove past Evans Used Car lot and continued for another block.

"Where are you going?" Myaisha asked, straining her neck to glance back at the car lot they'd passed a mile ago.

"We can't park out front if we want to work surreptitiously," Deniece hissed. "That would be like advertising, 'Please come in and catch us breaking in.'"

Myaisha eyeballed her friend then glanced up and down Wendover Avenue. *Please no police.*

Light snowflakes floated in the air before tumbling to the ground and coating the asphalt with a wet glow.

"Finish what you were telling me about Robin," Deniece said.

With her gaze rotating between the windows, Myaisha said, "A murderer couldn't expect to get away with poisoning Robin. If a healthy young woman dies suddenly, the medical examiner conducts an autopsy. Rat poison isn't hard to uncover if you suspect foul play. Also, the bruises and abnormal labs would instantly point to murder."

"I get it. You believe Robin ingested the poison intended for Donald."

"Yes."

"Okay, Easy. Who's the killer?"

"Terrence is out, as is Mrs. Jones."

"I didn't ask who the killer wasn't."

Myaisha frowned. "Unfortunately, René would still top the homicide department's list. She had motive to kill Donald."

At the stoplight, Deniece peeked at her. "And she was remorseful when her twin sister died by accident and decided to hasten Donald's demise with a bullet?"

"If we believe there is one killer, yes, that scenario would be plausible."

"Mrs. Evans, Junior, and the daughter are also on the list."

"Too bad we don't know more about the daughter," Myaisha mumbled to herself.

"What?"

"Nothing."

"Continue," Deniece said, observing traffic.

"Donald probably has a medical condition that would mask or resemble rat poisoning. Maybe a bleeding disorder, or he might have taken blood thinners. Yes, blood thinners. If a patient takes too much, the INR would be elevated. They would have bruising. A fall or other innocuous injury could result in massive bleeding. No one would be suspicious if he suffered an accidental death from a side effect of the medication."

Deniece chuckled. "No one would miss that bum."

At the signal light, the dark SUV completed a U-turn as Deniece headed back toward the car lot. "Here we go."

"We shouldn't be here at all. Todd can look over the photos tomorrow morning—legally—like a good police officer should."

"What's with you and this cop? You guys are real tight lately." Deniece winked. "You playing with two men?"

"Todd's a friend, who loves my desserts."

"I bet he does." Deniece laughed.

Myaisha glared at her.

"I'm joking. Goodness. You do need to get laid. Maybe then you'll relax."

Tightening her grip on the door handle, Myaisha grimaced. Todd wasn't exactly enamored with her at this moment. She wasn't sure even her chocolate bundt cake could soothe his ire.

"Are we doing this or not?"

"Yes." Deniece parked behind a chicken restaurant adjacent to but 300 yards away from Evans Used Car lot.

"Here?" Myaisha frowned.

"Yes, unless you want your boy toy to arrest us."

"It's freezing outside."

"Then move your butt."

Five minutes later, they exited Deniece's SUV and scurried up to the rear entrance of Evans' building.

"Now what?" Myaisha shivered, rubbing her gloved hands together, and scowling at Deniece.

From under her jacket, Deniece removed a gadget with one end resembling a screwdriver and the other a handgrip.

"What's that?"

"If I got my money's worth, it'll open this door," Deniece said, inserting the end of the instrument that looked like a screwdriver into the lock.

"Won't it break the knob?"

Deniece shrugged. "I don't know." The device made a whirling noise.

Myaisha scanned the area. "What if someone—"

"Shush. Come on." The doorknob turned under Deniece's grasp.

With one hand on Deniece's shoulder, Myaisha followed her friend inside. She closed the door and reached for the light switch. Deniece smacked her hand.

"Ouch."

"You'd make a lousy thief." A flashlight illuminated the flooring. Deniece tiptoed down the hallway. "Follow me."

Myaisha did as directed while rubbing the back of her hand.

A minute elapsed before her eyes adjusted to the darkness. The long hallway from the rear entrance continued up to double glass doors in front. Light from streetlamps provided sufficient illumination for Myaisha to gather her bearings. The linoleum flooring continued throughout the office. She counted four rooms off the hallway, two on each side.

The walls were shaded. She viewed picture frames but couldn't discern the images inside. No identifying labels distinguished the rooms.

"I believe from Tina's photos, Donald's private office was on the right," she whispered.

"Let's go," Deniece said, pointing her torch toward the closest room on the right.

Inside, Myaisha removed her winter gloves and slipped on disposable medical ones. She handed a pair to Deniece.

"At least you're not a complete moron when it comes to breaking in." Deniece slid the flashlight under her armpit while she slipped into gloves.

Myaisha scowled. "Let's get this over with."

Directed by Deniece, the flashlight floated over various photos of Donald and Robin aligned along the side of a large desk in front of a picture window.

One by one, Myaisha picked up each picture frame, examining them for secret compartments. She removed each photo, searching for anything hidden behind or between the frames.

"Nothing. Damn." She perched on the desk corner. "I thought there was something behind those photos."

"The man was a narcissist—not surprising for a serial philanderer. Let's check the rest of the rooms."

As Deniece sauntered out of Donald's office, Myaisha remained behind.

She'd been certain those photos were critical to solving the murders. If there wasn't anything hidden in the frames, maybe it was something within the pictures themselves. Since Deniece left with their light source, Myaisha used her cell phone light to review the pictures again.

In each photo, a smiling Donald had his arm draped around Robin, or in some way, he was touching her body.

"Ick." His picture made her itch. *Focus.*

One photo showed Donald's hand gripping Robin's shoulder. Another his hand on her thigh. Another ... *Wait.*

Myaisha scanned the pictures again. In each photo, Donald wore a wrist brace, but not always the same one. *Why not? How many wrist braces did he need?*

Like a cyclone, she searched inside desk drawers until she found a blue wrist splint behind a dozen hanging folders. As Myaisha removed the brace, her back stiffened.

The sound of jingling sparked her attention. She clicked off the cell phone light, stopped, and listened. The front office overhead lights snapped on.

"Crap." She surveyed the area. *Where could she hide?* She scuttled around to the back of the desk, considering how to fit her plus-size body underneath. Sweat dripped down her back as she slipped the splint under her shirt along her waistline.

Voices proceeded in her direction. Footsteps pattered along the sand-colored tiles.

There were no closets or cabinets to hide behind. She attempted to lift the window frame. *Dammit.* It wouldn't budge. Like hammer and tongs, her pulse roared in her ears. She had to decide. *Too late.*

Light flooded the room.

"Well, look what we have here."

Her dilated pupils constricted, throwing her into a second of darkness. As her gaze adjusted, Myaisha turned toward the door.

Please let it be the police. Because if not …

CHAPTER 41

Framed in the doorway of Donald's office, a stocky woman asked, "Doesn't the Hippocratic oath discourage stealing?"

Her vision still fuzzy, Myaisha said, "I'm not stealing." Incrementally, she recognized Donald Evans' ex-wife from newspaper photos.

The Evans matriarch gripped a sizable shoulder bag with a scowl nearly as large. Before Myaisha could formulate an excuse for her presence, another person arrived at the doorway.

"Why are you here?" the young man asked.

"I presume you're Mrs. Evans and Mr. Evans Jr.," she said with more confidence than her nauseated stomach had.

Junior grumbled. "We know who we are. I asked why are *you* here?"

"This is Dr. Douglas," Mrs. Evans said. "She arranged a memorial for your daddy's whore."

Myaisha bristled.

Junior strode into the room and within feet of the desk. "Why—"

"I was looking for a picture of Robin," she said, maintaining a distance from Junior behind the office desk.

"There're dozens of pictures of her here. My dad was obsessed with her. If that's what you came for, get it and leave."

She placed her hands in her coat pocket and proceeded toward the doorway. On the way, Myaisha glanced over at a table and a small refrigerator. A canister of protein powder sat beside two tall plastic cups. Protein. *Robin's smoothies.*

An idea came to mind. She hustled, determined to leave before—

"On second thought," Mrs. Evans removed a gun from her purse, "I've changed my mind."

Of course, you did. Myaisha's heart sank. She forced anxiety from her voice.

"What do you mean?"

"Why did you want a picture of Robin?"

"No specific reason. She's a—was—a friend. I figured you wouldn't miss one. Sorry for intruding. I'll be leaving." She lurched forward.

"No, you don't. Back up." A thick, stubby gun was thrust into her face. "I saw you glancing over at that table."

As ordered, Myaisha retreated toward the desk. "Look, I don't know anything. I simply want to leave."

"You should've thought of that before you broke in. I don't believe you came here for a picture." Mrs. Evans' bottom lip curled. "You know, I can shoot you and claim you broke into the office and surprised me. Before I realized who you were, I fired."

Myaisha retreated, reaching behind her back for the window. "That's a shaky excuse for killing someone."

Mrs. Evans inclined her head as if in thought. "Probably. But I'll give it a try."

"Ma." Junior bustled to her side.

Right then, Myaisha noticed his resemblance to the deceased—and not to his favor.

"What're you doing?" he asked. "Let her go. We came to get Dad's things."

"She broke in here to steal from your daddy. Now, I've got this. Go outside and I'll be there in a minute."

"Outside? Ma, what's going on? You can't kill her."

Taking advantage of their dispute, Myaisha inched toward the window, trying to lift it. "She's going to shoot me, Junior. Murder me like your dad."

Junior gawked at his mom. "What's she talking about?"

"Don't listen to her. I said go wait in the car—now."

Despite arguing with her son, Mrs. Evans maintained constant vigilance over Myaisha's movement.

In need of a distraction, Myaisha appealed to Junior. "When you leave, she'll kill me and claim self-defense."

"Shut your filthy mouth," Mrs. Evans snarled. "I bet you were one of his whores. Did you come here for a memento, something special from your lover?"

"Ma." Junior's face paled.

Though she directly faced Mrs. Evans, Myaisha peripherally scanned the room for a weapon or hiding place. The desk remained her single option. Behind her back, Myaisha's fingers searched for an object to throw.

"Fortunately, I never made your husband's acquaintance. But I did know Robin."

Anger scrolled along Mrs. Evans' forehead. Her jaw clenched. "That whore deserved what she got."

"Ma, this is insane. Let's go." Junior reached for his mom's arm, but she shrugged him off.

"We aren't going anywhere. If you love your mama, you'll go back outside and wait in the car."

"I understand why you killed Robin," Myaisha said, "but why Donald? You couldn't expect to inherit."

Mrs. Evans lurched forward, leading with the gun. "I didn't kill that bitch. She killed herself."

Myaisha frowned. "Suicide? Robin? Not likely."

"Not suicide."

Her brows lifted. "You *were* trying to kill your husband."

A tiny grin emanated from Mrs. Evans' otherwise somber face. "You'll understand if I don't answer that."

"Your husband was probably on blood thinners or a similar medication. Rat poisoning would have looked like an accident or complications from a medical condition."

Mrs. Evans growled, "Enough. Junior, leave."

"Ma—"

"Fine. Then, you'll see how much your mama loves you."

"Mouse!" Myaisha shouted and glanced toward the floor.

Both Mrs. Evans and Junior immediately searched the ground. Before Mrs. Evans glanced up, Myaisha dove behind the desk. As the gun rose in her direction, a large object slammed onto Mrs. Evans' wrist.

A bullet blew a large hole in the window above Myaisha's head. As glass shattered around her, she watched Deniece wallop Mrs. Evans in the head with a broomstick.

Junior rushed to aide his mom, pushing Deniece aside.

Racing around the desk, Myaisha entered the melee. She bear-hugged Junior around the chest as Deniece tussled with Mrs. Evans for the gun.

As they struggled, distantly, sirens blared.

Junior threw his head back and knocked Myaisha's chin. She increased her grip on his chest, dragging him away from Deniece and his mom.

The sirens' pitch increased.

Myaisha peeked toward the doorway, while bear-hugging Junior, and spied red and blue lights dancing along the hallway walls.

She recalled the wrestling shows she'd watched as a child. Myaisha wrapped a leg around Junior's waist, and they tumbled onto the ground. Fortunately, he cushioned her fall.

Junior landed face down, and Myaisha landed on his back. When she gazed upward a uniformed officer stood in the doorway palming a revolver.

"Freeze. Hands up."

She tossed her hands upward and glanced over at Deniece.

"Ma'am," the officer spoke with a flat tone, "get off that old lady and let her out of the headlock."

CHAPTER 42

Despite being an hour before sunrise, the downtown Greensboro police station was buzzing with activity.

Todd rubbed his temples in an attempt to push away a mounting headache.

"You want to speak with them." Ian glanced in the glass window of interrogation room two.

"No, I'd lose it," Todd said before turning away. "Release them. We can always interview them later."

"What if they run?"

He snickered. "Dr. Douglas and her writing group run toward murders, not away from them. We won't have trouble locating them when—if— they're needed." He exited the hallway into a spacious office area where the detectives' desks were located.

Beside the doorway but inside the office, Todd watched through a small window as Ian led Myaisha and the nurse—he believed the woman's name was Withers—from an interrogation room. Positioned near the doorway, he overheard their conversation.

"Okay, you two can go," Ian said.

Myaisha and Mrs. Withers glanced at each other, then Ian.

"What's going to happen to Mrs. Evans?" Myaisha asked.

"Ma'am, that's not your concern. Be glad you weren't charged with breaking and entering."

"Humph. She couldn't bring charges against us, the building doesn't belong to her," Mrs. Withers said.

"The *police* could charge you with trespassing."

"Why? We weren't bothering anyone," Mrs. Withers asked.

Todd chuckled. Only Myaisha and her friend could object to being told to leave a police station.

"You broke into an office."

"We were looking around," Myaisha said.

"That didn't belong to you," Ian said, his jaw clenching. "At night."

And almost got shot for trespassing. Todd observed Myaisha scanning the hallway before staring at the doorway. He scooted aside, hoping she hadn't spotted him.

"Where's Detective Gamble?" she asked. "I'd like to speak with him."

"He's busy, trying to solve a homicide—which we can't do if we have to rescue you two from a killer."

Mrs. Withers grunted. "Humph. Rescue who? We didn't need your help. The situation was under control."

"Lady—" Ian's fists clenched. He took a deep breath. "Ma'am, you had a killer in a choke-hold."

"Correct," Mrs. Withers said. "I had *her* in a choke-hold. And Myaisha tripped up the son. We would've called the police if we needed help."

Todd bit back a laugh, enjoying Ian's torture.

"You …" Ian's face flushed. "Please, go home."

"Your Tina's boy, right? You work out a lot. I like the biceps."

"D, let's go," Myaisha said, pulling her friend down the hallway and toward the exit.

"He's more attractive in person. Tina said he worked out a lot but did you see those muscles."

"Stop …"

Their conversation petered away with their departing steps. It was all Todd could do not to burst out laughing. Because Ian approached the office door, Todd hustled to his desk. Ian entered the room as Todd sank into his chair.

"So, how'd it go?"

"Shut up." Ian collapsed into a chair and pulled open his desk drawer. "Where's my candy bar?"

"You ate it."

"I thought I had another one." Apparently not finding it, Ian slammed the desk drawer shut. "Those ladies are crazy."

"Crazy smart."

"My mom needs to stay away from them."

"You think your mom's any different?"

Ian frowned and popped up from his chair. "I'm going to grab something from the machine. You want anything?"

Todd declined. During Ian's absence, he made two phone calls. When his partner returned, he filled him in on developments.

"The DA isn't ready to charge Mrs. Evans with murder, but we'll hold her on gun charges. Her revolver wasn't licensed."

"Where'd she get an unlicensed weapon?"

"Welcome to America, where you can buy a gun at a swap meet."

Ian shook his head and unwrapped his candy bar. "What else?"

"Forensics checked the canister in Mrs. Evans' purse. Apparently, it was in the staff break room. On the day of Mr. Evans' murder, it was searched for weapons and other contraband, but since his manner of death was a gunshot wound to the head—"

"Forensics didn't test food items in the break room."

"Correct."

"And now?" Ian asked.

"Rat poison."

"Prints."

"Mrs. Evans, Junior Evans, Mr. Evans deceased, Mrs. Jones-Collins, Ms. Howard, and an unknown."

"Who do we think the unknown belongs to?" Ian asked crunching on the candy.

"My bets are on an employee or the daughter."

"So, the ex-wife left it out where anyone could access the poison?"

Todd leaned back in the chair, gazing up at the popcorn ceiling. "My guess is she didn't think anyone else used the powder. From what I've been able to piece together from witness statements, Mr. Evans started adding protein powder to his drinks after he met Mrs. Jones-Collins."

"He was trying to get in shape to keep a younger girlfriend."

"Right. She created those smoothies. They were going to be part of her health and wellness business."

"When she made him a smoothie, Evans added the protein powder, thinking he would increase his muscles," Ian said. "Moron. You still have to exercise."

"Which he did little of. His medical doctor said Mr. Evans routinely missed office and lab appointments."

"The ex-wife would know about his medical problems. But how did she know about the drinks?"

Todd shrugged. "The son—or daughter—could have told her. She also still had a key to the office. Evidence of which is her entrance into the office last night."

"So, the theory is she went to the office last night to remove the protein powder and any evidence she planned to poison her ex."

Which she would've done if he hadn't gotten the idea of the protein powder from Ian.

"And motive?" Ian said, squeezing a muscle ball.

"Prevent Mr. Evans from disinheriting his children for his new girlfriend."

"This wasn't his first affair though. Why now?"

With a sigh, Todd reclined in the chair. "Good question. Something must have changed. Perhaps Mr. Evans was more serious about this relationship. He might also have contested continued child support. The son was in college—but also reached age twenty-one."

In a flurry of activity, Todd scanned folders on his desk. "I need to re-read the will."

"Did you hear about the anonymous caller?" Ian asked between chews.

"No."

"It came in last night while we were heading out to Evans' office. The caller said Ms. René Jones had incriminating papers at her home."

Todd frowned. "Were those the words the caller used?"

"I'm paraphrasing."

"Tell me exactly what was said."

Ian filled Todd in.

"Did the officer recognize the voice?" Todd asked.

"He thought it was a woman, but the caller was trying to disguise their voice." As if shooting a basket, Ian dunked the candy wrapper into a trash can. "What's next?"

A desk drawer shut, shaking the desks, as Todd regarded his partner. "We tighten the case against Mrs. Evans."

"Want to interview the son?"

"He lawyered up."

"The daughter?"

"Returned to Durham."

"She's not very attached to her family."

"Not much of a family," Todd mumbled. "Dad was a crooked businessman and adulterer. Brother frequents strip clubs and gambling establishments. And mom is a murderer."

"What's with that? The daughter hasn't come by to see her mom. I don't believe she's even called."

"Check with the front desk sergeant. Otherwise—" Todd grinned.

"Road trip to Durham."

While Ian dialed the front desk, Todd considered the Evans clan. Not an ideal family, by far. Mom fit the profile of a murderer—overbearing, determined, and short-sighted. She would do anything to protect her children.

The facts fit succinctly. Mrs. Evans laced her ex-husband's protein powder with rat poisoning. He'd sprinkle the substance on smoothies Mrs. Jones-Collins prepared. What the ex-wife hadn't considered was the girlfriend would also consume the poison. *Or had she?* Maybe she didn't care.

But Mrs. Jones-Collins' death brought immediate police suspicion. Whereas, if Mr. Evans had died from poisoning—instead of a gunshot wound to the temple—it would've resembled a simple case of a patient's irresponsibility in taking prescription medication.

Was Mrs. Jones-Collins' death an accident? Of course, it was. Stop second-guessing yourself. Myaisha said you needed more confidence. Myaisha.

He should apologize. Not because he was wrong. She was a meddlesome busybody certain to get herself killed one day interfering in a homicide investigation. But she had been helpful–in an irritating way. And she baked divine desserts. He'd speak with her later when his head cleared.

Ian ended his call. "Nope. Nothing from the daughter. And she was notified of her mother's arrest by the night desk sergeant."

Todd hopped out of the chair and put on his coat. "Let's go."

"You drive. My shoulder still hurts."

He laughed. "Right. Like you were going to drive anyway."

Outside the station, cold morning air smacked into Todd's face. It reminded him of his one interview with Ms. Evans. Her attitude regarding her father's death had been frigid. The young woman—

"Detectives."

Todd gasped. Ian halted.

A good ten seconds elapsed before Ian recovered. "Hello, Ms. Evans. We were—"

"We were on our way to an interview," Todd interrupted, "but if you have some information to share we can reschedule."

With an open hand, Todd directed her into the station. Ian caught his glance.

Three minutes elapsed while they removed their coats and were once more seated at their desks—but this time with Ms. Evans.

"It won't take long. I …" Her gaze faltered as she glanced at the desk. "My brother called. He said Mom was arrested?"

With a minute nod, Todd acknowledged her statement.

She breathed in and exhaled fully. "I see. Did she confess?"

After a slight peek at Ian, Todd asked, "What did you want to share with us?"

Ms. Evans glanced between them, then her chest sank. "I don't know if my mom committed murder—it wouldn't surprise me if she did. But the motive wasn't robbery."

Though a minute passed, neither detective responded. Biting her lip, Ms. Evans continued.

"I stole the money from my dad's overseas accounts."

Todd frowned. "Why?"

"Because dad was a fool—and a crook. He cheated people and spent money on … On someone that didn't love him. I knew he was about to waste a lot of money on that Jones woman, so I withdrew the funds to protect him."

Ian chuckled. "To protect him."

Her jaw tensed and she sat upright. "I knew what my dad was, but I still loved him. If he spent all his money on her, what would he have after she left him?"

"What made you think Mrs. Jones-Collins was going to leave your dad?"

Ms. Evans fiddled with her purse strap. "Because I followed her. She met up with her ex at his hotel."

Todd's gaze widened.

"Why did you follow her?" Ian asked.

"Because I worried about my dad. His health was poor. He was a crook past his prime. All he had was the money he stole. Robin carried on with other men, trying to launch a stupid smoothie business. She was dumb as dirt."

"And you stole the money to—"

"To protect my dad from himself." Her chin quivered. "I didn't come forward sooner because … When dad died, I thought it was my fault. I planned to explain what I did when he arrived Thursday night, but he didn't show up. And then I heard he was shot in the head. A suicide."

For a minute, she cried quietly into a tissue.

"Take your time," Todd said, glancing briefly at Ian, who was taking notes.

She wiped her nose. "Anyway, I have the information about his accounts. I never used any of the money for myself—and I didn't offer it to Junior when he asked for help with his debts."

Ms. Evans rose. "Will I … Am I going to jail?"

Todd and Ian shared a look.

"I'll call the DA," Todd said before picking up his desk phone.

"Have a seat," Ian said.

While waiting on the phone, Todd observed Ms. Evans. *Weird.* The Evans clan made the Addams family look normal.

CHAPTER 43

Light purple rays swathed across the burgeoning sunrise sky. Barry eased the SUV up the driveway and Myaisha jaunted from the car before he came to a full stop.

"Thank you," she said, closing the rear passenger door.

"Anytime Thelma and Louise get in trouble, I bail them out," he said with a smirk.

Deniece playfully smacked his arm. "I told you—Myaisha is Easy and I'm Mouse."

"Raymond Alexander," he said, in spirited repartee.

Myaisha had no interest—or time—for their romantic banter. It was nearly dawn, and she had a medical practice to take care of and probably a full roster of patients. With a wave to Barry and Deniece, she hustled inside the house.

Like a rocket, Boomer careened into her and gave a short bark.

"I know. I'm sorry. Mommy didn't know she'd be out all night."

He snorted and trotted away from her into the kitchen. He sat upright beside his water and food bowls.

"Sorry." She filled the bowls appropriately, then hurried into the bedroom to shower and dress.

***

291

Instead of driving straight to the office, Myaisha stopped by the hospital to examine two newborns. It was nine on the dot when she strode into her medical office. Once inside, she hung up her hat and coat.

At the weight scale, a mom tussled with a toddler. Phones rang. A medical assistant directed a patient into an exam room. The typical enterprises of a busy medical practice. She raced to the first exam room and allowed herself to be swallowed by the medical machinery.

Hours later, Myaisha trudged into her personal office at the rear of the building. She stumbled out of Birkenstocks and collapsed into a soft-leather chair behind her desk. It had been a long week—even without two murders.

While involved with patient care, she'd momentarily forgotten about Mrs. Evans being jailed. *How quickly things change?*

A year ago, having someone point a gun at her would have rendered Myaisha helpless. Now, she took threats against her life in stride and wrestled with murderers like it was a common occurrence.

Her gaze fell on the computer's clock. Six o'clock. She had also forgotten about her dinner date with AJ. *Should she cancel?* Although she didn't want to, she was completely exhausted. Not to mention twenty charts waited to be completed.

For five minutes, she considered her options. Charts could wait. Since she worked tomorrow morning, she would finish charting then. But if she intended to go ahead with dinner, she needed provisions. *A quick stop at the store to buy eggs and milk for cornbread. Check.*

Once she'd decided to proceed with her dinner arrangements, Myaisha again thought about the murders. Todd had locked up Mrs. Evans, which resolved one problem. But—

Two knocks on her office door preceded the entrance of her office manager.

"Mrs. Doctor," Yvette said, "two patients canceled for tomorrow, but three scheduled."

"No problem." Myaisha discussed weekend staffing with Yvette. Fifteen minutes later, she dashed out of the office to run errands.

***

Ding, dong.

Boomer scurried to his feet and raced for the foyer.

At a slog, Myaisha arrived at the door, wearing an apron, and carrying a metal spoon.

A peek in the peephole confirmed AJ had arrived.

She unlocked the door. Darkness shrouded the neighborhood. Myaisha viewed a single porch light on besides hers. She snuck a glance left, expecting to see Ms. Lula rocking on the porch and smoking. But Ms. Lula's porch was bare.

A large object approached the door. Myaisha leaped back as Zoey, AJ's brown Labrador, rocketed inside. While the Labradors chased each other around the living room, AJ pecked her cheek and entered.

Instantly, Myaisha detected a difference in his manner. His kiss was flat but his cologne tickled her nose. She reserved comment and allowed him to enter. He'd been there often enough to know his way around.

"The food's ready. We can eat now, or did—"

"I'm hungry. Let me wash up and I'll be right back." AJ hung his coat in the narrow foyer closet.

As he turned left toward the guest bathroom, Myaisha studied his back. He even walked stiffly. *You're imagining things. Projecting your own emotions.* With a shake of her head, she returned to the kitchen.

A minute later, AJ detoured around two frolicking dogs and entered the kitchen. The bar stool squelched as he plopped down at the kitchen island. He accepted the glass of wine offered.

"When were you going to tell me about last night?"

She glanced up from the plate of food she was preparing and into his stoic face.

"Things got busy—"

"Too busy to make a quick call?" As a demonstration, he extracted the cell phone from the rear pocket of his jeans and pretended to make a call. "Hello, AJ. Sorry to wake you, but Deniece and I confronted a murderer. No, don't worry. The police arrived in time, and I wasn't shot—almost—but not this time." He replaced the phone in his back pocket and glared at her.

"Who told you?"

"Barry."

"I'm sure he exaggerated," she said, sitting on a stool beside him.

"Deniece's husband didn't strike me as someone who embellished details. What were you two thinking?"

Myaisha grimaced. She wanted to argue with AJ but couldn't. "It was an impulse. A stupid mistake. We wanted to look at Evans' pictures."

"Why?"

She shrugged. "I don't know. Something about them bothered me. In the photos Tina showed me, it seemed he wore splints a lot."

"Donald Evans was an ass. Sorry for my language, but there's no better word to describe him."

AJ placed his glass in the sink. "I know it's unkind, but I'm glad he's dead. At least, he can't hurt anyone else."

"I'm sure he had some good characteristics."

"Hmm. Name one?"

"I don't have to."

Boomer whined and trotted up to her, pawing at her shoe.

She slid off the bench. "Mommy's sorry." She filled his and Zoey's bowls. AJ visited often enough that his dog had personal items at her house.

"Can we talk about something else?"

His light brown eyes regarded her. "Your choice." A smile twinkled at the corner of his mouth.

So handsome. With a determined look, she said, "I'd like to discuss us."

AJ's smile grew. "My second favorite topic—after you."

"I …" She struggled to choose the right words. "I believe we're both serious about this relationship."

He placed his strong hand on hers. Although it simply rested there, she sensed an embrace from emotions conveyed in his sparkling eyes.

She looked away, staring beyond AJ into the backyard. "Let me shut the shades."

It took a minute to close the shutters in the kitchen and living room, but Myaisha rambled slowly, giving herself time to summon courage. Back in the kitchen, she found her wine glass full and AJ eating collard greens.

"These are good," he said between bites. Juice from the greens glistened off his full lips. "Did you make them?"

"Yes, I had to ask my mom for directions. It's been a long time since I made greens. Josiah prefers cabbage."

For ten minutes, the only noises in the house were of jaws chomping and dogs lapping water.

AJ wiped his mouth with a napkin. "You ready?"

Myaisha blushed.

"Is this about Charlotte?" He pivoted on the stool, to face her.

"No, it's about more than that."

He laughed. "You want to talk about sex?"

She choked on a piece of cornbread. Because her coughing turned to choking, AJ patted her back and poured her a glass of water.

"I guess we'll approach that topic another day."

Having regained her breath—and composure—Myaisha said, "No." *Cough, cough.* "We can discuss it now."

"Okay." AJ lightly ran his fingers along her arm. "What questions do you have? Would you like me to explain the body parts involved? Or how babies are made?"

She laughed.

AJ's smile lit up the room. *Damn, he was hot.* Deniece was having a distinct influence on her.

"Thank you, but I'm familiar with the mechanics. I am a doctor."

"Oh. Want to play hospital?" He winked.

They climbed off the stools. AJ intertwined his fingers with hers as they retired to the living room.

"If we're going to have an intimate relationship, we need to discuss our sexual pasts." *How do you ask someone their sexual history? It's easier to tell patients how to do this stuff.*

"My sexual history isn't as long as I am."

She scanned all six feet eleven inches of him. "I hope not."

Over the next ten minutes, AJ shared his prior relationships. Myaisha listened. She had questions but didn't interrupt.

"Your turn." AJ grinned.

"First, I have a question. Have you been tested for sexually transmitted infections? And how recently?"

AJ clapped a hand over his mouth and pretended offense. "Oh, my. How dare you?"

Myaisha smacked his bicep, then regretted it. It was hard as a board. "I'm serious."

"After my last relationship." He gazed up at the ceiling. "That would've been three—no four—years ago."

"Would you be offended if I asked you to be tested again?"

"Not at all. But you too. I'm not buying this Miss Innocent story."

Her face fell and Myaisha turned aside.

"Hey, I'm sorry." He placed a hand on her shoulder. "I shouldn't joke about this."

"It's okay." After a deep breath, she swung around and glanced into his face but not his eyes. "I will get tested, but I've only had sex with one person."

AJ frowned. "Your husband, right?"

This time, Myaisha punched him in the chest. It also hurt. *He was built like a rock.* "Stop it."

He scooted along the couch and tucked her under his shoulder. "I thought you needed humor to lighten the mood."

"I did."

He kissed her cheek. A second later, his lips meet hers in a long embrace—until Boomer barked and sat on her foot.

"Really? You want a walk now?"

The black Lab barked and circled in front of her.

"How about a treat instead?"

He jerked his head away, barked once, and repeated the circle.

"I'll take him," AJ said, climbing off the couch.

In the foyer, he leashed Zoey. Before he could secure Boomer, the Lab darted away.

"Myaisha," AJ called from the front door.

She bustled to the front door and accepted the leash from AJ. "Boomer, if you want to go for a walk, you better behave."

The Lab snorted and glared at her.

"Fine. If you can't be good, then you stay home."

Zoey whined.

A moment passed before the Lab lowered his head and allowed Myaisha to apply the leash. When she handed AJ the lead, Boomer started to retreat.

"No," Myaisha said, eyeing the Lab.

A minute later, AJ jogged down her neighborhood street with two Labradors at his side.

Myaisha shut the door, resting her back against it. Her lips still tingled from AJ's kiss. *Sex talk done.* "I deserve a treat."

She entered the living room and turned on the stereo. As *Dim All the Lights* by Donna Summer played, Myaisha spied her cell phone on the coffee table. *Why not?*

Seconds later, Deniece answered. "Hey, lady. What's up?"

"AJ's out walking the dogs," she said, stretching her legs along the couch.

"Did he chastise you? Barry told me if I played amateur detective again, he would spank me. I can't wait." She laughed.

"D, something's wrong."

"What? Todd arrested Mrs. Evans. That crazy witch was about to shoot you."

"I know, but—"

"But what?"

"Mrs. Evans came back to the office to get the protein powder. That's what we believe, right?"

"Right, the protein powder she doctored to poison her husband."

"But Robin died instead, presumably by accident."

"No argument from me. Robin ingested the poison meant for Donald. Some couples drink after each other, which I find disgusting."

Myaisha stared into the kitchen, ignoring her friend's last comment. "That's possible."

"Of course, it is. They lived together. Robin drank after Donald. He spooned rat poison-laced protein powder into those smoothies. She suffered a pulmonary hemorrhage and died."

"In Donald, the rat poisoning would've resembled an overdose of his blood thinner medication. Tina said the medical examiner discovered he had an arrhythmia."

"There you go. So, what's the problem?"

What was the problem? Why was she fixated on those wrist splints?

"Those wrist splints. Todd was curious about those different wrist splints. Then all those pictures." Myaisha stared off into the distance.

"That proves Donald couldn't have committed suicide. His carpal tunnel prevented him from pulling the trigger. Again, Mrs. Evans, the jilted ex with an unregistered handgun and no morals, is the murderer. When poison didn't kill him, she finished him off with a shot to the temple."

"Do you believe she could have shot her husband in the temple?"

"The. Chick. Tried. To. Shoot. You," Deniece said, separately enunciating each word.

Why was she arguing? Deniece was right. Mrs. Evans was more than capable of murdering someone point-blank without a qualm. But still … Contemplating the murders, Myaisha missed what Deniece had said. "What was that?"

"I asked, what's up with you and the skinny detective? He's cute."

"It's not what you think. He likes chocolate."

"I bet." Deniece laughed.

"You've got a dirty mind."

"Speaking of dirty, when are you and AJ gonna get it on?"

"None of your business."

"Prude."

"Pervert."

"Well, I gotta go. I'm expecting a spanking. Hope you get your groove on."

Deniece hung up before Myaisha could deliver a snappy retort.

She glared at the phone. A minute passed before she returned to the kitchen. Ten minutes later, after cleaning up and making a snack for her and AJ, she remembered something.

"Wait a minute."

Rushing into the foyer, she scooped up her purse. Nothing. She unzipped the center pocket—also empty. With the purse on her lap, Myaisha reflected on last night.

Mrs. Evans entered the office. Lights came on. The gun came out. She yelled for Deniece then jumped behind the desk. The desk drawer.

The foyer closet door swung open. She searched her coat pockets. "Bingo." A blue wrist splint rested in her hands. "I forgot to give it to Todd."

In the living room, she made another call. After the fifth ring, voicemail clicked on.

"Hello, Todd. I forgot to give you the wrist splint I found in Donald Evans' office desk drawer. I slipped it into—anyway, I'll drop it off—"

With a beep, the call ended.

"Oh well. He knows how to reach me."

She collapsed on the sofa and inspected the splint.

Why would Donald Evans wear different splints? Maybe it had nothing to do with the murders.

Mrs. Evans had enough hate to kill her husband, and she definitely had a financial motive. Maybe Deniece was correct. Donald Evans had a penchant for photos, and he did have carpel tunnel syndrome. Patients could still experience pain following carpal tunnel surgery.

Myaisha started to toss the splint on the table when her finger bumped against something solid. She examined the splint as her ears alerted.

What was that? It sounded like a stick or twig breaking. She sat upright without moving. Minutes passed without a sound. She returned to examining the splint until another noise distracted her.

She'd definitely heard something. Still carrying the splint, Myaisha inched toward the sliding glass doors leading out to the backyard. At the window, she peeked around the curtains.

"Who's there?" *Idiot. Do you think an intruder will say, "It's me. Let me in."*

For a minute, she gazed into the night. Along the edge of her property, trees swayed in the wind. Unable to detect a presence, she clicked on the outside lights. Her stomach clenched.

Down along the stone patio pavers were wet footprints.

CHAPTER 44

With the rhythmic fluidity of an accomplished typist, Todd completed his report, summarizing interviews he'd conducted. He saved the document and glanced across the desks at his partner.

"What about dinner?"

"Maybe tomorrow," Ian said, rubbing his shoulder.

"Tomorrow's Saturday. I plan on—"

"Detectives." A uniformed officer strode up to their desks. "There's a woman out front, a Ms. Jones. She asked to speak with you—said it's about the Evans murder."

For a second, Todd and Ian exchanged a glance.

"Thanks. Bring her back," Ian said, adjusting the shoulder brace.

"On second thought," Todd said, "place her in interrogation room one."

In under three minutes, the officer escorted Ms. Jones into the interrogation room, where Ian was already seated at a small square table. At the door, Todd greeted and invited her inside.

Ms. Jones looked older than her stated age, a significant change from their last interview. Deep, dark circles cradled her eyes. Creases furrowed deep into her forehead. The door clanked shut as Todd offered her a seat.

"No, thank you," she said, scanning the room like a trapped animal. Her gaze remained in motion. "I only wanted to drop off these letters."

Todd accepted the package and again directed her toward a seat. "We need to read these. It'll take a few minutes. Please." He held the chair out for her.

She regarded it a moment, then perched precariously on its edge.

Once she sat, Todd considered the letters. He removed gloves from his pants pocket and handed a pair to Ian. Carefully, he extracted each letter from its respective envelope. With a nod to his partner, Todd read the letters while Ian questioned Ms. Jones.

"Tell us about the letters. Where did they come from?"

"I ..." She hesitated and scanned the room once more.

"It's okay. This isn't being recorded."

Her head inclined slightly. "The first letter came the day after Robin died."

"In the mail?" Ian asked.

"No. Someone dropped it off at my townhome."

While they conversed, Todd read the first letter again. It was crude. An amateur attempt to appear uneducated and young. He studied the second letter.

"Why didn't you bring it in then?" Ian slid his chair closer to her.

"I thought the police suspected me of murder. And the letter suggested I was involved in Robin's death."

Ian nodded. "And now?"

"My cousin told me you arrested Mrs. Evans. So, I figured you realized I couldn't be involved in my sister's death."

Still regarding her, Ian peeked at Todd, who gave an infinitesimal nod.

"There was an unknown DNA sample on your sister's hand. We requested a second blood and tissue sample from you."

The unstated question lingered. A full minute elapsed.

Ms. Jones swallowed. "Robin and I had a fight. I slapped her in the face. We ..." Tears streamed down her face.

Ian thrust a tissue in her hand, then slid the entire box across the table in front of her.

Todd handed Ian the letters. While his partner read, Todd said to Ms. Jones, "Take your time."

"I got scared," she sputtered. "When Robin started seizing, I thought I hit her too hard."

"She didn't die from a punch in the nose."

Doe-eyed, she regarded him. "It's still my fault. If I hadn't introduced her to Donald, none of this would've happened."

"Did Mrs. Evans know about your affair with her husband?"

Ms. Jones stared at the wall as if considering the question. "I always thought she did, but I can't be sure. Donald certainly wasn't discreet."

"And you?"

Her shoulders stiffened.

Todd detected a slight retraction in her body. *Go slow.*

"I'm not proud of having an affair with a married man." She sniffed. "But I didn't chase after him. I met Donald at a meeting for Greensboro business professionals. He invited me out for drinks. He never wore a wedding ring. It was about six months later when I discovered he was married with kids."

"But you didn't end the relationship."

She scowled. "I loved him."

"That's what Junior Evans said. You were the one person who truly cared about his dad."

She didn't respond.

"Are you and Junior Evans friends?"

"You better call him Junior. And yes, we're friends."

"Nothing more?"

The chair scraped along the linoleum as she sprang up. "He's a child."

"Not much younger than you."

Her chest heaved. "There's nothing indecent between us."

"You helped pay his debts."

Her gaze darted.

Todd's eyes narrowed. He prepared for a lie.

She placed the used tissues on the table. "Yes, when I could."

"His dad wouldn't."

"Donald cut Junior off because of a strip—a young lady."

"Dad didn't approve?" Todd asked.

"The young lady was a professional dancer. Donald wanted Junior to make better associations."

"Humph. Mr. Evans was a mass of contradictions. A philanderer with higher moral standards for his kids."

"Donald was complicated."

"And he kept secrets." Todd observed her shoulder flinch. "We know about the money."

Her fists clenched. Though she lowered her face, Todd observed her eyes. She was searching for an answer, wondering how much they knew.

"We know you didn't kill your sister but withholding information pertinent to a murder is accessory after the fact."

Ian squirmed, a grin on his downturned face. Todd frowned but knew his partner wouldn't let on about his overreaching statement. What mattered was Ms. Jones didn't know he exaggerated.

"I knew Donald hid money from his wife."

"You helped him."

Her jaw clenched. "I wanted you to have the letters. It might help convict Mrs. Evans."

Ian placed the letters aside. "You don't like her."

A flash sparked in Ms. Jones' eyes. "She murdered my sister."

"Did you like your sister?"

She glared at Ian. "No, but I loved her." She stood and hurried to the door.

Todd met her and knocked twice.

A uniformed officer opened the door.

"Thanks," Todd said to the officer before accompanying Ms. Jones from the room. "Listen, I don't want to trap you—and this is off the record. But we need more information on Mrs. Evans to secure a conviction."

"What more do you need? She was jealous of Robin."

They passed several police officers as they traversed the hallway and exited the station.

Cold air flowed right through Todd's clothing and into his chest. *Should've grabbed a coat.*

"Mr. Evans Sr. cheated before. There was no reason for his ex-wife to be jealous of your sister."

"I see." Ms. Jones stopped and sized him up. "Then it had to be about money."

"I believe so. Did she know about the money he hid?" Todd shivered, trying to focus on the interview and not on how long he had before his toes developed frostbite.

"I don't know, detective. She didn't learn about it from me."

They spoke for another minute before Todd dashed back inside the police station. He returned to his desk, rubbing his hands to revive circulation.

"Where'd you go?" Ian asked, fiddling with his shoulder brace.

"Outside. I had a few more questions."

Ian chuckled. "Without a coat? I hope the answers were worth it."

"What did you do with the letters?"

"Sent them to forensics. Probably won't be any probative evidence on them or prints. The first letter was juvenile and useless. The second hinted Mrs. Evans planned to kill Ms. Jones over the stolen money."

"If the letter writer was concerned for Ms. Jones' safety, why not meet her in person or call the police?"

"You think it was a ploy?"

"Don't know, but the letters were from two different writers."

"Or one person masquerading as two people," Ian said.

Todd's fingers drummed along the desk. "Mrs. Evans could have written the first letter. But I don't see a reason behind the second."

"Throw Ms. Jones off-balance, frame her for murder, or a prelude to a third murder."

"Killing her husband's lovers. Why now? No, I think it's about money. The forensic accountants discovered embezzlement in Evans' businesses."

Ian readjusted his splint. "They haven't started on the overseas accounts yet."

"I believe there are two different thefts involved. The daughter admitted to withdrawing money from the overseas accounts, but adamantly denied removing money from the business accounts."

"The son could've stolen it."

"If so, where did he hide it? And if he had embezzled from his dad, why did he need to borrow money from Ms.

Jones? The accountants have found over nine hundred thousand dollars missing." Todd stared up at the ceiling.

"He might have lost the money in a dancer's cleavage."

Todd grimaced. "Or he blew it gambling. The Jones woman tensed up when I asked about the money. Maybe she knows where it's located and is waiting for things to cool off before she retrieves it."

"She's smart … and cagey."

"Yes, we need to keep an eye on her. Let's go. It's late." A rumbling in his coat pocket alerted Todd to his cell phone. He frowned. "Hell."

"What?" Ian asked, fumbling with the splint.

"The doctor. Dr. Douglas."

"What is it with you guys? I think she has a thing for you. Some women do, you know. Cops turn them on." Ian grinned.

"It's not like that. She's a nice, nosy, pain in the behind." *Who often has good information and better desserts.* Todd silenced the phone and let it go to voicemail. *Call her back later.*

"Come on." Todd stood and put on his coat and gloves. "Are you still messing with that splint?"

"It's too tight. The doctor showed me how to adjust it, but it's not working."

"You're a klutz."

"Then you try it." Ian hurled the splint at Todd.

"Ouch." It struck him on the chin and dropped onto the desk. "That hurt."

"Sweet cheeks."

"Seriously, what's in this? I thought splints were Velcro." Todd retrieved the splint and examined it.

"They are, but there's a rod inside to provide stability. It keeps the joint immobile."

Like a dawn cresting over the horizon, Todd's face lit up. He grabbed his service revolver and car keys. "Let's go."

"Where? It's Friday night. I thought we were calling it a day."

"We were, but I figured it out."

"It what?"

"I'll tell you in the car."

They hustled out of the station.

After buckling into his seat, Ian asked, "Well?"

Todd frowned, thinking out loud. "I wonder where Ms. Jones went." He sped out the lot.

Chapter 45

Leafless tree branches braced against the December wind. After staring into the darkness for another minute, Myaisha abandoned the window and rested on the couch. She placed her cell phone on a side table. There was no one in the backyard. *Must be nerves.*

Again, she examined the wrist splint, appreciating a slight difference in the stitching. The splint had separate holes for the thumb and fingers. Adjacent to the thumb opening, Myaisha scrutinized interrupted stitching, unlike the rest of the splint. Her fingers prodded a thick metal strip. Trailing along its side, she picked at the threads.

"This must be for added support."

Myaisha slipped to the splint over her wrist. With a grimace, she rotated her wrist. The splint fit uncomfortably and appeared bulky.

"No one would want to wear this."

She teased apart the threading and discovered a hidden pocket. Using her thumbs, Myaisha pushed against an object. Although she could have sliced apart the stitching, she wanted to preserve the pocket and cause as little damage as possible. Like an earthworm poking up from the dirt, a thin metal bar poked out. Taped to it was a USB drive.

Myaisha gasped. "Hello, what is this?"

"So, you found it."

Her head spun around. Intent on inspecting the splint, she hadn't heard the front door open.

"What are you doing in my house?"

"I guess your friend forgot to lock it." Gradually, the person entered the living room, surveying the area. Although they wore a ski mask with only the areas around the eyes and mouth visible, Myaisha recognized the voice as female—not to mention she detected breasts under the dark brown peacoat.

"Give me the USB drive and I'll consider not killing you," the woman hissed. With a gloved hand, she pointed a gun a Myaisha's chest.

"Why did you kill Robin?"

"I didn't kill her," the woman said.

"Who are you?"

"Doesn't matter. Give me the drive."

Myaisha shook her head.

The woman cocked the gun. "Don't make me kill you."

"You're going to kill me anyway." From the lesson on guns Grace had given the Greensboro Women of Color Writing Group, Myaisha recognized the weapon as a revolver. It held six bullets. *How many would the woman be able to shoot before Myaisha ran and hid?*

"I don't give confessions, and I have no interest in sticking around here longer than necessary." The gun flicked to the side as the woman motioned Myaisha to approach. "Let's go. Give it to me before your friend comes back."

Stall.

"How did you know about Donald Evans' hiding place?"

"He always wore those ridiculous splints—even after his carpal tunnel surgery. There had to be a reason. Too bad I didn't figure it out earlier."

"And the money? Did you guess about it too?" Myaisha had her back to the kitchen. As the woman entered the living room, she'd been making a slow retreat toward the island. *Give him time. Keep her talking.*

"I knew he hid it offshore, but I needed the codes."

"That's why you killed him."

"Shut up," the woman growled, advancing toward Myaisha. "Give it to me."

In a rush, the woman stormed toward Myaisha. The latter hurled the USB drive into the kitchen. It bounced off the island and disappeared near the refrigerator.

"You crazy … Where'd it go?" The woman thrust the gun toward Myaisha, grabbed her right arm, and dragged her into the kitchen. "Since you like playing games, get in there and find it." The woman flung Myaisha into the island then bashed her with the butt of the gun.

"Ow," Myaisha cried, touching her chin where the gun smacked her face. "I don't see it."

She shoved Myaisha forward. "Check over there by the fridge. Find it."

"Did you mean to poison Mr. Evans? Was Robin's death an accident?"

"I didn't touch her." The woman grabbed a handful of Myaisha's thick wavy hair and pulled her along the ground. "Hurry up or I'll shoot you and look for it myself."

Myaisha fell to the ground on her knees at the same time she reached up to release the grip on her hair. "This isn't necessary. I'll—"

"Ouch," the woman wailed.

In her peripheral vision, Myaisha saw the gun crash onto the ground near her leg. She reached for it as the woman stomped on her hand.

"Dammit," she yelled, glancing up at a familiar face before—

Smack.

"Stop it," the masked woman moaned, cradling her arm, and bustling away.

As the intruder examined her wrist, Myaisha retrieved the gun. She kicked Myaisha in the abdomen.

"Now that wasn't nice," Ms. Lula said, before pummeling the woman's shoulder again with the bat.

The woman's body was hunched and her face contorted as if she prepared to attack Ms. Lula.

"No, you don't." Myaisha assumed the stance Grace had taught the writing group and leveled the gun at the intruder.

Right then, the front door burst open. Three uniformed officers sprinted inside from the foyer. Todd rushed in from the kitchen side of the house while his partner entered through the sliding glass door.

"Hands up," an officers shouted.

Myaisha assumed he meant her and placed the gun on the kitchen island. Pain prevented her from fully raising her right arm.

Officers surrounded Ms. Lula and the masked woman. Todd intervened and directed the officers to stand down.

"This is Dr. Douglas." Without hesitation, he ripped the mask off the intruder's face. "And if I'm not mistaken—"

Simultaneously, Todd said, "Cynthia Howard," as Myaisha said, "The office manager."

A police officer handcuffed Ms. Howard around the back.

"Wait," Myaisha said, "I think her shoulder's broken."

The officers regarded Todd, presumably for instructions.

He nodded. "Cuff her in front." Todd glanced at Ms. Lula. "You're pretty dangerous with a bat."

"If y'all were faster, it wouldn't have been necessary," Ms. Lula spat before weaving around Todd to sit on the couch.

Todd smiled.

Detective de Jesus corralled Todd and another officer on the opposite side of the living room, conferring beside the entertainment center. A separate officer directed Ms. Howard into a high-back chair near them.

Amidst the chaos, in trotted two Labradors, followed by AJ.

"What's going on?" AJ asked, his gaze circling the room, beginning, and ending on Myaisha, who stood beside a couch. "There's a half-dozen police cars outside."

He started toward her when he glanced down at the couch. "Oh, hello, Ms. Lula."

The senior citizen rested the bat at her side. "Hello, young man. You've been a long time coming back."

"I guess I have."

"Is someone gonna help me?" Ms. Howard groaned, rubbing her injured shoulder against the back of the chair. "That old bitty broke my arm."

"An ambulance is on the way, ma'am," Todd said.

"Let me help." AJ bustled over to the woman. He paused a second, glancing up at Todd. "Uncuff her. I can't examine her shoulder like that."

With a wave, Todd directed an officer to remove the handcuffs.

Beside the chair, AJ kneeled down and examined the woman's shoulder. "What happened?"

Hesitant at first, Ms. Howard released her arm and allowed AJ to inspect it.

"I'm a firefighter, paramedic," he said with an engaging smile.

Myaisha wondered how many women had been comforted by those same words. *Don't worry. His true smile is reserved for you.*

"What a minute." AJ gasped. "You work for Donald Evans. I've seen you in his office. What's your name again?" His head pivoted upward as if in thought. Seconds later he said, "Cynthia something."

The woman snapped her jaw shut and glared at AJ.

"Cynthia Howard," Todd said.

On the couch, Ms. Lula petted the dogs. "At first, I thought it was your friend sneaking inside. But when I didn't see her flashy SUV, I knew something was wrong. That tart's too good to walk, so I decided to stop by."

"And you brought a bat?" AJ asked, tending to Cynthia Howard's shoulder.

"Son," Ms. Lula said, stretching back into the pillows, "I always carry a weapon."

CHAPTER 46

Paramedics arrived. AJ assisted them in treating Cynthia's shoulder.

Ms. Lula, using the bat as leverage, hauled herself off the couch. "Well, I'll be going. You should be safe with these police officers. Half the people on our street are probably outside watching this place. I better go and tell them what actually happened before that gossip next door spouts a trail of lies."

Myaisha smiled. "Thank you, Ms. Lula." She kissed the woman's wrinkled cheek.

"Now enough of that," Ms. Lula said, waving her off. "Your young man like those greens?"

"Yes, ma'am. He did."

"I knew he would. No good man can turn down my collard greens. If a man doesn't like those greens, he's mean evil."

"Um, ma'am," Todd called after the departing Ms. Lula, "we're going to need a statement from you."

"Y'all don't need nothin' from me. The doc can explain everything." Ms. Lula exited the house providing more proverbs about how to know you have a good man.

Behind the septuagenarian, patrol officers and the detectives also departed.

After accompanying her neighbor to the door, Myaisha returned inside and collapsed on the couch.

Boomer barked.

"Seriously?" She crawled back to her feet. "This was your fault. If you didn't want to go for a walk."

Myaisha slid the sliding glass door open, and Boomer and Zoey bounded outside.

AJ returned from assisting the EMTs with Ms. Howard. "Well, this was quite the evening."

He kissed Myaisha lightly on the lips. She winced.

"What's wrong?"

"I got hit in the face with a gun."

Frowning, AJ examined her chin. "I see a slight bruise. In the morning it'll look like a rainbow."

"Great."

He glanced around the room.

"What?"

"I wanted to make sure we were alone. No cops spying on us." He smiled.

She pecked him on the lips and ambled into the kitchen.

"You want me to stay the evening? Protect you from prowlers."

Myaisha started to smile, but her jaw ached. "No, I'm good. Todd will probably be here a while."

"Todd?"

"Detective Gamble."

"You call him Todd. Should I be concerned?" AJ's eyebrow arched.

She frowned. "My face and shoulder hurt. I'm not up for jokes."

He walked over and gave her a big, deep hug. "Seriously, I can stay the night. Platonic. I'll sleep on the couch."

"It's fine. By the time I finish answering questions, it'll be morning." She closed the refrigerator after removing a pitcher of juice. "You want some?"

"I'm good. Where's Zoey?"

Over the next ten minutes, AJ retrieved Zoey, said his goodbyes, and departed.

Police circulated outside the house for another hour. Todd conversed with them, telling Myaisha he would speak with her later.

She felt hollow after the evening's drama. Wind howled in the woods behind the house. Boomer stretched along the floor before the sliding glass doors. His snoring reminded Myaisha of how tired she felt. Once she finished her juice and cleaned the kitchen, she headed for her bedroom.

A knock at the door sent Boomer scurrying into the foyer with barks and growls.

What now?

Before answering the door, she followed Ms. Lula's dictum and got the bat out the foyer closet. Through the peephole, she viewed Todd. She'd forgotten he wanted to speak with her. It took a good minute to remove the chain, deadbolt, security lock, and stash the bat before she welcomed him inside.

"I won't keep you."

She stood aside. "No problem. Come in. It's freezing outside."

After removing his coat and gloves, Todd followed her into the living room.

As Boomer started to growl, Myaisha whistled and directed him away. She entered the kitchen, preparing a tray of cookies.

Todd stayed in the living room. "What made you think about the wrist splint?"

She handed him a glass of lemonade and set the cookies on the coffee table. "You."

"Me?" Todd's voice rose as he accepted the glass.

Boomer growled and eyed Todd, who glowered and sat on the couch.

"Yes, you piqued my interest by mentioning how often Donald Evans wore wrist splints. Then I remembered those pictures where he wore a splint, even while lounging with Robin."

"I thought he was still having pain from the surgery."

"That was a possibility, but I found it curious. At first, I thought something was hidden in the picture frames. That's why Deniece and I went to his office. Then I remembered René mentioned Donald hiding money from his ex-wife. And I recalled different colored wrist splints in the photos. I can't claim to have worked it out before I found the USB drive, but it makes sense now."

"Yes, it does." He drank lemonade and accepted another cookie, which hovered before his mouth as he spied Boomer creeping up toward him. He tossed it at the Labrador.

Boomer sniffed it, gingerly picked it up between his teeth, carried it a few feet away, and ate it while eyeing Todd.

"What the hell type of dog is that?" Todd asked, taking another cookie.

Myaisha laughed. "A good one to have."

He readjusted himself on the couch. "Unfortunately, we didn't get a lot off the cell phone audio recording. Thanks for trying."

"Sorry. I tried to get her to talk but she wasn't interested in confessing. When I saw the gun, I forgot about the recording app."

"It was worth a try, but I wouldn't want you to get hurt trying to obtain a confession."

"Do you have enough to charge her?"

"With murder?" He swallowed the remaining lemonade. "Not yet. We have evidence against Mrs. Evans and Ms. Howard."

"I hadn't considered her. René mentioned her once, I believe." Myaisha's brow furrowed in thought. "Anyway, Mr. Evans had quite a few lady friends. All of them had potential motives."

"He has a lot to answer for." Todd rose. "I guess, in a way, he's paid for his sins."

"I suppose." Myaisha followed him to the door.

Because he spun around suddenly, they stood less than a foot apart.

Up close, she appreciated haggard lines etched in his dark thin face. He looked older and tired. "You should rest."

"I will. A few things need my attention, then I'll head home."

Seconds passed.

He stammered, "I want to apologize for my behavior the other day."

"Don't—"

"No, I was out of line. You're a pain, but …" His somber face rose. "You're a good friend."

Her shoulders lifted. "Thank you, Todd."

He turned to leave. "But stay out of my homicide cases."

Myaisha laughed. "I will."

"Sure, until the next time."

She secured the door before returning to the living room. As she cleared away snacks, Myaisha wondered how Todd would prove who killed Donald Evans.

CHAPTER 47

Myaisha sighed—her attention momentarily diverted by the café's aromas. *Don't even think about it. You need to lose weight.* She continued into the rear conference room and discovered she wasn't the first to arrive.

"Hey, lady." Deniece rose, kissed her cheek, and gave her a hug.

"Careful." Myaisha winced. "My jaw hurts."

"I should be furious with you. How come you didn't call me last night?"

"A woman tried to kill me for a USB drive." She returned the greeting but didn't mention Ms. Lula and a bat saved her life.

Myaisha placed her tote bag and purse on a chair in the front row. "Sorry if I forgot to call you."

Deniece smacked her arm. "Selfish. You hog all the fun."

"Having a woman thrust a gun in your face isn't fun. It was a horrid night. I'm glad Grace gave us those lessons about guns."

"Nonsense. You should be used to it by now."

Did one ever get used to having their life threatened? All this drama because I can't let go of a mystery.

"You have issues." Myaisha watched as other members of the group entered.

"Hey, Tina, Mary. Anyone else coming?" Deniece asked, taking a seat in the front row.

Tina placed a large backpack on the seat beside Deniece and sat in the next one over. "No, this is a secret meeting between the four of us."

Mary closed the conference room door. "We wanted to talk about the murders." She dragged a chair over from the second row, and they formed a circle.

"Tina hasn't locked down the rights to the story yet." Deniece smirked.

"Stop it," Tina said, tapping Deniece lightly on the hand, "this is serious. The police still have Mrs. Evans under arrest for both murders."

"I believe she's only been charged with a weapons violation so far," Myaisha said.

Waving a hand, dismissively, Tina said, "Particulars. They haven't charged the Howard woman with anything but attempted robbery."

"Did she confess to anything last night?" Mary asked, her cherubic face lit up in delight.

Were they ghouls to take so much interest in murders? Myaisha spent her free time writing murder mysteries. *How big a leap was fiction to reality?*

"No, she's been tight-lipped—but did mention she hadn't killed Robin."

"She could've killed Donald though," Mary said.

"I didn't get a chance to ask her anything except about the money and USB drive."

The four ladies gazed at each other without speaking. Minutes passed.

"How can we help?" Mary asked.

"Help who?" Myaisha asked. "René is off the hook."

"According to whom?" Deniece asked, inching forward on her seat.

Myaisha frowned. "She turned the letters over to the police. They don't consider her a suspect as far as René knows."

"I didn't hear about a second letter," Mary said, frowning.

Tina filled in the details about the two separate letters René had received.

"What's this?" Deniece asked, pulling a manila folder from Tina's open backpack.

"Oh, those are newspaper clippings and other miscellaneous information about the murders," Tina answered.

"Already doing your research?"

"Never too early." Tina grinned.

Mary opened a plastic container—releasing a delicious aroma of chocolate and cinnamon—and passed it around. "You know, I've been thinking this over. We should publish a true crime mystery novel as a group. We can share in the work, then publish it under a pseudonym."

"That's an interesting idea," Deniece said, handing the container to Tina.

"How's your erotica book going?" Tina asked Deniece, declining a brownie but passing the container over to Myaisha.

"Fine, but self-publishing is a marketing nightmare. I'm thinking about switching to clean, wholesome romance. The market's bigger."

"I thought you loved erotica." Myaisha smirked. "You have so much real-life experience to share."

"Jealous prude," Deniece sniped.

"Not at all, nymphomaniac," Myaisha slapped back.

"We'd have to work out the details," Mary said, ignoring their banter. "A group collaboration should be carefully ironed out—to avoid conflicts."

"Brownies." Myaisha accepted one, closed the lid, and placed the container on a chair beside her. "I should get some tea." As she departed for the café, Todd entered the conference room.

"Hello, Todd," Tina shouted. "You've been working my son too hard."

Did Todd blush?

"Well, Mrs. de Jesus, things have been busy downtown."

"I know." She tittered. "It keeps him out of the gym. Have you seen how big he's getting? He's built like the Hulk."

"He is," Deniece said, "but it looks good on him."

"Dr. Douglas, may I speak with you for a moment?"

Myaisha joined Todd at the doorway.

He lowered his voice and leaned in close. "I need you to come to the station to sign your statement—about what happened last night."

"No problem." She lowered her voice too. "How did you know I was here?"

He chuckled. "Ian. He said his mom was meeting with her writing group. The group's meeting location is posted online. I knew you couldn't resist despite last night. You're drawn to murder like a moth to a flame."

This time, she blushed. "Humph. But you could've called."

"Gave me an excuse to leave the office and get something to eat."

His head tilted right toward the three women observing them. "Have you ladies figured anything out?"

She smiled. "And if we do …"

He stood up straight and raised his voice to a normal speaking level. "The police always appreciate the assistance of the community."

Before he could leave, Myaisha lightly restrained him by the arm. "Is Cynthia Howard under arrest for murder?"

"Right now, the charge is attempted burglary with a weapon. That's why I need your signed statement. We're still developing a case."

Myaisha turned her back to her friends and lowered her voice again. "And what do *you* think?"

"Now, that would be cheating, doctor." This morning, his face appeared youthful, revitalized. As he exited, he gave her a goodbye wave.

She watched him depart.

"What did he say?" Deniece yelled from the front of the conference room.

"Nothing," Myaisha said. "I'm going to get tea. Anyone want anything?"

***

An hour later, they were unable to break the deadlock about who had murdered Donald Evans.

Mary stood and stretched. "I still vote for Mrs. Evans. She meant to kill her husband to protect her children's inheritance. Robin died by mistake. She shot her ex-husband to finish him off. The letters were smoke screens."

Though she listened, Myaisha had tuned out the discussion. She studied the newspaper clippings in Tina's folder.

"Smoke screens are meant to disguise something. What purpose did these letters serve?" Tina asked.

"They're confusing the case. The police haven't identified the author yet."

"Maybe we're wrong about Mrs. Evans. Junior might have tried to poison his dad. He had gambling debts, remember."

"What about …"

Their voices ran together and vanished into the distance. Myaisha examined a newspaper clipping from the morning of Donald's murder—or the morning his body was discovered. Todd didn't clarify the time of death.

"Ladies." Myaisha raised her voice. "Hey. Wait a minute. When was Donald Evans murdered?"

For a minute, the noise from the café filled the room because none of the women spoke.

Deniece glanced at Tina. "Well, you should know. Didn't you find the time of death in your son's work papers?"

Tina grimaced. "No. He left them at the office the last time he came by."

"He's gotten wise to your snooping?" Deniece winked.

"It's important. Look at this." Myaisha showed them a photograph of the front of Evans Used Car lot on the morning Donald Evans' body was discovered.

They rose and surrounded Myaisha, staring down at the clipping. Everyone spoke at once.

"I don't see anything."

"What are we looking for?"

Myaisha stabbed the photo with her index finger. "Right there. Under the car."

Deniece shrugged. "Unless you see a gun, I've got nothing."

"Does anyone have a magnifying glass?" Mary asked, rubbing her eyes. "I don't see anything but dry gravel."

"Exactly," Myaisha said, gazing up at them with twinkling eyes.

Three women gazed at her like she'd lost her mind.

"I remember it rained early Friday morning because I got drenched walking Boomer around the block. It made me late getting to the office, but my first two patients were late too. There were several accidents because of the slick roads."

Tina nodded. "Yeah, I worked late the night before. My supervisor asked me to take a morning shift, but I refused. No way I was driving in that mess after working twelve hours—"

"Tina, focus," Deniece said.

Mary eyed Myaisha. "What does it mean?"

"Someone arrived at the lot before the rain started."

"When did the rain begin?"

"It had to be before eight," Tina said, "because the nurse supervisor called—"

"Check online," Deniece said, interrupting Tina's remonstrations about her job.

"I've gotta go pick up my kids," Mary said, giving Myaisha a peck on the cheek. "Let me know what y'all find out." She hugged Tina and Deniece. "We'll discuss our collaboration later."

The conference room door closed behind Mary as Myaisha continued to study the photo, and Tina called the newspaper for last week's weather reports.

"Oh, thank you. I appreciate it." Tina ended the call.

"Yes?" Deniece asked, extending her legs forward.

"News reports documented rain started at 7:30 Friday morning."

"Now, we need to know when Donald was killed." Deniece glanced at Myaisha. "Call your friend."

Myaisha beamed at Tina. "Call your son."

Tina said, "We'll call them both."

"Or we can walk over to the station. Scratch that. Let's drive." Myaisha shivered.

***

"See," Myaisha said, again pointing out the dry spot under two cars in front of Evans Used Car lot last Friday morning.

"That's significant, isn't it?" Tina asked, regarding her son.

"Yeah, Mom," Detective de Jesus said, "but we need more than that."

Deniece reclined against the desk where Todd sat. "We can't help unless we know the time Donald Evans was murdered."

"Your assistance is appreciated," Todd said and rose. "We can take it from here, ladies."

Myaisha brought out the plastic container of brownies Mary had left them. She popped open the lid and placed them in front of Todd. "Can't you simply give us one little clue?" She smiled meekly.

Todd shook his head. "You're a wicked woman."

"And a good baker," Ian said, leaping across the desks and grabbing the box.

"Hey." Todd snatched the container from Ian and palmed two brownies.

Tina's son retrieved the container and helped himself to three.

Tina smacked his hand. "Look how you behave. Like you're starving. Don't I feed you?"

Myaisha bit her lip to hide a smile. Deniece laughed out loud.

"Mom, don't. Not here." Crumbs tumbled from the detective's mouth full of brownies.

Todd looked at Myaisha. "I won't tell you the exact time, but he died Friday morning."

"And the cars?" she asked under lifted brows.

"Donald Evans' and Ms. Howard's."

"She did it."

Todd's eye sparkled before he regained his seat. "Now, if you ladies don't mind. I need to call the DA."

CHAPTER 48

Spices clung to the smoky air inside the dimly lit restaurant. Myaisha wiped her mouth and sank into the cushioned booth next to AJ. From his stern flat countenance, she discerned something amiss. However, he couldn't dampen her mood. She was dining at her favorite Indian restaurant in Charlotte with her best friend and …

Wasn't she too old to call AJ her boyfriend? He wasn't exactly her partner. *How did older women refer to the special men in their lives?* He appeared upset, but she didn't care to explore it right then.

"Well, Mya," Deniece said, reclining against her husband, "you definitely know how to bring the drama."

"This wasn't my fault," she said, drinking the last of her mango lassi. "I'd forgotten about the wrist splint until I got home and found it in my coat pocket. I guess Ms. Howard followed me home from Donald Evans' office."

"So, she knew about his overseas accounts?" Barry asked, stretching his arm along the headrest behind Deniece's neck.

"I guess so," Myaisha said, sneaking a glance at AJ. She noticed his face hadn't softened. He continued to stare out across the restaurant.

"If we hadn't gone to the office, Cynthia Howard would've found his wrist splint, retrieved the USB drive, and escaped with the money."

Myaisha nodded.

"Why didn't she go earlier?" Barry asked.

"The police had the place cordoned off," she said. "Then the estate lawyer sold off all the cars. She waited until activity around the place died off. Besides, she didn't understand about the splints. In photos, Donald wore a black splint, but the one with the USB drive—the one I found in the office—was blue."

"You still shouldn't have gone," Barry said, gazing at his wife.

"Why did you go to the office?" AJ asked, glaring at Myaisha.

Caught off guard, she stuttered, "I … well. We—"

Deniece slid forward and placed her hand on AJ's. "Don't blame Mya. It was my idea."

"Where one goes, so does the other?" AJ asked, a tiny grin peeking at the corner of his lips. "Do you always follow Deniece's example?"

Unsure of the meaning of his taunt, Myaisha remained silent.

Laughing, Deniece rose. "Unfortunately for you, she doesn't."

Barry accepted the check from the server and assisted Deniece from her chair. "Well, Ms. Howard is locked up now. It's hard to believe she was behind all this."

"What about the letters?" Deniece asked Myaisha.

"Todd said Mrs. Evans admitted to writing the first letter."

Deniece grinned. "Oh, is Todd confiding in you again? What did you bake for him this time?"

"A tart."

"What about the second letter?"

"He didn't say, but I bet it was Cynthia."

"Why?"

"I don't know. Maybe to sow discord between René and Junior. Maybe to frame René. The police believe Cynthia killed Donald Friday morning. When Junior unexpectedly arrived at the office, she slipped out the back door. Todd said Junior mentioned seeing it unlocked in his original statement."

Deniece nodded. "So, while Junior discovered his dad dead in the office, Cynthia sneaks out the rear door, slips around the front, and enters the showroom as if she just arrived."

"Exactly."

The two men discussed the check, while Myaisha slipped behind AJ and out of the booth.

"She didn't kill Robin though," Deniece said, sliding into the arms of a coat Barry held for her.

"No?" Barry asked.

"No. Cynthia killed Donald, but Mrs. Evans killed Robin. Right, Mya?"

"That's right," Myaisha said, as AJ helped her with her coat. She followed Deniece and Barry out of the restaurant.

Outside, Myaisha paused, recalling the woman she'd barely known. "Robin's death was an accident. Mrs. Evans doctored her ex-husband's protein powder with rat poison. She believed the symptoms would resemble a side effect of his blood thinner medication."

"She hadn't realized Donald would pour the powder into his smoothies," Deniece said.

"Robin inadvertently drank the contents—"

"During the fight with René, she suffered a massive pulmonary hemorrhage," Deniece interjected. "Poor René."

"She probably feels guilty," Barry said, opening the car door for Deniece.

"Well, we'll get her spirits up. It's only been a week, but she'll heal in time," Deniece said.

Hugs were exchanged and Deniece and Barry departed.

***

Inside AJ's truck, Myaisha reflected on the past two weeks. *Was René devastated by the death of her sister?* The two hadn't been close, but they were twins. Everyone said twins carried a special bond. Close proximity breeds contempt. *Was that the saying, or—*

"Thanks for coming," AJ said, observing the congested Charlotte evening traffic.

"I enjoyed it." Myaisha sank back into her reflections—or at least tried to—as the radio played *Faerie*, from *The Nutcracker* by Mannheim Steamroller.

"*The Nutcracker* is special to me. It was the first ballet I watched as a child. My parents thought I was crazy because every year for Christmas, I asked to see *The Nutcracker*."

"And they took you."

AJ chuckled. "Hell, no. My dad wasn't going to a ballet. My aunt took me."

Myaisha admired AJ's profile, chastened for thinking about death when she had an exceptional man beside her.

"What?" AJ sneaked a peek at her. "You want to go home?"

"No, it's not that."

"Deniece and Barry are going to check on the dogs."

"I know."

"Then what? Are you having second thoughts? We don't have to spend this weekend together in Charlotte."

Myaisha reached across the truck and squeezed his hand. "I'm looking forward to this evening."

"That's it. Not even excited."

She spied a grin in the curl of his lips. "I don't like being teased."

"Yes, ma'am. Tonight, we do whatever you want."

Although she laughed, Myaisha wondered what she did want.

***

AJ swiped the key card across the reader and held the hotel room door open for her.

Inside, Myaisha inspected the furnishings.

They had reserved a suite. The communal area appeared clean. Myaisha peered into the bedroom and decided the bed comforter, with its splashes of blood red against a flowery background, had to go. A vision of Robin's head surrounded by—

She startled when AJ tapped her shoulder.

"Sorry. Let me take your suitcase."

As he deposited their luggage in the bedroom, Myaisha strode over to the window in the common area and viewed downtown Charlotte. She detected AJ's return from the bedroom and abandoned the window.

He reclined on the couch.

Myaisha detected a sudden tension between them. Though she presumed to know why, she would let AJ speak. A minute passed as he frowned distractedly. She scrutinized his face, wondering if she should broach the topic first.

"Is this how things are going to be with you?" he asked.

Myaisha joined him on the couch. "What do you mean?"

He sighed and gathered her hands in his. "Why do you risk your life for these murder mysteries?"

"This wasn't some paperback novel," she huffed.

"No, it was an actual murder." His lips tightened.

"I didn't mean to get embroiled in Donald Evans' murder."

"Only Robin's?"

Her body stiffened. "René's a friend. She asked for my help."

"And what am I?"

Here we go. The conversation she wanted to have, but not right then.

"What do you want to be?" Her breath caught. The hairs on her arm stood at attention as she awaited his reply.

"Do people our age call each other boyfriend and girlfriend?"

She tried to exhale without being too obvious about her relief. "We can call each other whatever we want. What matters is what we understand between ourselves."

He scooted along the couch until their bodies touched. "I want to be a meaningful part of your life."

Her body trembled. "I understand."

AJ bent forward. Their lips brushed up against each other when the hotel phone rang. Myaisha's chest relaxed. She detoured around AJ and went to the bathroom while he answered the call.

"Everything okay?" she asked on her return.

"The hotel clerk asked if we wanted to stay an extra night. They have some sort of weekend special."

He held his arms open. "Want to stay an extra night?"

She smiled. "Let's see how the first one goes."

"Um. Sounds good."

***

The room was dark, but sunlight trickled around edges of the curtains. Myaisha's lashes fluttered. Groggily, she peered through a haze of unconsciousness. *Where was she?*

A loud inhale confirmed she wasn't alone. As the fog lifted from her vision, she viewed the outline of a form beside her on the bed. Light cologne reminded her …

She smiled. Memories of the prior evening flittered around her mind. The ballet. Dinner afterward. It had been near midnight when they'd returned to the hotel. Her hand reached out to touch AJ's side. His deep exhale reassured her.

Carefully, she slid across the bed, not wanting to wake him.

The details of their first night together were brief and completely G-rated. In short, they had fallen asleep. A laugh rumbled in her stomach as she glided up beside him, resting her head on his chest. She lay still listening to his rhythmic heart and symmetric breathing while inhaling his cologne.

Myaisha jumped when his hand wrapped around her waist and drew her closer.

"I thought you were asleep," she said, afraid to speak too loudly and break the spell of their romance.

He stretched his head back along the pillow. "I was until a minute ago."

They cuddled, silently, for several more minutes.

"Did you enjoy *The Nutcracker*?" he asked before yawning.

"Yes." She curled into his side. "I've seen it before, but this was memorable."

"For me too." He planted a short kiss on her forehead.

She pushed off his chest. "AJ, about last night—"

"Oh, hey." He fumbled amongst the covers to roll over and face her. "Look, I'm sorry about falling asleep. I had a long week."

"No, don't worry about that. I meant—"

"I promise, I'll do better." AJ's grin reached his ears.

She trusted his promise. "I want us to be friends above—"

"Lovers."

Their eyes locked.

Breaking off, Myaisha nestled onto his chest. *How long had it been since she'd cuddled into a man's embrace?* She wanted this moment to last. Enjoy AJ's company without having to explore—

"What time is it?" he asked, reaching over to the bedside table, and reading the clock.

"I don't know," she said, stretching, and sitting up. "Probably still early."

Ping.

"What's wrong now?" *I hope it's not the office.* Myaisha reached across to the opposite bedside table to check her phone.

AJ's name popped up on the screen. She frowned and opened the message. A folder was attached. While she opened the attachment, AJ's hands encircled her waist. His lips trailed along her neck, nuzzling against her ear.

Inside the folder was a song file. Her finger tapped play.

Lyrics from Boys to Men's *I'll Make Love to You* filled the room.

Myaisha grinned, turned around, and met AJ's lips. Maybe she had learned something from Deniece. One way to find out.

About the Author

Born in Illinois, as a military dependent, Michelle moved between San Diego, California and Charleston, South Carolina. She enrolled at the University of California Santa Cruz before attending Michigan State University where she completed a pediatric residency program. After over twenty years in clinical medicine, Michelle now works as a medical consultant. As a member of Crime Writers of Color, Sisters in Crime, Capitol Crimes, Alliance of Independent Authors, and Science Fiction & Fantasy Writers Association, her writing interests cover many genres—mystery, fantasy, and thrillers. If not writing, you can find her baking, gardening or bicycling.

Thank you for reading *Murder In Gemini*. As a self-published author, I depend upon reviews to increase my visibility and credibility. Please post an honest review. Visit my website for book reviews and resources for writers.

If you missed the first book in the series, read *Murder Is Revealing*. The third book in the series, *Murder Between Neighbors,* is also available. Sign up for my Write Club Mysteries newsletter and receive bonus content, information on new releases, and resources to assist the writing community.

www.MichelleCorbier.com